MW00471856

GALAXIES AND OCEANS

N.R. WALKER

"May the stars forever guide us, and may this lighthouse bring us home."

COPYRIGHT

Cover Artist: Cover Affairs
Editor: Labyrinth Bound Edits
Publisher: BlueHeart Press
Galaxies and Oceans © 2018 N.R. Walker
First Edition: June 2018

All Rights Reserved:

This literary work may not be reproduced or transmitted in any form or by any means, including electronic or photographic reproduction, in whole or in part, without express written permission.
This is a work of fiction, and any resemblance to persons, living or dead, or business establishments, events or locales is coincidental, except in the case of brief quotations embodied in critical articles and reviews.
The Licensed Art Material is being used for illustrative purposes only.

Warning

Intended for an 18+ audience only. This book contains material that maybe offensive to some and is intended for a mature, adult audience. It contains graphic language, explicit sexual content, and adult situations.

Trademarks

All trademarks are the property of their respective owners.

Galaxies and Oceans

N.R. WALKER

CHAPTER ONE

I STOOD in the middle of the cabin unable to speak. Last night had been the worst one yet, and I felt disoriented, worthless. Anton put the bag of groceries on the kitchen counter and made sure the fridge was turned on, then came and stood in front of me. He raised a hand to my face, and I instinctively flinched but then made myself stay still.

He made a deliberate show of tucking a long strand of my hair off my face. "Why don't you get undressed and get into bed. I'll grab you some Tylenol."

I did as he said, biting back a groan when my shirt brushed my face.

"It's warm here." Anton turned the ceiling fan on before sitting on the bed beside me, holding the pills and a glass of water. "Here. Sit up," he said. "Take these."

I did, and he smiled. My stomach rolled. "See? I look after you," he murmured in that sickening way he did when he pretended to be sorry.

I lay back down and pulled the covers up despite it being the beginning of summer. I shouldn't have been cold...

"I'll be back on the weekend to get you. Get some rest."

I swear I didn't breathe until I heard his car pull away. I sat up, took photos on my phone, and saved them to my online storage file like I always did. It was a mechanical reaction now. Despite the pain, I was numb to it all. I switched my phone off and threw it toward the foot of the bed, lay back down, and closed my eyes.

I was alone again, which I was both thankful for and resentful of in equal measure.

I pulled the blankets over my head, and only then did I allow myself to cry.

———

I'D BEEN at the cabin for two days when the fire started. I hadn't known about it because I hadn't turned the television on, or my phone. I couldn't see out of my left eye anyway, and the throbbing in my jaw below my right ear was enough for me to stay in the dark and quiet with the blinds drawn, hidden from the rest of the world.

I hadn't eaten. I'd gotten out of bed to vomit once, only to crawl back under the covers wishing for a different life. A different me, waiting for sleep to numb me.

I'd heard helicopters but didn't think much of it. I didn't think much about anything at all. But I smelt smoke on day three and finally went out onto the front veranda that over-looked the Brindabella Mountain valley, and that's when I saw the horizon to the northeast was a curtain of black smoke.

Oh my God. The whole of the Brindabella National Park must be on fire...

I raced back inside and switched on the TV. It was on every channel.

"A massive bushfire is razing the national parks west
    of Canberra, countless homes lost, five fatalities
    already, experts are saying the worst is yet
    to come."

Holy shit.

The sound of an approaching vehicle on the road below
sent a chill through me, thinking it could be Anton coming
to get me. Out the window, I could see a New South Wales
fire services patrol truck crawling down the road, siren
wailing and a loud speaker declaring, "Mandatory evacuations. Leave now. You must head south to Brindabella
Valley Road and Snowy Mountains Highway. Take any
pets and all the water you can carry. You have half an hour
until you are in the red zone. Mandatory evacuations. Leave
now. You must head south..."

Holy shit. Red zone. Half an hour.

I was struck with fear, unable to move, panicked and
scared: emotions that were second nature to me now. You'd
think I'd be used to it, resigned, but I never was. It struck
the fear of death in me every time. But now that wall of
black smoke, of fire, was coming straight toward me. And for
a few minutes, I just stood there.

A stark realisation occurred to me.

If I stayed here, it'd all be over. I could sit on the couch,
open the red wine I was never allowed to touch, raise my
glass, and toast the end of my days as the fire came to
greet me.

It wouldn't be a terrible way to die. Not really. No,
living my life as it was a terrible way to die. If I drank
enough wine, maybe I'd pass out before the flames reached
me. Maybe the smoke would kill me first.

It wasn't as if anyone would actually miss me. Anton

would grieve more for his lost cellar of French and ageing Barossa wines than he ever would for me. He'd get to play the part of the grieving boyfriend politician who had brought me to "his mountain retreat for a week of rest and creativity" like he often did. No one knew the real reason he brought me here. No one was inclined to drop in unannounced and find me beaten black and blue... Oh yes, he'd play the part of the grieving politician so well. He'd score sympathy and the insurance for his house, of course, and his political career would skyrocket. Voters loved a sob story...

Then something cracked in my head, like a sheet of ice finally melting, expanding, shifting. Then fear dissolved into something else. An eerie and cold calm crept over me. Something my grandfather had told me once...

If there were mandatory evacuations, it meant the fire was uncontained. And in this forest, that meant it would raze everything in its path to the ground. That meant, with heat so intense, identifying bodies would be unlikely. I remembered that from the massive bushfires when I was a kid, watching horrified with my grandad, sometimes they couldn't determine human remains at all. Even dental records weren't much use against the intensity of a raging bushfire...

So Anton only had to *assume* I never made it out.

I didn't have a car. I was here alone. I had no way to escape; that much was true. The police would deem it unlikely I ever got out. It would all be very tragic...

A spark of hope flickered in my chest for the briefest second, and I felt alive for the first time in years. I pulled my hair into a ponytail and shoved some clothes into a backpack and the bag of food that still sat untouched on the kitchen counter. I threw in as many bottles of water that would fit and dressed in jeans and a long-sleeved shirt, despite the summer heat. I pulled my hiking boots from the back of the closet and snatched my phone off the bedside table. The battery was almost flat. I had no missed calls, no messages. Surely Anton knew about the fire. Surely.

Then a chilling thought occurred to me. What if Anton was seconds away from pulling up to get me?

Oh God. I really was out of time. The thought of him turning up was worse than the impending fire.

Trying not to panic, I hit his number, and he answered on the fourth ring. "Ethan," he said smoothly. It sounded like he was in his office.

Relief flooded through me. "There's a fire," I said flatly. "Mandatory evacuations. I have to leave."

He'd once threatened me if I ever tried to leave that he would find me. He would make me sorry...

"Ethan, I've been in meetings," he started giving one of his many excuses. "I've only just seen the news. The fire's changed direction. You should leave. Get to safety. I'll come to you. If you—"

"I hate you. I *hate* you." I sounded cold and calm and was surprised my voice didn't shake. I'd wanted to say this to him for years. "I hate you for everything you've done to me. For everything you turned me into. I was strong before I met you." I couldn't even cry; there were no more tears left. "And the worst part of all, I hate that I let you."

Silence.

I took a deep breath. "I'm about to walk into the path of a bushfire because you stranded me here alone. My death is on your hands."

I hit End Call and surprised myself by smiling despite wanting to scream and punch something.

I could do this.

I took as deep a breath as my lungs would allow and shook off any lingering moments of doubt. I could do this. I grabbed my backpack, but something red near the stove caught my eye. A fire hydrant and a fire blanket. I grabbed the foil blanket, and just as I got to the door, I saw it. My telescope. It was an old brass Broadhurst and Clarkson telescope and leather case that had been my grandfather's. There was no way I was leaving it behind. It was the only thing I had from the man who raised me and the only thing left in my life of any value. I didn't care about anything else I'd have to leave behind, but I was taking that. If I made it out.

With a last look around, I bid goodbye to my life as I knew it and ran out the door.

The wall of black smoke toward the east was huge, billowing, and closer than it had been just five minutes ago. I followed the drive that ran south along the dirt fire trail, isolated, lined with tall eucalypts. The whole area was deeply forested. This part of the world was made famous by *The Man From Snowy River* movie, but it was also renowned for experienced hikers getting lost and perishing, even with supplies. With that in mind, I left the road and stumbled into the underbrush.

After making my way far enough in, I took all the cash out of my wallet, leaving behind my licence and credit cards, and stashed the few fifty dollar notes in my pocket. I threw the wallet and my phone on the ground and wrapped them in the foil blanket. All going well, when they searched this charred land, they'd find this and assume me dead. For good measure, I took off my watch—a gift from Anton after he'd once lost his temper—and tossed it near the blanket.

And that was it.

That was all I could do. If I made it out of this alive, I would no longer be me. Regardless if I survived or not, Ethan Hosking would die here today. God willing, I would have a new life.

With no time to waste, I said a silent goodbye to everything I'd ever known, and instead of running back toward the road, I went southwest, away from the fire, but deeper into the forest.

I kept the fire trail to my left and always in sight. A few four-wheel drives and rural fire trucks roared past, but I stayed out of view. If this was going to work, I had to remain unseen. I just kept heading south. I never stopped. The underbrush was dry and dead, gone too long without rain, and it was pure kindling for the coming fire. Even for early summer, this was not good. And with the fire rolling in fast behind me, panic really kicked in.

I didn't want to die.

So I ran. In blistering heat with the wall of fire at my back, through scrub and trees. Even as darkness fell, I kept on going. I didn't have time to fuss over being scratched by trees or my black eye or how my jaw still ached. I fished rice crackers out of my backpack and a bottle of water, but I never sat down. I couldn't afford to.

This was my one and only chance.

I scrambled over rocks, slid down embankments, into shrubs, and around trees. I scraped and scratched myself from head to foot.

I had no idea how far I'd gone or how far I had to go. I'd never gone south of the Trail Road before. I'd only ever gone to the cabin from the north when Anton drove me. I had no clue where I was going, but it was away from the fire —away from Anton—and that was all I needed.

My water was gone, though I still had some food, and I

was thankful for the full moon. I couldn't even imagine where I'd be if it weren't for the moon. Lost and disoriented, I took a moment's pause.

What had I done? Walking into the forest was a stupid, stupid thing to do.

Despite all the wishing I'd done for this life to be over, I didn't actually want to die. I wanted my old life to die. I wanted my life with Anton to be over. But I wanted to live, and something more than panic squeezed my lungs as I realised I might actually die in this forest.

I wanted to cry. I wanted to collapse to the ground and weep. I considered giving up. The wall of orange fire was closing in; the smell of smoke was acrid and dry.

I tried to think of what Grandad would do. He'd take a second to regroup and catch his breath; that's what he'd do. He'd get his thoughts in order and work out a plan. So that's what I did. The forest was dark and eerily silent, as if the animals had known a fire was coming and fled. I looked up at the sky, and that's when I saw it. Like a sign from my grandad, he'd shown me the stars.

I remembered him teaching me about the constellations and his words came back to me. "If you're ever lost, look for the Southern Cross. The tail points south, always."

Of course!

"Thank you, Grandad," I whispered with new purpose.

Using the Southern Cross as my compass, I went south, and sometime later—I didn't know how long—I found a dirt road. A fire trail, by the look of it, and it made my going easier.

I stayed to the side of the road and half a kilometre on, a small cattle truck was parked off an old driveway, heading south, engine rumbling, headlights on. A man, older, grey hair, climbed out. He quickly closed the gate he'd just driven through and did one last check on the sheep in the back of his truck. "Hold on, girls. Just need a quick pit stop and we'll get you all to safety," he said as he walked to the far side of the truck, into the opposite tree line and proceeded to take a piss. I took it as my one opportunity for a free ride out of the forest. I snuck up behind the truck and, as quietly as I could, climbed into the back tray. The sheep bleated, and the man replied with, "Okay, okay, I'm done."

I slid in amongst the flock and ducked down and held my breath, just as the man climbed back into the cab of the truck. The old engine coughed into life and I almost laughed as we began to drive. I lay in sheep shit, got trod on, shoved and bleated at, but I was safe. The view behind me was a smouldering amber against the darkness, and only then did I realise just how close the fire was. I clutched my backpack to my chest, ignoring the stink and shove of sheep, hardly believing I'd made it. I was overcome with a wave of new tears; relief this time.

I was free.

———

I TRIED to keep track of time, but my eyes struggled to stay open. The loud engine and jostle of the truck were putting me to sleep, but every time I'd nod off, a bump jolted me awake, and I was grateful. I couldn't afford to fall asleep and be found out. At some point, we'd taken a turn onto the Snowy Highway, and from the passing road signs, I deduced we were headed toward Cooma.

Good. Small towns worked for me.

As we came into town, the truck pulled off at the first

service station. It was a two-pump dive, and as soon as the driver disappeared inside, I climbed out, took my backpack, and headed down the footpath. Thankfully, there were no passing cars and streetlights only on every other corner.

I found a small superette and bought some more water and a pair of scissors; the man behind the counter was too busy yelling at some kid about how to stock shelves properly to pay any attention to the state of me. Next stop was the public toilets in the park to freshen up the best I could in the small sink and poor overhead light. I washed my face, careful of my eye. My hands stung, and it was then I noticed the scratches and cuts.

But I still had to make Ethan really disappear. So I pulled my hair out of the ponytail and proceeded to give myself a haircut. I'd always thought it was ridiculous in the movies that someone cutting off all their hair would make any difference to people recognising them, but I was known for my long hair. In all the publicity shots with Anton, my long, wavy hair was the first thing people noticed. So I took the scissors to it, cutting it off, barely half an inch from the scalp. It was absurd and surreal to hack it all off, and I barely recognised myself in the mirror. I obviously couldn't see the back of my head and could only go by feel, and it was, at best, a hack job, but in the end, I just didn't care.

I wrapped all my cut hair in a plastic bag and disposed of it into a public bin, hiding it under takeout containers, and then walked to the smallest, shittiest motel I could find. All I wanted to do was shower and sleep. The reception was empty, save a small TV on the wall, and of course, the news was on.

"The bushfire west of Canberra, with a wall of fire fifty-kilometres wide and up to sixty-metres high, ripped through the Brindabella National Park leaving nothing in its wake. The official death toll now stands at seventeen, but with dozens of people unaccounted for, experts are expecting the death toll to climb. A late change in wind direction saved the Snowy Mountains National Park, and rain forecast tomorrow will bring with it welcome relief. Only then will emergency services be able to move into the area and start what is expected to be the grisly task of recovering bodies."

If the fire made it all the way to the Snowy Mountains National Park, then Anton's cabin was most definitely gone. I expected my name, Ethan Hosking, to be cited as missing, followed by a distraught-acting Anton, Canberra's only openly gay politician lamenting the loss of his long-time boyfriend... but thankfully it never did.

A lady with a hard, deep-lined face appeared through a staff-only door. She didn't even look twice at my black eye. "What can I do for you?"

"I need a room."

"Sure thing. It's forty dollars if you're here for an hour or a night. Card or cash?"

"Um. Cash." I took out the folded money in my pocket and handed a fifty over.

"What's your name, love?"

My name.

Jesus. What was my name? Ethan Hosking sat on the edge of my tongue, but he was, for all intents and purposes, dead. I eyed the TV screen, showing the number of fatalities in the chyron under images of raging fires.

My next thoughts ran to the only person in the world I

would have killed to still have in my life. My grandfather. And somehow, it seemed to fit.

"My name's Aubrey Hobbs."

CHAPTER TWO

PATRICK CARNEY

HADLEY COVE WAS A SMALL, practical town on the most southwest tip of Kangaroo Island, South Australia. Remote and rugged, the wind from Antarctica was blustery on a good day. It could cut you in half on a bad day. It was those winds that shaped the coastline, carving out rock over aeons of time, and left the shoreline on this side of the island mostly inaccessible.

The island itself was only a hundred and fifty kilometres from east to west, barely sixty clicks north to south. It took forty-five minutes to get the ferry from Adelaide to the east side of the island, then almost another two hours to drive to Hadley. Tourists rarely came this way anyway, preferring the east or north coast for their beautiful beaches and idyllic towns that thrived on tourism. And that was how we liked it.

With a population of sixty-three people, Hadley—as it was known—barely survived, let alone thrived. Locals who sought solitude and privacy kept it going, though. Most were retired or pensioners or self-employed. Some worked and went to school in Vivonne Bay, thirty kilometres away.

Hadley boasted a small shop that doubled as a post office and a liquor store, a takeaway store that did a pretty good fish and chips, a childcare mum who doubled as a hairdresser, a rundown caravan park, and a one-man police station.

Oh, and a lighthouse.

Which I looked after.

Hadley Cove Lighthouse had stood proud since 1821 and was made electric in 1981. For one hundred and sixty years, it had had a keeper who kept ships safe in the Great Australian Bight that was infamous for being more rock than water. But now it had me, someone to maintain it, make sure it was all in working order, keep the grounds tidy, and occasionally play the tour guide should anyone stay long enough to ask.

Most people walked up to it, around it, looked out to sea, took photos, and went on their way. Hadley was mostly just a pit stop for tourists.

Which was why a new stranger in town didn't go unnoticed.

I made my Monday morning walk to the store to collect my mail and buy a newspaper and found resident post-mistress, store owner, and barista extraordinaire, Penny, whispering quietly to Collin. Or Sergeant Collin O'Hare as he was otherwise known.

"Morning, Patrick," Penny greeted me brightly. "How was your weekend?"

"Fair," I answered with a smile. I liked Penny. A plump woman in her fifties with short grey hair and a penchant for a chat.

Collin gave me a nod. "Patrick."

"Collin." I glanced back to where they were looking, or rather, who they were looking at. Outside, there was a silhouette of a man in jeans and a blue parka, hood pulled up, leaning against the handrail that overlooked the sea. It was windy and cold, unsurprising given it was winter. Even late winter, it was still cold here. The man held a coffee cup in both hands and sipped it.

I didn't have to ask because Penny quickly filled me in. "Young fella. Came into town on Saturday. Staying at the caravan park and is looking for work."

I frowned thoughtfully. "If he doesn't freeze to death staying in a caravan first."

Penny nodded seriously. "Seemed a nice young fella."

Collin sighed. "Might ask him how long he intends to stay."

I resisted rolling my eyes. Asking him how long he was sticking around for usually meant moving them along. "What's his name?"

Penny shrugged. "Didn't think to ask."

"Maybe he's got a trade or something," I offered. "Lord knows we could use an electrician or plumber."

Penny smiled fondly at me. "Always looking for the good in people, hey, Patrick?"

I shrugged and Collin scowled. I ignored him and aimed a smile at Penny. "I try."

"Usual coffee this morning, love?" she asked.

I came in for the same thing every morning, but every morning for the last five years, she'd ask if I wanted a coffee, and every morning I'd add, "And the paper too."

Just like clockwork.

Collin stood to the side, and I finally offered him a small smile. "They reckon there's a cold front moving in this week. Southerly up to eighty k's coming straight off the cap."

Collin nodded. "Yeah, wind warnings came through this morning."

And that was about as interesting as conversation between Collin and I got. After I moved here and everyone heard I was gay, he told me he could possibly be interested in me. I told him I wasn't on the market. That was six years ago, even before Scott... Then after Scott, he hung around a bit, never asking outright, but he didn't have to. The timing was so wrong, and besides that, while we might be the only two gay men on this side of the island, we had nothing in common. Collin was a decent man, but he and I would never be more than friends.

Penny put the paper down on the counter, front side up. The headline from *The Adelaide Times* was a spin on the energy crisis, but the second headline at the bottom of the page read *Grief and Empty Caskets. Canberra Bushfire Exclusive.*

Penny tapped it with her finger. "Can you believe it's been six months?" She put my coffee on the counter. "Where does the time go?"

Six months. Wow. I sighed. "Just seems like yesterday."

I skimmed the first paragraph of the article. Politician Anton Gianoli was interviewed about the death of his boyfriend.

> The worst part is not knowing. An empty casket funeral didn't feel like goodbye.

I swallowed hard. *No, no it doesn't.*

Taking a deep breath, I folded the paper and tucked it under my arm and sipped my coffee. "Wonder what story he's got to tell," Penny said.

I realised then they were back to looking at the guy

standing across the road who was still watching the ocean.

"I'm sure it's not good, whatever it is," Collin mumbled.

"Not everyone's a bad guy," I offered.

Penny frowned and nodded. "True. But everyone who moves to Hadley's running from something."

Her statement hung heavy and cold in the air. It hung true.

Collin glanced at me before going to say something, so I quickly beat him to it. "Well, I'll be seeing you tomorrow," I said, walking out the door. Only I didn't duck around the corner out of the wind and head home. I stopped, looked toward the lonely figure still watching the ocean below, and with a deep breath and nothing to lose, I crossed the street and walked toward him.

"Hi," I said, still a few metres away so as not to scare him.

He spun regardless, his eyes wide. He had dark eyes, pale skin, and I could see short brown hair poking out from under his hood. He looked three days unshaven, and the bump on the bridge of his nose gave his handsome face a rugged edge. "Oh, hi."

"Didn't mean to scare ya." I nodded toward the tumultuous, tumbling ocean. "She's upset today."

He looked back out to the rough seas and gave me a quick smile. "It's actually kinda pretty."

I scratched at my beard. "I've heard it called cruel, cold, rugged, hellish. The only people who call it pretty are the ones who end up staying."

He looked back out to sea and smiled. The wind caught his hood and tousled his hair. His cheeks were pink from the cold as was the tip of his nose. He was handsome, no two ways about it. And possibly fifteen years younger than me.

I made myself look away. "What brings you here?"

"Looking," he answered without turning to me.

"For?" I stared out across the stormy waves with him. "Work? A new beginning?"

He shot me a look. "Something like that."

I sipped my coffee. "There's not much work here. Well, that's not true. There's a tonne of work; this whole town is weather-beaten and old. Just not much work that pays."

His lips twitched.

"But you can try the caravan park." I didn't let on that I knew that was where he was staying. "Old Frank Hill who runs the place would never say no to help. Maintenance, that kind of thing."

He turned back to the water, to the wind. "I've asked him already."

"Frank's just a grumpy old man who thinks anyone under thirty's a hooligan. I'll have a word with him if you like."

"Why would you do that?"

I smiled and gave pause. Why was I offering to help this guy? I didn't know him from Adam. Sure, he was good-looking, but there was something in his eyes. Something deep, hidden, and burning. Something horrendously painful. Something I recognised.

I faced the angry sea alongside him. "Because you called this ocean pretty."

Neither of us spoke for a while. I drank my coffee and he turned his empty cup in his hands.

"Anyway," I said, realising I couldn't stand around all day. "My name's Patrick. I live at the lighthouse."

That made him look at me. "In the lighthouse?"

"No. Not in it. In the residence."

"Oh. Cool."

"Well, it's almost two hundred years old, made from sandstone, and it's tiny. But yes, it's cool." I smiled as the wind whipped around us. "I should go. I have work to do, but I'll call around and see Frank after lunch." I pulled the newspaper out from under my arm, and his eyes darted to the front page.

He stared so long I turned it around so he could read it, but he shot me a look that I couldn't place, and it was gone so fast I'd wondered if I'd seen it. He stepped back. "Yeah, um, thanks. That'd be great."

It wasn't until I got home that I realised what the look on his face was. It was fear. And I realised I didn't know his name.

———

CHORES DONE, I set off to find Frank Hill. Apparently Frank had owned and run Hadley's caravan park since the '80s. There were only four permanent vans on-site and an ageing amenities block, so there wasn't a lot of work, but Frank's arthritis overruled his ambition and capabilities. He needed help, and even if he couldn't pay this kid much, maybe he could get reduced rent.

I didn't know why I was doing this. I was putting my neck on the line for a guy I didn't know, but something about him spoke to me. If it went pear-shaped, Frank would tell me to sod off, and chances were that was exactly what he was going to say from the get go. The weather had turned nasty. The biting wind felt like sleet, so I drove up close to Frank's house, pulled my beanie on, and made a dash up to his front door. I knocked, and I could hear Frank grumble as he got closer. He pulled the door back and greeted me with a harrumph.

"Hi, Frank."

Frank was probably in his late seventies, around five foot eight, wiry, and wore a permanent scowl. "What do you want?"

"Well, I was hoping to talk to you about the young man who's staying in one of your vans."

He narrowed his eyes. "What about him?"

"Nothing bad. Just the opposite, actually. I was hoping you might have some odd jobs he might be able to do for you."

He grumbled something I couldn't make out and turned, hobbling back into his lounge room. "Well, don't just stand there. You're letting all the warm air out," he barked. Stepping inside and closing his door behind me, I followed him into his small kitchen and stood beside him at his sink window. He nodded to the outside.

There he was, the young guy, in the sleeting, howling wind, his hood pulled around his face, crouched down hammering plywood sheeting to the underneath of one of the vans. "Already told him yes," Frank said. "He's a worker, that's for sure. Soon as I agreed, he went to it. Found a bunch of stuff in the old shed and put it to good use."

I smiled, more to myself than to anything else. I noticed he was out there working with his hands, without gloves. God, he was going to freeze to death. I had an old pair somewhere I was sure I could give him...

"Well, I'm glad," I said to Frank. I turned to leave but stopped. "Um, he didn't by chance tell you his name, did he?"

Frank ran his gnarled hand over his face. "I got it written down somewhere." Then recognition flashed in his eyes. "Hobbs. Aubrey Hobbs."

CHAPTER THREE

AUBREY HOBBS

Aubrey

I DIDN'T KNOW what made me choose Kangaroo Island. Maybe because it was so remote. Maybe because it was the last place anyone would expect to find me.

Not that anyone was looking.

But it was the southern tip of South Australia, and every time I looked at the stars, they pointed their way here. So here I came.

I'd only caught a real quick look at that nice guy's newspaper, but I saw enough. I saw Anton and the words *empty casket*. So they'd finally buried me... I didn't know whether to feel relief or grief.

It had been six months since I'd walked out of my life. Six months since those bushfires swept through the national park and burned everything to the ground. Six months since Ethan Hosking died and Aubrey Hobbs rose from the ashes.

It hadn't been easy. In fact, sometimes it had downright sucked. I made my way through Victoria and ended up in

Melbourne where I'd managed to score a few cash jobs here and there. The thing was, smaller towns were easier than cities. Country people were more trusting, and quite often a handshake agreement still meant something. City people needed ID and tax file numbers, and that was something I just couldn't give.

I made enough cash to eat most of the time. Sometimes not so much. And I'd spent more nights living rough than I cared to remember. There were some nights I considered walking into a police station and telling them who I was, claiming amnesia or something. But I couldn't go back. I would never go back.

So when I'd had enough of Melbourne or when people asked too many questions, I headed west. Following the seasonal fruit pickers, I spent some time in Geelong, then Warrnambool. Then I crossed into South Australia and spent some time at Mount Gambier before finding myself in Adelaide. Wine country was good for some cash grape picking and cheap accommodation with the backpackers who came for the work as well.

I had enough cash to last me a little while if I was smart with it. And the one thing being essentially homeless without an identity made me, was smart.

Street smart, anyway. I could tell who to trust and who to avoid just by looking at them. And where Ethan Hosking couldn't do much more than cite designer catalogues, Aubrey Hobbs could muck out stables, pack shelves, clean toilets, mop floors, pick fruit, and train grape vines. I could start a job completely clueless, with the mentality of 'fake it until I make it,' and I got by okay.

Not long after the fire, I kept a close eye on the news, when and wherever I could. And my ploy of leaving my wallet and phone under the fire blanket had gone exactly to plan. They'd found them, melted but still identifiable as mine, not too far from Anton's house.

They never found my remains, but it wasn't too uncommon with such intense heat, the news reporter had claimed. Four days after the fire, my name, well, the name of Ethan Hosking, was officially added to the victims list.

Anton turned it on for the media, sobbing in his freshly tailored suit and dark sunglasses as it was announced, and the nation wept alongside him.

That poor, poor man, people said. *How terribly tragic.*

LGBTQI+ groups across the country used him as their poster child for how professional gay men were upstanding community leaders, and he was still their face of gay politics.

God, how he had them fooled.

He was a lying, manipulative, violent piece of shit. I still had nightmares about some of the things he did to me. I'd slept on park benches, under bridges, in cardboard boxes. I'd been threatened by ice addicts and sneered at by shop owners for being unwashed, and still it was nothing, *nothing* compared to the hell he put me through.

But I was stronger because of him.

And I had a good feeling about this town. As soon as I arrived on the island, I knew I wouldn't be staying in the bigger towns. I stayed two nights in Penneshaw, but I found myself wanting to go west. Drawn to the isolation, to the brutality, I bummed a lift and arrived in Hadley Cove to a turbulent ocean, howling southerly wind, and dark and foreboding, low-hanging clouds.

And I felt at home.

I wasn't sure I'd ever feel at peace again, but by God, I could almost taste it here. And I wanted it. I wanted to find a place where I could stop running.

If I could find *that* here, only time would tell.

That Patrick guy seemed nice enough. His hair was brown but his beard had flecks of silver and red. His eyes were blue, like faded denim, and he looked a little weathered, as though he'd spent his time outdoors. I'd have to guess his age to be a year or two over forty. He was as rugged as the town he lived in, and the fact he lived at the lighthouse was interesting to me. I was certain he had a story to tell.

And that was the problem.

Everyone had a story to tell, myself included. And if I let myself get too close to anyone, they were bound to ask questions I couldn't ever answer. I hadn't allowed myself the luxury of even looking at guys this last six months. Not even the backpackers. I couldn't risk anyone getting too close.

It was the price I had to pay.

"Thought you could use these?"

I was fixing the last panel of sheeting to the underside of the van when someone spoke behind me, and I damned near leapt out of my skin. I spun around to find Patrick. "Holy shit," I said, putting my hand to my heart. "You scared me."

He put his hands up and looked honestly sorry. Or like he was trying to tame a wild animal. "Sorry," he said quickly. "I didn't mean to startle you."

I still couldn't catch my breath. "It's all right." Yeah, so maybe I still had to work on my game face, because I knew I'd gone pale; all the blood had rushed to my heart, and I could feel it slowly colouring my cheeks. "I didn't hear you come up."

He produced a pair of gloves. "Thought you could use these," he said again, smiling like he was nervous. "I called in to see Frank before, but you were already working. Your fingers'll freeze off if you don't wear something."

"Oh. Sure." I swallowed hard.

"You can just have these." He handed the gloves over, still watching me as if I might turn and bolt. "I've had them in the back of a drawer for a while. They're too small for me."

It'd been so long since anyone had done anything nice for me, it felt foreign. "Um, thank you. I wasn't expecting it to be so cold."

Patrick waved his hand to the wind. "It can be fierce here."

I nodded, not sure what else to say. I was certain he was about to ask me questions... So I turned back to the panelling and made it the focus, not me. "I was almost done on this one, but I'll be sure to wear them tomorrow."

He made a face and twisted his hands together nervously. "Frank said you worked all morning. Have you had lunch?"

I stared at him, not sure what to say. Not sure what his motives were, and not sure why I found his nervousness sweet. "Um."

"It's no big deal," he replied, looking into the wind. "Just thought some hot fish and chips sounded good."

Oh man. Hot food. Fish and chips sounded like heaven wrapped in newspaper.

He smiled. "Come on. My shout." He turned and it was pretty clear we were walking to the takeaway shop. It wasn't far away; nothing in Hadley Cove was far away. I fell into step beside him and he looked at my hands and shook his head. "Those gloves won't keep your hands warm if you hold 'em."

I chuckled and pulled them on, feeling warmer instantly. "Thanks again for these."

"No problem. Like I said, they were just lying around. I've got an old beanie you can have as well. Actually, I've got about ten. Mrs Stretzki—she lives up on Portside Street —she knitted me a whole bunch of them because I fixed some busted pipes for her." He stuffed his hands into his coat pockets. "A lot of people around here work on a bartering system. I got a free hair cut for changing a tyre once. And the Hollies, who have the world's loudest rooster, will trade eggs for fish. Or bread, or anything really. I thought it was kind of weird at first, but it's how things work here."

"Old Frank's giving me free rent for as long as I'm fixing up his place," I admitted.

"See? You're almost a local already." We'd walked to the takeaway store by now and Patrick opened the door for me. A bell tied to the door announced us, and a waft of fried food and oil made my stomach tighten.

Or maybe it was Patrick's smile.

I stood back from the counter and looked up at the chalkboard menu, and Patrick soon stood beside me. He was taller than me by a few inches, but bigger and broader by a mile, though not in an intimidating way. It was more of a pillar of strength kind of way. He was quiet for a moment, then asked, "What do you feel like? The grilled fish and chips comes highly recommended."

Ugh. It wasn't like I could order up a storm. He was paying, so it kinda felt rude. "Um, whatever. I'm good with whatever. The grilled fish sounds great."

"Oh hi, Patrick," the girl behind the counter said. She was short and robust, had a soft face with chubby cheeks, a silver stud in her nose, and a clump of pink hair in her otherwise black messy bun. She glanced at me, then back to Patrick. "What can I get for ya?"

He held up two fingers. "Usual times two, thanks, Cassy." He looked around at me, then back to her. "We'll eat it here if that's okay? Bit fresh out today."

"Sure thing," she replied. I slid into the second booth seat and they chatted about the weather for a bit and about someone named Davey who had a bus that was apparently an inside joke, because Cassy rolled her eyes and Patrick laughed. It was pretty clear that Patrick was a likeable guy, and I guessed when you lived in a small town like this, everyone knew everyone's business. Everyone either liked you or avoided you, and I wondered which of the two I'd be.

Avoided, for sure.

That wasn't a bad thing. As much as I wanted friends and longed for conversation or just company to hang with, I couldn't.

It wasn't like I was in some witness relocation program where I was given a new identity, with associated paperwork and records to match, should someone get nosey.

I had nothing. No Medicare card, no tax file number, no bank accounts. No history.

Jesus, I didn't even have a phone.

Which seemed crazy, because not even a year ago, I was glued to it. Social media, news, texts. But Anton had taken care of most of that; isolating me from my friends, my work, my dreams. So giving up a phone hadn't been too hard. In fact, in the beginning, it was a blessing.

"Aubrey," Patrick said, standing at the drinks fridge, and from his tone and the look on his face, I wondered how many times he'd called my name. "Coke or Sprite?"

"Um, Coke, thanks."

Wait a minute. How did he know my name?

Patrick sat opposite me and handed me the bottle of Coke. "You were a million miles away."

"Yeah, sorry." I pulled off my new gloves and opened the bottle, taking a nervous sip. "Um, how did you know my name?"

"Frank told me. Don't worry, by tomorrow, everyone in town will know your name. It's how the Hadley grapevine works. Frank will go into the store for his two bottles of beer at four o'clock, and he'll tell Penny, and Penny will tell, well, everyone."

"Oh, right." I snorted. "Is everyone in this town so predictable?"

Patrick barked out a laugh. "Oh yeah. Once, the national time administrators lost power, and they came here to reset their clocks." He winked. "Frank gets his beer at four, on the dot. Collin O'Hare, the local sergeant, does a five-kilometre jog starting at five thirty in the morning exactly, passing the lighthouse at five forty-two." Then he sighed. "Not that I'm one to talk, really. I get my morning coffee from the store every day at eight fifteen. I guess we're all creatures of habit."

I turned the Coke bottle one half-turn. "Oh yes, I met the policeman yesterday."

Patrick gave me a bit of a smile. "He's a nice guy. Just likes his rules and likes his town to stay exactly as it is. Did he ask you what you were doing here, how long you planned on being here?"

"Yeah, kind of."

Patrick waved his hand, dismissively. "Ignore him. He did the same to me when I first arrived, but he's okay."

"Is he a friend of yours?"

He shifted in his seat. "Kind of. Not really. It's complicated."

Just then, Cassy delivered two takeout containers that each held a mountain of food. "Here you go, boys," she said. Boys? She was younger than me and maybe twenty years younger than Patrick. She paused and gave me a blatantly appreciative once over and smiled. "And you are...?"

"Um, Aubrey," I answered.

"Well, nice to meet you, Aubrey. I'm Cassy." She stood there, smiling until it became awkward.

"Thanks, Cassy," Patrick said, and thankfully she took the hint and left us alone. "Sorry about that. Don't get new folk in town very often."

"I can tell," I said with a smile. He stared at me, his blue eyes delving into me a little deeper than I should allow. There was something there. Something familiar and warm.

Needing a distraction, I took the plastic fork and stabbed the white, flaky fish. The smell was incredible and I couldn't help but moan with the first bite. "Oh my God, that is so good."

Patrick was staring at me, his fork stopped halfway to his mouth before he blushed and squirmed a little, blinked a few times, then proceeded to eat. "Yeah. It really is."

Okay, so I might have moaned a little louder than I thought, but I couldn't help it. God, it had been so long since I'd had real food. Not just cheap cups of noodles or bread or black tea. Patrick ate his lunch between glances at me, and if there was any interest in his eyes, it soon gave way to something that looked more like pity.

Like he was watching a guy who didn't eat real often.

I put my fork down slowly and offered him a smile. "It's uh, it's really good."

He smiled. "Told ya. Cassy puts some secret seasoning on the fish before she grills it. Her dad runs one of the fishing boats that leave the cape every morning, brings her back a fresh catch every day."

"I've never tasted fish so good."

He nodded toward the food in front of me. "Keep eating." Then he kind of ignored me while I finished it so I probably wouldn't feel bad for demolishing the whole thing. Well, not ignored me, but he certainly pretended I wasn't some starving guy he fed out of pity.

When I couldn't fit in another bite, I washed down the grease with a mouthful of Coke. "So what's involved exactly with the upkeeping of a lighthouse?"

Patrick's face lit up, and he pushed his half-eaten lunch to the side. "Well, it's all electric now and the lamp is automated, so it's more maintenance than anything else. The salt and the wind make for a lot of work."

"That's still pretty cool though. Not many people can say they work in a lighthouse."

"No, there's only about three hundred and fifty of us nationwide. I'm actually employed by the Australian Maritime Safety Authority, or the AMSA. It's just a permanent part-time job, so living here in Hadley, where living isn't too pricey, kind of works for me."

"It seems like a nice town," I offered. "The bartering thing is a bit quirky, gotta admit."

He smiled. "Have you seen the penguins and seals yet?"

"No, but I want to." According to the tourist brochures I'd seen, it was an incredible sight. "Whereabouts do I go to find them? Is it walkable from here?"

"I can show you one day if you like?" He shrugged like his offer meant nothing. "I'm a bit of an expert on the location. And yeah, it's walkable. Everything in Hadley's walkable."

"Why? I mean, why are you an expert?"

"It's on my front doorstep."

"Oh. Makes sense." I took a sip of Coke and steeled my nerves. "Why are you being nice to me?"

Patrick's eyes flinched and his smile faded into something tinged with sadness. "Because you look a bit lost, and you remind me of..." He sighed. "You remind me of me."

I swallowed hard, and my full belly tightened uncomfortably. "I, um..."

When I didn't offer anything else, he did. "I know what it's like to need someone around who doesn't ask questions. Because the only thing worse than having no one around, is having some well-meaning but nosy person asking all the wrong kind of questions."

I let out a slow breath. God, he actually got it. I didn't know what led him to say that, but clearly, he understood. But maybe he was someone I didn't have to be defensive with. "It's tiring being on the back foot all the time."

"It is." Patrick gave me a kind smile. "Which is why you won't hear questions from me. Unless it's about mundane things like, have you seen the penguins and seals, or do you like your fish grilled or fried?"

I chuckled in what felt like the first time in forever. "I can handle questions like those."

"Good. So, what are your plans for tomorrow?"

"Another question."

"Yes, but another mundane one."

I smiled. "I'm going to start on the communal shower block. I don't think Frank's done anything to them since he bought the place."

He snorted quietly. "Please tell me there's hot water."

"Barely." I gave him a smile. Or maybe I was still smiling. I wasn't sure anymore. "But it's not that bad."

"Am I allowed another question?"

"Depends."

He smirked. "It'll be mundane, Scout's honour."

"I was a scout, you know."

He did the salute. "Then I will dutifully uphold my promise to only ask mundane questions."

I laughed. "Then please, ask away."

"If you're free tomorrow night, I could show you the penguins returning to land?"

He wanted to meet me again. I wasn't sure that was a great idea, but the warmth of his eyes and the kindness of his smile and the longing to connect with another person—especially with someone who promised not to ask questions—wouldn't let me say no. "Sounds good. What's the catch?"

"No catch. Unless you think walking down to the cove in the freezing cold at night is a catch. I promise it's worth it."

CHAPTER FOUR

PATRICK

IT WASN'T A DATE.

I told myself that, probably a dozen times. But nerves warred with guilt and I almost drove around to see him and cancel.

I wasn't ready. I wasn't prepared to move on. I wasn't capable.

Memories of Scott's touch, his hands, his smell, his taste swirled around me. His photo on the mantel made the ache in my heart heavier. Some days it was bearable; some days it burned. Grief was like the great Southern Ocean; it moved in ebbs and flows, often turbulent and rough, or peaceful and settled, and even over time when I could navigate the waters, the tide never stopped.

Four years was a long time. I'd now grieved for him longer than I'd known him, so while four years felt like a lifetime, and everyone said 'he'd want you to move on,' or 'he'd want you to be happy,' four years still didn't feel long enough.

But something about Aubrey spoke to me. Something about his eyes and his lips when he smiled. He was watchful, cautious, and I knew he had a story to tell, but I didn't want to push him. Stories were better told over time, anyway, when allowed to unfold only when they were ready to be written.

I wouldn't push him, and I promised him I wouldn't ask questions, as much as I wanted to know what brought him here or why he was so nervous and jumpy. I couldn't imagine it was a happy story, and that spoke to me as well.

Something about him made me want to know him, protect him. Something in me longed to touch him, to feel him in my arms and pressed against me. Which was absurd, because I'd only just met him, and I wasn't ready to be meeting anyone new.

But it wasn't a date.

I didn't know if he was even inclined that way. I'd like to think I could tell, but the truth was, I didn't know if he was gay or bi, straight, or anything in between. And in all likelihood, given he turned up here in Hadley and looked around himself like a scared rabbit, he wasn't in a good place. Emotionally, he was probably about as ready as me to be thinking about such things. Even if he was on the rainbow scale somewhere, chances were he wasn't on the market.

Because I wasn't on the market either. So what did it matter?

It's not a date, Patrick.

So why was I nervous? Why did I tidy up and dust my place, and why did I make extra pasta on the off chance he might want dinner? Because if eating lunch with him was any indication, I got the distinct impression he didn't eat very well or often. He was skinny, or more wiry than thin, and although he looked healthy enough, he could do with some more weight on his bones.

So why, above everything else, did I want to take him in

and care for him? Why was I so drawn to him?

I told him I'd pick him up at five, and at four thirty, I was pacing my small living room. Tabby the cat, my resident master and mouse catcher, watched me with judgement in her eyes from her spot in front of the fire. "It's not a date," I told her. She stared at me in the superior way cats did.

At twenty to five, I was standing in my kitchen, trying to convince myself to cancel, or not to cancel, see-sawing so bad I was getting motion sickness. Or maybe that was nerves. Or guilt.

At ten minutes to, I stood in front of the mantel and ran my finger down the frame of Scott's photo. He was looking right at the camera, laughing. Forever young and handsome. "It's not a date," I whispered to him, and I both cherished and hated the silence that replied whenever I spoke to him.

But then the wind howled outside and rattled the door as though the island was telling me it was time to go. I took my coat off the hook by the door, slid it on, and pulled the door closed behind me. I made myself get into my car, and I'd arrived at the caravan park before I could convince myself that this was a terrible idea.

I realised then I had no idea which van Aubrey was staying in, except only one had a light on, so I assumed that might be his. But no sooner had I got out of the car, did he walk out. He wore his blue jacket with the hood bunched at the back of his neck, jeans, and boots; the only clothes I'd seen him wear. He was holding the gloves I'd given him and a black rucksack.

"Hey," he said, stopping two metres in front of me. It was a wary distance, and I felt foolish for even thinking this could be some kind of date.

"Evening," I replied, trying to smile for him. "Ready to

see some penguins?"

He nodded, then looked up at the sky. "At least it's not cloudy."

I was about to say clouds didn't make much difference for penguins but decided not to. "It's windy though, and the southerly off the ocean can be pretty harsh." I opened my car door, but he seemed hesitant to get in. "You okay?"

He jolted into motion. "Yeah. Sorry." He opened the door and got into my car. I was sure he tried to make himself take up as little room as possible, and he was pretty quick to get out once I pulled up at home. But he looked up at the lighthouse and grinned.

I stood next to him and looked up at it too. The red and white stripes were still visible against the darkening sky, the beacon pulsing light out to sea.

"It's impressive close up," he said.

"It is. I can take you up in it if you want? The view is amazing, even at night."

His gaze shot to mine, full of excitement, but something stopped him; like he had to remind himself to be wary. "Maybe another time."

"Okay." I shrugged, trying for indifference. Then I nodded toward my house. "Give me a sec to grab you that beanie. It'll be colder down on the shoreline." I didn't really wait for him to object, because I was pretty sure he was about to. It was just a beanie. It didn't mean anything.

I unlocked my door and went inside, then when I realised he was still standing at the car, I stopped. "You can come in," I said from the doorway. I went back inside, leaving it up to him whether he wanted to or not. I wouldn't push him. He clearly had some self-preservation issues, and he was probably out there seeing which of his fight-or-flight instincts would win.

When I came out from my room into the living room, he was at the doorway. Not exactly inside but close enough. I held up the beanie. It was a dark grey, basic knitted thing that I'd been given. "Try this on. I've never worn it. It's literally been in a drawer for years."

He took a tentative step inside. "Nice place."

I looked around the small living room, which opened up straight to the kitchen. It was small but very cosy. One three-seater lounge, one recliner, a rug, and a TV fit in the living room, plus two small side tables. The kitchen had a row of cabinets under the window, made from old 50s laminate, a fridge in one corner, a stove in the other, and a small table sat square in the middle with two seats.

"I told you it was small," I offered.

"It's perfect," he whispered. "Feels like a home."

It was such an odd thing to say. "It does."

The cat stretched from a ball to her full length, showing her tummy to the fire. Aubrey smiled at her. "You have a cat."

"Ah, Miss Tabby. She graciously allows me to be her slave."

His lips twitched. "Cats will do that."

I handed him the beanie and went back to collect the torches from on top of the fridge. I held one up in each hand. "Penguins!" I nodded over Aubrey's shoulder. "Shall we?"

He stepped back and kept a few metres between us as I led us down to the spot where the penguins came in to nest. The lighthouse itself stood about thirty metres back from the rocks that met the ocean, but if you followed the edge a hundred metres or so further down, there was a small sandy beach that was peppered with boulders and shrubs; a perfect home for fairy penguins' burrows.

I stopped at the usual spot and jumped down to the first rocky ledge. It was only two metres long and barely one metre wide but it gave the perfect view. "We sit here and wait," I said. "They'll come in right below us."

The sun had just disappeared and the sky was a rich black, the moon was bright, and the wind was whipping right up the coast. I hunkered down, back against the wall of rock, trying to escape the brunt of the chill.

Only then did Aubrey jump down beside me, and he sat an arm's length away. He sat with his small rucksack on his lap, both hands on it like he might up and run at any second. His trust issues were really evident by the space he put between us. I knew it wasn't anything I'd done, but I had to wonder what he'd been through to make him so guarded.

"Thanks for the beanie," he said.

I glanced at him then. He had the beanie pulled down low, his hair and ears hidden. His nose was pink against the cold, and even with just the moonlight, I could see he was trying to smile. Trying to be brave.

"That wind will cut right through you. We won't be here long though. You're not too cold, are you?"

"No, I'm okay," he replied.

I fixed the red filter to the torch and handed it to him. "White light scares them and they won't come in. Red light doesn't affect them at all."

He switched it on, casting a red glow over us. "Thanks."

I fixed mine and switched it on too, shining it down where the water met the rocks. "They shouldn't be long. They've been out fishing all day so they need to come in and rest."

"And they wait for dark to avoid predators, right?"

"Yep."

He was quiet after that, and about five minutes later, he switched his torch off and opened his bag. He pulled out a cylinder-type thing and at first, I thought it was one of those aluminium water bottles, but then he unclipped something and pulled out a... telescope?

It was one of those extendable ones, and he pulled it to its full length, put it to his eye, and pointed it skyward.

Okay, so I was surprised. And impressed. Out of all the things I thought he might have been, a stargazer was not one of them. "Now that's cool," I whispered.

He shot me a look, and when he realised I was talking about him, he smiled and seemed to relax a little. "It was my grandfather's," he murmured. He smiled at the telescope, or at a memory. I wasn't sure. "He used to take me camping and we'd spend all night looking at the stars."

I don't know how I knew, but I was certain that was a part of himself he didn't share with just anyone. "Sounds wonderful."

"He taught me the constellations."

"He sounds like a great man."

He shot me a fervent stare before looking away. "He was. The greatest."

I was just about to tell him I was sorry—he'd used past tense, so I assumed his grandfather had passed—when I heard a disgruntled shuffling sound and the familiar squawk of penguins. I leaned forward and shone the red light to the rocks. "Look, here they come."

Down below us, a colony of fairy penguins began to emerge out of the water. They timed the tide to shoot from the waves and land, still rather awkwardly, on the rocks. From there, they hopped up, climbing the steep incline toward their burrows.

Aubrey was sitting forward, leaning on one hand and

holding the torch in his other, looking down beside me. He was grinning, and I wasn't sure which sight was more spectacular. Was he a little closer to me? Or was I imagining it?

"Oh my God," he whispered. "They're so cute!"

And they were. They were the smallest breed of penguin in the world and a permanent feature here on the island. Most places they only returned to breed, but these colonies stayed on the island all year round. It was easy to get used to seeing them, and I'd forgotten what the thrill of seeing them for the first time was like.

"They really are," I agreed.

And for the next half an hour or so, we watched as they all made their way from the dark depths of the ocean to waddle up to their burrows. I kept a rough count of colony numbers, and when the last few stragglers came to shore, I switched off my torch. "I forgot how much fun that is."

Aubrey chuckled. "I'm really glad I got to see that, thank you."

"You're welcome. Any time."

He began to pack away his telescope. "Did you want to stay a while and look at the stars?" I asked. "It's not very often you get a clear night here on the island."

"You don't mind?"

"Hell no. I have to say, I'm impressed. I wasn't expecting you to be an astronomer."

"Well, I'm not really. It's just a hobby."

"Anyone who studies the stars and planets is an astronomer, are they not?"

He smirked. "I guess so." Then he sighed and held the telescope in his hands as if he was testing the weight of it. "I like the consistency of the stars. They never fail, regardless of the rotation of the earth. It's fascinating to me that each star holds the possibilities of other worlds. Space is just so vast and dense, it makes everything else seem insignificant." He stopped abruptly, like he had to rein himself in. "Sorry, I just…"

I couldn't look away from him. "Don't apologise."

We both seemed to realise at the same time that the wind had stopped. It was silent, save for the crash of the ocean below us.

"I guess I study the ocean," I allowed. "Not the whole thing or the animals within it or the science of it. I need to study the wind and tides, the currents, and how the weather plays its part."

"Does that make you an oceanographer?" he asked. "If I'm an astronomer, by definition."

I chuckled. "Well, not really. I'm just a lighthouse keeper. Keeping an eye on the ocean is part of the requirements. Like just now, I did a rough count of penguins. I keep track of numbers, only roughly, to help with conservation. Every month or so I send a quick report to the penguin centre in Penneshaw. It's not an official report; it's not really my job, more of a helping hand, really. If there's a significant change, like if there were only ten, then they can look into it further."

"Was there? A change, I mean?" he asked, genuinely concerned. "Were the numbers okay?"

"They look good, actually. I counted over forty. That's good. Means they're healthy and the ocean is in good supply of food for them, and they're breeding well."

He smiled at that. "I'm glad."

"Yeah, it's a good sign." I nodded to the telescope he was still holding. "So, are you gonna use it or just hold it?"

Even in the dark, I was pretty sure he rolled his eyes. But he put it back to his eye and looked up. He stayed like that for a while, slowly panning an arc across the southern sky, and I leaned back and watched the white caps break against the rocks below us.

The ocean was calmer tonight, there were no angry undertones, and it was times like this that I could imagine it wasn't a force to be reckoned with, that it was a peaceful beast, gentle, providing refuge for all that lived in it. Some days it beat like a heart, the earth's pulse, giving life to all things.

Some days it took life.

There was a reason for the adage to never turn your back on the ocean. It was an unforgiving beast. I preferred when it was rough and choppy, grey and cold, because it was easier to remember what it was capable of.

"You okay?" Aubrey whispered beside me.

He'd packed his telescope away and was watching me. I was as many million years away as the stars he'd just looked at.

"Sorry. Lost in thought." I gave him the best smile I could muster. "You ready?"

He nodded and got to his feet. He put his bag on the ledge, then both hands, and nimbly pushed himself up. Jesus. And I kept in reasonable shape, but the days of leaping a metre off the ground that effortlessly were well and truly behind me. My face must have said as much because Aubrey laughed and held out his hand. "Come on, old man."

I took his hand, and his strength surprised me. He was wiry, yes, but he was strong. He pulled me up easily. "I'm not that old, I'll have you know."

He picked up his bag, slung it over his shoulder, and dusted his gloved hands on his thighs. "So, out of curiosity, how old is not that old?"

"I'm forty-one."

He nodded thoughtfully. "I wondered, that's all. The grey in your beard made it hard to guess."

I instinctively put my hand to my beard. "You saying this makes me look old?"

He laughed. "Distinguished."

I rolled my eyes. "Yeah, right. And how not old are you?"

"Twenty-seven."

Fourteen years. I'd guessed as much. We started walking back to the house. Fourteen years. That wasn't so bad, was it? I sighed, not liking where my thoughts had taken me. Why was I even considering this? I needed to get back on track. "I'll have you know, the beard is functional. It keeps my face warm against the wind. I spend most of my days outside."

"I wasn't criticising," he said quickly, and with a side-step, he put another metre between us.

God, he really was like a scared rabbit, or like a puppy that'd been kicked.

He shoved his hands in his pockets. "I actually like it. I meant it when I said it makes you look distinguished."

I smiled at him, wanting to show I wasn't mad or upset with him. "I'll take distinguished. A compliment's a compliment, right?"

He appeared to relax a bit and afforded me a small smile. Then when we got to my house, he was struck again by the size of the lighthouse. "It's just gorgeous," he said, looking up at it.

"It is." Then I had a thought. "Did you want to go up to the gallery to use your telescope? I bet the view of the stars is even better from up there."

He smiled like he considered it. "Sure. Another night though. I've taken up enough of your time."

"You're not an inconvenience, Aubrey," I said, staring right into his eyes. "But we can do it another night. I don't mind." Then I remembered that I'd driven him here and should drive him home, but I wasn't quite ready to say goodbye just yet. "Have you eaten? I made plenty of pasta. It's just a tomato-based vegetable throw-together. Nothing fancy, but it'll warm you up."

He opened his mouth like he wasn't sure what to say, like he wanted to but didn't want to impose. Or like he was really hungry but wasn't sure about coming inside with me.

"Or I can put some in a bowl and you can take it home," I offered. "I really did make too much."

"Oh, I um..." He looked at my front door and let out a slow breath.

"Or I can just take you home. Whatever you want. I'm all for mundane questions and not making you uncomfortable, remember?"

He gave me a half smile. "I remember. And I guess I could eat."

I hid my smile as I unlocked my door and went in. Normally I'd hold it open for someone, but I didn't want him to feel pressured. I just walked inside and said, "Pull it closed behind you," letting him come in when he was ready.

I took off my coat and hung it up, then peeled off my gloves and beanie. It was nice and warm inside, but the fire was getting low, so I opened the fire door and threw on a small log. Tabby gave me a cranky glare because I dared wake her, so I gave her an apologetic scratch behind the ear. She went right back to snoozing, and I considered myself dismissed. I waved her off. "No, please, don't get up."

Aubrey was now inside the doorway smiling at me. "Talk to your cat often?"

"All the time."

He closed the door and took off his coat and gloves, then pulled off his beanie. His hair stood up at all ends, and I imagined mine looked the same. I ran a hand through mine and went into the kitchen. "Um, thanks for the beanie," he said. "And the gloves. And for lunch yesterday, and for showing me the penguins, and now for dinner, I guess."

I gave him a smile. "It's no problem." I opened the fridge. "I have bottled water, beer, tea, coffee...?"

"Oh, um, water is fine. Tap water is fine."

I grabbed two bottles of water and held one out to him. It was only three long strides for him to take it, but it was as though he needed to make himself walk closer to me. He took the bottle and quickly took a step back. "Thanks."

God, he was honestly scared, and I couldn't even imagine what it took for him to even say yes to coming inside with me.

"You're welcome." I took a drink of my water while I grabbed some plates and got dinner sorted, then said, "Take a seat anywhere."

He surprised me by sitting at the table. I would have assumed he'd take a sofa, given his need for distance, but maybe because he was going to eat? I didn't know. He was a conundrum, that was for sure.

"So, if you're wondering why I'm helping you out—"

"I don't do that," he interrupted quickly, frowning. He shot up from his seat. "I mean, yes, I'm gay. But I don't put out for favours or money. I'm not a hooker."

I blinked, plate of pasta in hand, stunned. A hooker? Did he think I thought he was a hooker? That thought hadn't even crossed my mind. "What?"

He froze, then took another step backwards. I wasn't sure which of us was more horrified.

"I should go."

CHAPTER FIVE

AUBREY

MY HEART FELT TOO heavy for how fast it was beating. I didn't want to leave. Patrick was the first person I'd spoken to in what felt like forever, and I thought he was kind and genuine. He'd taken me to see the penguins and waited patiently while I looked at the stars. And for a moment on that ledge beside him, when he didn't know I was looking at him, he'd looked sad like he carried the weight of the world on his shoulders.

Like he knew how much it hurt.

And I thought for one stupid moment that he could be a friend. But then when I said out loud everything he'd done for me, like a list of favours, I realised then he might expect something in return.

I knew from the second I said I wasn't a hooker that I'd misread everything. Because the look on his face was shock, horror. Appalled.

I'd offended him by assuming he wanted that. That he would use me, *for that*.

And I'd just outed myself as gay to him.

Maybe that's why he was so appalled.

"Don't go," he said, and the look of hurt on his face stopped me. He slowly put the plate on the table. "I don't want that from you," he whispered. He swallowed hard and his eyes were glassy. "I would never ask that of you."

I stood in the middle of his living room, not sure what to do. I felt like I should leave, but his pained whisper stopped me. "Sorry."

"Jesus. Please don't apologise." He pulled the other seat at the table out. "Please sit down and eat. There are no strings attached, Aubrey. I was just going to say I was being nice to you because I know what it's like to be new in this town. Most everyone was born and raised here, except me. And now you." Then he went back to the stove and dished up another plate of hot pasta, and man it smelled so good. He took a block of cheese from the fridge. Not just any cheese, but real Parmesan cheese. "If you want me to take you home, I will. But please take some food."

"Is that Italian Parmesan?"

His lips twitched in an almost smile. "Of course." He turned to the drawer and took out some cutlery, then sat at the table. He put a fork and spoon next to my plate. "For what it's worth, Aubrey, I'm gay too. You shared that about yourself with me, so it's only fair I'm honest with you about that as well."

I took a slow step forward, then another, and sat down slowly, feeling foolish and guilty. So he wasn't horrified at my announcement. Well, not at the gay part, anyway. Patrick grated some cheese onto a small plate, and I had to say something... I had to clear the air. He'd been nice to me out of the kindness of his heart, it was the least I could do.

"I spent some time in Melbourne," I said, deliberately choosing what not to say. "I was staying at a hostel-type thing, and the owner said I could stay if I helped out fixing stuff. I just didn't realise he expected certain favours in return. And I spent some nights on the streets after that, and guys would offer me money for... It was kind of expected, you know? That I was so desperate I'd do anything for some cash. But I didn't. I mean, I don't begrudge anyone for decisions they make in desperate times. You gotta do what you gotta do, right? But I didn't do that, no matter how much they insisted..."

Patrick frowned and set his fork down. "I'm sorry they did that. I'm sorry you went through that."

"Me too." I sighed. "But it wasn't all bad. Some people were good. I got some odd jobs and people were kind."

"But you didn't stay in Melbourne long?"

"No. Big cities aren't for me."

I was certain there were a thousand questions he could have asked me after I'd just dumped that info on him, but he simply slid the plate of cheese toward me and said, "Me either."

The mood between us relaxed, and I took a deep breath and tried for more pleasant conversation. "Hadley seems like a nice place," I said as I sprinkled some cheese onto my pasta which, from the looks of it, was full of zucchini, eggplant, and tomatoes, and a whole bunch of spices. "Though I imagine the gay scene isn't really happening."

Patrick snorted and swallowed his mouthful of food. "Ah, no."

I took a spoonful of pasta. "Oh my God, this is good," I said with my mouth full. So I swallowed it down and tried again, this time with manners. "Sorry. This is really good. You made this from scratch?"

Patrick smiled warmly. "I did."

"Well, it's very good." I couldn't even be embarrassed. I was too hungry, and this food was just too damn good.

"I'm glad you like it." He stared right back at me, and after a while, he waved his fork at my plate. "Did you want to keep eating?"

Oh right. I was stuck staring at him. I tucked in and demolished the whole plate. I tried not to eat too fast so he wouldn't look at me like I was starving.

"Would you like seconds?" he asked, pushing his plate away.

"No, thanks." I patted my belly. "Carbs. Whooo." I let out a breath. "I'm full."

He smiled in a warm way that made his eyes shine. "Well, I'm glad I made extra."

I stood up and took both plates. "Let me clean up."

Patrick joined me at the sink, but not too close. "You don't have to do that."

"It's only fair." I filled the sink with hot water and found the detergent under the sink. Patrick picked up a tea towel, and we had it done in a matter of minutes. I realised, standing side by side with him, that he smelled nice, but most importantly, that even though he was way bigger than me, I felt totally at ease with him. He gave off a feeling of comfort and warmth that had nothing to do with the knitted sweater he was wearing.

"Thanks," he said when we were done.

I leaned my butt against the counter and gave him a smile. "Thank you. For everything."

"Any time." He folded the tea towel neatly and put it beside him. And before he could say anything else, Tabby walked into the kitchen, stood in front of us, and stretched. Then she glared at Patrick and meowed loudly at him.

"Oh, stop whingeing. You have plenty of food," Patrick said to her. He rolled his eyes and scooped her up, cradling her like a baby in his arms. Yeah, she wasn't spoiled at all.

She looked over at me with a smug satisfaction on her face, which said *His attention will be on me, not you.*

I couldn't help but smile and give her a pat, letting her nudge my hand. "She has you well trained."

Patrick chuckled. "I know, I'm a sucker. But she's good company."

Having my hand on Tabby, brushing ever so slightly against his chest, felt strangely intimate. Especially in the quiet of his house and how close I was standing to him. I reluctantly pulled my hand away and stepped back. I missed the closeness immediately but thrilled at the way my heart thrummed in a good way. I hadn't felt that in a long, long time.

"I should probably go," I murmured.

Patrick stared right into my eyes and it made my blood sing. "If you want."

I didn't want to, but staying any longer was too risky. Making myself break eye contact, I walked over to where I'd thrown my bag and coat on the sofa and picked them up. "I can walk. It's no problem."

He picked up his keys. "Please let me drive you. I picked you up, so it's only right I take you home."

Like a date.

It would have seriously taken me all of ten or fifteen minutes to walk, but I liked Patrick. I felt safe with him, and he was offering. "Okay."

His smile was immediate, so he gently put Tabby on the single sofa and walked over to grab his coat. It was kind of close, but I thought he could tell I didn't like people crowding me, so he gave me as much room as he could. I liked that he could read me, and I liked that he wanted me to be comfortable. Anton never gave a shit about what I wanted...

I shook any thoughts of *him* out of my head and pulled on my new beanie but kept hold of the gloves. I collected my bag, and when I looked up at Patrick, he gave me a smile. "You ready?"

With no more than a nod, he opened the door, and a bitterly cold wind met us outside.

"Is your van warm enough?" he asked as we walked to the car.

"Yeah, it's fine." It really kind of wasn't, but the small heater and blankets kept me warm enough at night. But I wasn't telling him that. It was my problem, not Patrick's. And anyway, I'd stayed in worse. I spent some cold nights on the streets, so by comparison, the van was a palace. I got into the passenger seat, grateful to be out of the wind, and buckled up. "I mean, it's not huge and it's probably older than me, but it's clean and dry."

Patrick put on his seatbelt and started the car. He turned up the heat and gave me a smile as he reversed out. He had to put his hand on the back of my seat so he could look over his shoulder, and it made my belly tighten. He was almost touching me...

The truly frightening part was, I wanted him to. It had been so long since I'd been touched or even held a conversation with someone. Maybe that's what it was; my loneliness was making me desperate.

I hadn't wanted anyone to even look at me in what felt like forever, let alone touch me. But something inside me wanted to lean against Patrick's chest and have him hold me. I bet those big strong arms felt like heaven...

"Aubrey?"

I shot him a look. "Yes? Sorry." Then I realised we were already at the caravan park. "Oh." I'm sure the disappointment in my tone didn't go unnoticed.

He smirked a little, so yeah, he noticed. "I asked if you wanted to see the fur seals one day? They come in a little south of here, so we'll need to drive."

"Oh, sure. I'd really like that."

He let out a slow breath and it was then I noticed he was wringing his hands like he was nervous. "Okay, then we'll work out a day."

I nodded. No pressure. He was really good at not making me feel pressured. "Sounds good. I have to start on fixing the amenities block tomorrow, and I'm thinking it'll take me a few days."

"I'm sure Frank won't mind if you take an afternoon off. Not much happens real fast around here, so he probably won't even notice." He looked out his window, so I couldn't see his face. "And if you drag it out a day or two longer, then you'll stay longer, right?"

Did he want me to stay longer? It sure sounded like it.

"I'd like to stay here," I admitted. I wanted to find a place I could stay forever. I wanted to feel a sense of normalcy and stop looking over my shoulder. I hoped one day that would be a reality for me, even though I knew deep down it wouldn't be. I'd chosen this life. At the end of the day, it had been my decision to run. "You probably think I'm crazy for saying that."

He turned to face me, and his smile was more genuine now. "This little town isn't so bad. It's far enough removed from the rest of the world to make it perfect."

"It's kinda why I chose it," I said, then realised I probably shouldn't have.

He took that little sliver of information, and again, with a perfect opportunity to ask more questions, he didn't. "Are there any days of the month that are better for star gazing? Like moon phases or something?"

It took me a second to change gears. "Uh, yeah. A new moon is best for looking at the stars."

"So, no moon at all." Patrick considered that for a second, then made a face. "Makes sense, I think."

I chuckled. "But truthfully, any time is okay. Just some are a little better than others."

"There'll be a new moon next week," he said.

"And you know this off the top of your head?"

"Tide charts."

"Oh, of course." I rolled my eyes at myself. "I should have known."

"So, how about I check the weather forecasts, and if we're lucky enough to have some clear nights after the new moon, I can take you up to the gallery."

"The gallery?"

"The top of the lighthouse."

"Oh." I was sure I blushed. "Of course."

Patrick laughed, and I noticed with the lack of light, a dimple shadowed his beard when he smiled like that. "I don't expect you to know the terminology."

"You can teach me," I said. "When you take me up there next week."

He smiled again and gave a nod. "Okay. I'll make us a picnic dinner and we can eat up there. You can look at the stars for as long as you want."

"That sounds... incredible. Thank you." I put my hand on the door handle to get out but stopped. I wasn't sure what the etiquette was; he'd given me dinner and driven me home, so did I kiss his cheek? I didn't want to lean across the centre console, which was awkward anyway, only for him to push me away or something as equally horrifying. So I settled for saying, "Thanks again, for dinner and the beanie.

And I'm looking forward to seeing the seals. And the lighthouse."

"Me too," he replied, but then he looked kind of sad, so I was very glad I hadn't tried to kiss him.

"I'll see you soon." I didn't wait for a reply. I just opened the door and dashed out into the blustery wind and ran to my van. I unlocked the door and quickly climbed the steps and pulled the door shut behind me, my heart pounding.

The smell was a familiar, dank odour of old bedding and dust. It was clean, though; I'd cleaned it myself as soon as I'd walked into it. It was dry, that wasn't a lie, but the wind hammered the outside, and cold crept in through the thin walls and windows. I cranked up the heater and took off my coat, hanging it in the small and only wardrobe. I put my gloves on the small table but kept the beanie on my head. I was already warmer because of it.

Because of Patrick.

Oh man, tonight had been interesting. I'd been nervous before going, but he soon put me at ease. He was a nice guy, very generous and kind, and he was as ruggedly handsome as the coast he called home. And he was gay.

After I'd outed myself and disastrously announced that I didn't have sex for favours, he wasn't offended or even questioning. His only concern was for me. He didn't push, he didn't pressure me.

But there was an underlying sadness in Patrick's eyes, and even though I wanted to know what his story was, I wouldn't push him either.

I waited until the heater had the van at a bearable temperature, undressed, and slipped into bed. The mattress was hard and I had to sleep diagonally to fit on the bed at all, but it sure as hell beat some of the places I'd slept.

Sleep eluded me for a while. The wind howled outside,

and my thoughts drifted back to Patrick. I imagined him in his warm little house; I bet his bed was big and soft and comfortable, and I bet he was snuggled in a mass of blankets. I wondered if Tabby the cat slept at his feet, and I wondered if he slept in pyjamas or if he slept naked. And for the life of me, I couldn't decide which would be sexier.

The fact I was even thinking of these things should have raised alarm bells in my head. It should have had me running as fast as I could in the opposite direction. But the only thing that sounded in my mind was his warm chuckle and his kind eyes when he smiled. And the only place I wanted to run to, was his place.

I imagined I was in bed with him. I imagined his warmth, his strong arms around me. The hair on his chest would be warm and would tickle my nose as I lay my head in the crook of his arm. But he'd wrap me up tight and rub my back, and he'd be gentle. He'd touch me like he was afraid I would break, and he'd never, ever, raise his hand in anger.

I fell asleep warmed by those thoughts alone.

———

I SPENT MUCH of the next two days fixing the amenities block. Which was mostly cleaning, removing broken tiles, and putting new tiles in their place, and I even fixed a broken tap. I removed some dodgy latticework and replaced it with some wood panelling in some kind of attempt to bring the place into the twenty-first century.

If I could tell anyone from my old life what I was now capable of doing, they'd laugh. The old me, Ethan Hosking, could barely replace a light bulb without incident. Now I could use cordless drills and saws, do basic plumbing and carpentry. It was incredible what I was actually capable of when I had no other choice.

I'd started on the garden bed that ran alongside the back of Frank's residence when I heard a deep rumble of laughter. I turned to find Patrick talking to Frank, and Patrick clearly found something funny. I sat back on my haunches and took a minute to stretch my spine, feeling every crick as I straightened.

Patrick noticed me and gave me a smile. Frank pointed his arthritic finger at the garden bed. "What's wrong with my weeds?" he asked, a smile at his lips. "Took me years to get that soil as hard as rock, and just when I finally get them plants to learn to live without being looked after, you're gonna rip 'em out."

Those plants were nothing but weeds, grass, and thistles. "I've heard of native gardens, but this is taking it a step too far."

Frank smirked and shuffled off, leaving Patrick smiling at me. "Hey."

I tried not to smile too hard in return. "Hey to you too."

"Been busy, I can see," he said, looking toward the amenities block and the newly oiled wood panels that formed a walkway into the men's side of the building. "Looks good."

I dusted off my hands. "Thanks."

"So, you're good with your hands," he said. The innuendo twinkled in his eyes.

I played along. "Amongst other things."

He grinned and looked away. He was particularly handsome today; he wore navy work pants and a dark grey woollen sweater that matched the flecks of grey in his beard. There was no beanie, so the wind played with his short hair, but the blue sky highlighted his eyes. "Apparently the seals have all come in. The sea's a bit rough today."

"Well, if the wind is anything to go by," I said. Then I remembered his invitation. "Oh, should we go today?"

He nodded. "If you're busy here, it's no big deal. The seals come in every day, but apparently they're in good number today."

"No, I'm not too busy." I looked at the garden. "One more day won't make a difference here, believe me."

Patrick walked over and inspected it. "Looks like a lost cause."

"Nah, it'll come good. Just needs some TLC."

He nodded slowly. "Yeah. Like all things, I guess."

I met his gaze. I was pretty sure he was talking about me. Or maybe about himself. "Yeah. I guess."

"So? Shall we go see the seals today? Or another day?"

"Today. But I'm not ready."

He shrugged. "That's okay. I'll wait. Or I can come back in an hour or whatever..."

God, he said that like it was no big deal.

Patrick's not Anton.

"Gimme one sec to get cleaned up." I dashed into the amenities block, washed my hands and as far up my arms as my sleeves allowed. Then I scrubbed my face and neck, washing away dirt and sweat. It was two o'clock; I'd done a full day's work already, only stopping for a quick sandwich and an apple. So when I ducked into my van, I changed my shirt, reapplied some deodorant, downed a glass of water, pulled on my sweater, grabbed my beanie, gloves, and coat, and pulled the door closed behind me.

Patrick was leaning against his car, waiting, and he smiled when he saw me. "Ready?"

"Yeah. Sorry for keeping you."

"It was no problem. You took all of two minutes." He got in behind the wheel and I was glad to get out of the cold when I climbed in beside him.

He didn't even care that I'd made him wait. *So very different from Anton.*

"My God, that wind is brutal today," I said.

Patrick immediately adjusted the heating vent so it faced me, then turned it on high. "Are you warm enough?"

I didn't mean for him to worry, but I kind of liked that he did. "Yeah, thanks."

He turned the car at the ocean intersection, heading left, and followed the coastline south. Just as Patrick had said, the ocean was a choppy, murky grey with whitecaps; it looked cold, rough, and dangerous. No wonder the seals weren't in it. "Jeez. It's not so pretty out there right now."

Patrick laughed. "Yeah, she's got a bee in her bonnet today."

That made me smile. "Do boats go out in that? You mentioned Cassy's dad was a fisherman."

Patrick's jaw bulged and his eyes tightened. "Yeah. Not from Hadley. The rocky cliffs make it impossible. Fishing boats leave north of here, closer to Stokes Bay. Or further south, toward Vivonne Bay. But yeah, they go out most days. Though it has to be worse than this to stop them."

Now, I learned a lot from living with Anton for four years. Physical reactions always said more than words. I learned that Anton could tell me he loved me, tell me he was sorry, tell me he'd never hurt me again, but the coldness of his eyes or the set of his mouth told me otherwise.

Patrick could talk about stormy oceans and fishing boats all day long, but it pained him to do it. There was a rip in his waters, an undertow that belied the calm surface.

And, through all those years of living like that, I was an

expert in changing topics to avoid confrontation or conver-
sations I wasn't ready for. "So, these seals... what kind
are they?"

Patrick let out a relieved breath, as much as he tried
to hide it. Then he launched into a description of fur
seals and sea lions, explaining migration and breeding
habits and feeding patterns. "Most tourists will be
heading to Seal Bay because access is better," he said. "So
we'll cut in north of them and get more of a private
viewing."

He turned on to some goat track of a road and followed
it for a few minutes before pulling up at a dead end. "This is
the access the park rangers or conservation students use," he
explained. Then he grinned at me. "You ready?"

I nodded, and we got out. Ready to see the seals, yes.
Ready for the biting wind, not so much. "Holy hell," I
mumbled, pulling on my gloves and beanie.

Patrick was doing the same. "Yeah, it's a bit like that."
He pointed to a sandy path that weaved through the low
shrubs. "This way."

I followed him through a carpet of hardy greenery, no
higher than our knees. Actually, there weren't any trees at
all on much of the southwest coast. And from the strength
and temperature of the wind, I wasn't surprised. It seemed
everything in this corner of the island, plants, animals,
people, hunkered down to protect itself.

But soon the sound of crashing waves broke through the
howling wind, and when we reached the edge of the land-
line, Patrick started to climb down onto the rocks that met a
small pocket of sandy beach with large flat boulders, worn
down by the ocean and time. He found one boulder large
enough for the both of us and sat, smiling at me to do the
same. It was slightly protected from the wind, but not much,

though it didn't really matter—because in front of us was a herd of fur seals.

"Wow," I said, sitting down beside him. Our shoulders touched, but he didn't seem to mind.

The small beach and surrounding rocks were splattered with fur-covered lumps. Some had their heads up, trying to catch some semblance of sunshine, but most were just plonked any which way. "It looks like the tide left behind a mess of furry blobs."

Patrick chuckled. "It does. They have no appreciation for neatness."

One more seal came out of the churning ocean, walked on its flippers up to some random spot, and collapsed.

"Is it all right?" I asked. But before Patrick could answer, the seal rolled over, waved its flipper, and barked.

"Oh."

Patrick laughed.

Then another one barked, then further up, one must have got too close to another because there was a noisy scuffle and the offender backed off. Then one on a closer rock sat up and made a loud howling bark noise, another flapped its flippers.

I breathed in deep. "What's that smell?"

Patrick laughed again. "They stink, yeah?"

It was a strong fishy, ocean smell that wasn't exactly pleasant. I nodded. "And they're louder than I imagined."

Patrick sat back and happily watched the performance in front of us, and for a long while, I watched him.

It was as though he was the personification of this coast, this ocean. He was browns, blues, and greys, just like the scenery behind him, with a spark of life in his eyes but a sadness too. A little worn, rugged, weathered, but beautiful all the same.

I had to make myself look at the seals. And I had to remind myself to breathe.

"Look," he said excitedly, pointing. "A pup."

He pulled his carryall around and took out a digital camera and a notepad. He snapped a dozen different shots and tucked his camera away again, then flipped open the notepad. "I'll just take some data down," he said. "And I send it to the seal conservation people in Kingscote."

"Like the penguin people in Penneshaw?"

He grinned at me. "You remembered."

"Of course I did. I love that you do that."

Patrick shrugged. "Whether the information is helpful or not, I really don't know. But I figure it can't hurt." Then he said, "If I'm going to sit and stare at the ocean for so long, I may as well do something useful."

I was quiet while he jotted down numbers and whatever other things he noted, thinking about what he said.

If I'm going to sit and stare at the ocean for so long...

He'd mentioned before about watching the ocean and studying it. I'd never really paid that much attention to it before. Sure, I loved the beach as much as the next person. Sun, sand, and surf were always fun, and I loved going to the beach for holidays as a little kid. But I'd never loved it. I'd never longed for it or wanted to know its secrets. Not like the stars. No, I rarely studied the ocean because I was always looking up.

I knew that most people just saw dark skies when they looked up at night, they didn't appreciate the stars, the galaxies, the infinite vastness of space. The endless possibilities, the significance and insignificance of life. Most people just saw a few stars and the moon and didn't care. Much like how I viewed the ocean.

So instead of watching the seals, I cast my eye out to sea for a bit, trying to see what he saw.

Did he see mystery and power? Did he see strength, or was it frightening and limitless?

"Are the seals boring you?" Patrick's voice startled me, and when I looked at him, I saw he was smiling.

"Oh no, not at all. They're incredible actually. It's hard to reconcile them with being wild animals."

"Cute, adorable, fairy penguin killers," he said. My mouth fell open and Patrick laughed. "It's true!"

I looked out over the herd of seals, then back to Patrick. He nodded, and I frowned at the seals again. At all of those cute, adorable fairy penguin killers. "I'll never look at them the same way again."

Patrick chuckled and nudged my shoulder with his. He was quiet for a while, then he said, "Are you okay? You were lost in your thoughts there for a bit."

"Yeah, I'm fine," I answered reflexively. "I was just thinking..."

He bit his bottom lip as if wrestling with pushing for more. "About?"

I think he was expecting some secret from my past because my answer seemed to surprise him. "About you, actually."

His gaze shot to mine. "Me?"

I swallowed hard, suddenly nervous. "What do you see when you look out there?" I asked, nodding toward the ocean behind him. "I was trying to understand what someone who studies the ocean sees. I mean, I know what I see when I look at the night sky. I just wondered if it was the same."

He turned and stared at the ocean for a long while. So long, in fact, I wondered if he would answer me. He spoke to the wind. "I see something that's beautiful and ancient. That's unforgiving and unyielding."

Those were strong words, as I imagined the emotion behind them was too. "Unyielding? How so? When it bends and breaks."

He looked at me then, smiled, and shook his head. "It's not the ocean that bends and breaks. You think those rocks down there are unmovable and a solid force because the water crashes around them, but it's the opposite. The ocean shapes them and breaks them down. It moves them, not the other way around. The ocean is a constant force of energy. It yields for nothing."

He spoke of it with such intimacy, with such raw honesty it scared me. It scared me so much, I took hold of his gloved hand and squeezed it. He held onto mine just as tight, and neither one of us spoke.

I was sorry I'd asked, yet so glad I did.

It was like with every question I asked, with every answer he gave, I just unearthed more questions. I wanted to know more but was terrified of finding out, terrified of getting close to him, to anyone. It wasn't fair that I wanted to know everything about him when I couldn't tell him the truth about me.

I dreaded him asking me questions I couldn't answer, and maybe he somehow knew because he didn't ask. We just sat there, holding hands, watching the seals until the sun began to set and the temperature plummeted and the wind soared.

A violent shiver ran through me and Patrick rubbed my hand in both of his. "You ready to go?" I nodded. "Come on then, let's get you home."

And even though our hands were both gloved, the second he let go, I missed the contact. I got to my feet and couldn't stop shivering; the chill had seeped into my bones. I wrapped my arms around myself. "God, it's cold."

Patrick looked horrified. "I'm sorry. I should've realised."

"'S not your fault," I said, my teeth chattering. "Should've realised what?"

"That it'd be colder than you're used to. Come on, let's hurry." He stepped up to the top of the rock and turned around to offer me his hand.

I took it and smiled. "I see the tables have turned. I helped you at the penguin watch, now you're helping me."

"Without the old man comment too."

I laughed and he pulled me up easily, and when he let go of my hand, there were barely two inches between us. I met his gaze, so close I could have kissed him, and I saw the blue fire of want in his eyes. But he blinked it away quickly and took a step back. "Uh, right. The car... this way," he mumbled, again leading the way.

The walk back to the car seemed to take longer, or maybe it was the failing daylight that made us tread carefully, slower. Or maybe I was dreading being alone with him in an enclosed space.

Maybe I was looking forward to it.

We climbed into the car and I noticed the silence first. Then how my skin burned from where the freezing wind had been. Then how my whole body was shaking. Patrick turned on the engine and cranked up the heat, pointing the vents at me. "Please don't take this the wrong way, but I'd really rather you came back to my place."

I rubbed my hands along my thighs. "Why?"

"Because I'd imagine it's warmer than yours."

"My place ain't so bad. I mean, it's not the Taj Mahal, but it does me just fine."

"I have endless hot water and I made enough soup to last a week. You'll need a shower to warm up. You're chilled to the bone."

I tried to reply but my teeth chattered, and apparently that was enough answer for him. He put the car into gear and drove me to his house. I was warmer by the time we got there. The car heater was pretty thorough, but the idea of a steaming hot shower and warm soup was too good to pass up.

Patrick drove up to his place, grabbed his bag, and got out. He opened the front door and waited for me to walk in first. He was right; his house was warm. Not the kind where a heater took the chill out of the air, but warmed right through, like heat seeped into the walls and everything in it.

Patrick knelt in front of the fire and threw on another log. Tabby, who was curled into a ball in front of it, meowed in thanks. He gave her a quick pat, then stood up. "Shower's this way." He went down a small hall and stood at the open door. "Clean towels are in there. Have the water as hot as you can stand it for as long as you want. It's a natural gas unit so it won't ever run out."

He pulled the door closed, leaving me alone in his bathroom with my blood pounding in my ears. Maybe I was colder than I realised. I pulled off my gloves and coat, then stripped right down and turned the shower taps on.

The water felt like pins and needles at first, scalding hot or freezing cold, I couldn't quite tell. But soon enough, I relaxed as I heated up from the inside out. I could have stayed in there forever. It'd had been so long since I'd had the luxury of unlimited hot water and time, but then I remembered that I was at Patrick's house. Naked, in his shower. I quickly scrubbed myself with soap and rinsed off, dried as quick as I could, and redressed in my clothes.

I came back out holding my socks, gloves, coat, and beanie. Patrick was in the kitchen, his back to me. "Thanks for the shower."

He looked at me, at my unbrushed hair and bare feet, then met my eyes. "Feel better?"

I nodded. "Didn't realise I was so cold."

He smiled, probably pleased that he was right. "Soup won't be long. I'm just reheating some bread. Sound okay?"

My God, it sounded like heaven. "Sounds perfect."

I sat on the sofa and pulled on my socks, grateful I'd worn a pair without holes. And just when I'd pulled on the second one and was about to stand up, Tabby jumped up onto my lap. She meowed loudly at me, yelling at me for reasons only she knew of. I patted her head and gave her a scratch behind her ear, and she leaned into me, nudging my hand and purring, then she turned herself in a circle and plonked herself down for a nap.

When I looked up, Patrick was standing in the kitchen with a plate in his hand, staring at her like he couldn't believe his eyes, but not really in a good way. Like his cat sidling up to me wasn't a good thing. "She just jumped up on me," I said quickly. "I didn't pick her up or anything."

He swallowed hard. "No, that's fine. It's just not like her. She doesn't like people, generally." Then he frowned. "Well..."

I scratched under her ear again, which became a scratch under the chin. "Well, she seems to think I'm okay."

Patrick nodded and put the plate on the table. "Yeah, she does." He went back to the counter and collected two bowls and put them on the table. "Um, dinner's ready."

"Sorry, Tabby," I said, gently picking the cat up. "But I got a better offer." She gave me a death-glare as I put her on the sofa and took my seat at the table. Patrick had put out two bowls of minestrone-style soup and what looked like home-baked bread. "Do you make your own bread?"

Patrick sat down quietly opposite me. "Only when I make soup."

"Well, this looks incredible." It really did. Being cold and hungry, it didn't get any better than homemade soup and bread. I tasted a small spoonful of the soup. "Okay, wow."

He finally smiled and relaxed. "Thanks."

"You're a really good cook."

"Just for the homely stuff. I'm not much good at that fancy kind of cooking."

"This," I gestured to the food he'd put on the table, "is better than any of that fine dining crap I've ever had."

He had some soup and a mouthful of bread and pretended like it was no big deal when he asked, "Eat a lot of fine dining food?"

Oh crap. "Uh, yeah. A lifetime ago."

He nodded thoughtfully and tucked that little sliver of information away before he changed the subject. "So, about old Frank's garden, need a hand with it tomorrow? I have a mattock you could borrow. That soil's going to be like concrete."

"Nah, the soil's okay, but I could use a hand lifting one of the old washing machines. It's one of those real old types, and it weighs a tonne."

"Sure thing. After lunch okay?"

"Perfect. I don't know what's wrong with it. He just said it hasn't worked in years."

"Like most things there, I suppose." He smiled. "Frank's a funny old guy."

"He is. I think he pretends to be cranky so people leave him alone, but he's not really." I bit into the homemade bread and proceeded to moan like a bad porno. "Oh my God, this is so good."

Patrick stared at me with darkened eyes before he looked at his bowl and shifted in his seat. "It's been a long time since I've cooked for anyone."

I tucked that little bit of information away, tit for tat. I could have asked why or how long, but we had some kind of agreement not to push for information. "Well, they don't know what they're missing out on," I said, instead. Then, for reasons I'll never know, I followed up with, "Because this is better than sex."

His gaze shot to mine, heated and all too brief. He swallowed thickly, and his tongue swept across his bottom lip. "I don't think it's quite that good."

I took another spoonful of soup, surprised my hand didn't shake. "Well, it's been a long time in that regard too."

His voice was husky and barely above a whisper. "Or maybe you just weren't doing it right."

And like a bolt of lightning that earths too close to home, memories of Anton doing unwanted things to me flashed through my mind. My stomach squeezed and I swallowed down the urge to vomit. Hoping Patrick couldn't see the change in me, I picked up the bread. "So maybe my memory's a little fuzzy, but this bread is delicious."

He put his spoon down and frowned, and I knew that whatever emotions flittered across my face didn't go unnoticed. "You don't have to tell me anything, but I assume whatever happened to you wasn't good."

I put my spoon down as quietly as I could and put my hands in my lap. I couldn't bring myself to speak, so I gave him a small nod of my head. This game of tit for tat had swayed in his favour, I'd given him more information than I'd meant to, and I felt off-kilter because of it. There was something about Patrick that made me want to tell him everything. I wanted to crawl into his lap where he'd keep me safe, he'd rock me back and forth with my head on his chest, and I'd tell him all my secrets, then he'd say magical words that would fix the mess my life had become.

"I don't know what brought you to Hadley or why you chose to come here," he said. "But I have a feeling you've come to the right place." I looked into his eyes then, not sure what to say to that, and found his eyes were glassy. "The knots we get ourselves tied into," he murmured, "seem to unravel here."

"Did it work for you?" I asked.

He stared right back at me like he wasn't sure if he should tell me the truth, if this game of tit for tat was worth the heartache. "Two weeks ago, I would've said no. But now, I'm not so sure."

CHAPTER SIX

PATRICK

WHAT THE HELL was I doing?

Why was I offering him parts of myself that weren't mine to give?

And what the hell was it about this Aubrey Hobbs that upended my comfortably numb life?

I wasn't prepared to feel anything again. I wasn't *supposed* to. When hearts are broken so utterly beyond repair, they're not supposed to beat again, right?

So why did my chest get all tight when I saw him? Why did I want to pull him against me to bear the weight of his troubles? Why did I want to protect him, hold him... kiss him? God, I wanted to kiss him.

And that scared the hell out of me.

I dropped him home, and there was a moment before he opened the door, that will-he, won't-he say something or do something moment. And I didn't know if I was more grateful or disappointed that he did neither. He simply held my gaze for a long moment before thanking me and getting out of the car.

I don't think I breathed until I got home.

I finished cleaning the kitchen, fixed the fire, and found Tabby on the sofa. "Well, you were a surprise," I said to her, giving her a pat. "What are you trying to tell me, huh?"

Of course, she didn't answer. She just purred a little louder and closed her eyes. Maybe that *was* my answer. But I couldn't believe it when she'd jumped up on him. Tabby had been Scott's cat. She'd adored him, followed him everywhere, and had—without one iota of shame or care—made her preference for him over me very well known.

After Scott... well, she wouldn't come near me for the longest time. She only tolerated me because I fed her. She'd sit across the room, or under the table, or in the hall, and look at me as though she blamed me because her Scott was gone.

Well, my Scott was gone too.

I walked over to the photo of him, and my heart squeezed again. This time for a whole slew of other reasons. Loss, grief, and now guilt.

"I don't know what I'm doing," I said to him.

I could almost hear him laugh and say, "You're navigating uncharted waters, Patrick."

I blinked back tears. "I don't know how," I replied.

And the answer was as clear as a bell.

By following the stars.

I gasped back a breath. "Oh God. Aubrey."

Scott's eternally-smiling face smiled now as if I'd finally clued in to what he'd known all along. I could just imagine him shaking his head at me, laughing. *Trust the waters, Patrick. The ocean was mapped out from the stars.*

———

I IGNORED Penny's probe for information when I bought

my morning coffee. She dropped hints like *haven't seen that Aubrey around much* or *wonder what brought him here*. She meant well, she always did. But Aubrey wasn't gossip fodder, his past or his reasons for being here. Not that I could have given her much information if I'd wanted to. I didn't know specifics, but I knew enough.

Whatever brought him to Hadley wasn't good. If I could read him right, I'd guess it was an ex. Ex-boyfriend, ex-friend, ex-partner, ex-family; I didn't know. But someone had hurt him. The mention of bad sex, which I'd meant as a joke, sent a horror show of fear flashing in his eyes. People only reacted like that when they'd been hurt in the most horrible of ways. Someone he'd trusted would explain why he'd found himself at the edge of the country.

"Keeps to himself," Penny said. "Seems friendly enough. He's polite and speaks kinda quiet. He's come in here a few times, just to buy some bread or cups of noodles, tinned spaghetti, that kind of thing."

Well, that explained why he loved my home cooking so much.

"He is a nice guy."

She was just about to hand over my coffee but held it hostage. "Sounds like you got to know him?"

"I took him to see the fairy penguins and the seals," I admitted. "Just to show him around a bit."

Penny put the coffee on the counter next to the newspaper. "Mm-hmm."

"It's not like that," I replied. "Whatever you're imagining right now, you can stop. He's in need of a friend, and I know what it's like to be new here and to have everyone stare and whisper."

"Oh, we were never like that with you."

I raised an eyebrow.

"Okay, well, maybe a little bit. But your circumstances were different."

I sighed. "I dunno, Penny. I kinda get the feeling him and I aren't that different at all."

"Has he told you anything?"

I shook my head, having already said more than I'd wanted to. "No. Not a word. But sometimes you have to listen to the silences. When things aren't said. That's where the truth is."

Penny frowned and nodded sadly. "I guess you're right."

"Anyway, you have a good day," I said, taking my usual score of coffee and newspaper.

"Patrick," Penny said, stopping me before I got to the door. "You said 'it's not like that,' and that's fine. But if it was like that, that'd be okay too."

I swallowed down the lump in my throat, but I still couldn't speak. I wouldn't have known what to reply with anyway. I gave her a half smile and nod and went on my way. I had lawns to mow and my usual maintenance logbook to go through. My job was never demanding or stressful, just a few hours per day to make sure the lamp hardware was functioning, all batteries and backup systems were primed, and all structural mechanisms were in good order.

I'm sure anyone else would have found it boring, but I loved it.

And once I had all my chores done for the day, I fixed myself some lunch and headed around to give Aubrey a hand with that washing machine. I'd never been inside the amenities block, so I was curious what I'd find.

What I did turn up in time to see was Aubrey wearing jeans and a T-shirt, shovelling, lifting, and stretching as he toiled in the garden. When I got out of the car, he let the shovel fall into the soil and lifted the hem of his shirt to wipe his forehead, giving me a very good view of his belly. He was thin but not unhealthy, more lean and sinewy. A happy trail of dark hair ran from his navel to disappear underneath his waistband. I'd wondered if his complexion was from too much time spent outdoors, but he was olive all over.

"Hey," he said by way of introduction, a small smile on his lips.

Did he know I'd just checked him out? Or was that display of skin and body deliberate?

"Hey." Needing a distraction, I nodded toward the garden. "It's looking good."

He groaned and stretched his back. "You weren't wrong about the concrete analogy. I broke it all up and keep coming back to turn it over. Not sure it's good for anything but weeds."

"We can go out to the Whittaker's," I suggested. "They have bags of chicken manure to give away."

"For free?"

"Happy to get rid of it, I think."

He smiled. "Reckon Frank'll like the smell?"

"Probably not, but he'll love the price."

Aubrey chuckled and wiped his forehead with the back of his hand, smearing dirt as he did. It was cute...

What the hell, Patrick? Stop noticing him.

"Where would I find the Whittaker's to get some chook poo?"

"They're like five k's out of town. I can drive you if you want?"

"I don't expect you to keep driving me all around town."

"I don't mind. And I'll get some for my place if that makes you feel better."

He looked as if he wanted to object but settled for a smile. "Deal."

"So, about that washing machine," I said. "Shall we do that first?"

He brightened, like he'd forgotten the reason for my being here. "Yes, this way." He turned quickly and headed toward the far end of the amenities block, and I followed. The laundry room, as it turned out, was quite a decent size. There were two washers, two dryers, and a built-in ironing board and countertop that both appeared to have had recent modifications.

I put my hand on the countertop and tested its ability to hold weight. The countertop itself was the original, but there was new bracing and brackets underneath. "Did you fix these?"

He turned to look at what I was talking about. "Oh, yeah. They were just about to fall off. I'm surprised he hasn't been sued by someone staying here. Everything's a bit of a shambles, to be honest."

I chuckled. "You've seen Frank, right? He's the picture definition of shambles."

He grinned. "True." Then he turned to the washing machines and tapped one in particular. "This is the one that won't go."

"Right, then," I replied. "Let's get it out and see if we can take the back of it off."

He took the far side and I stood opposite him, and together we heaved it out from where it had stood for the last thirty years. God, it was heavy. And the dust and crap behind it was disgusting.

"Have you got a face mask?" I asked. "Frank should give you a face mask."

Aubrey snorted. "You've met him, right?"

Yeah, fair enough. Stupid question. "Well, you don't want to be breathing this shit in."

He waved me off, took a screwdriver out of his pocket, and had a look behind the machine. In just a few minutes, he had the back plate off and pulled out a broken rubber belt. "Well, I'm not a washing machine expert, but I'd reckon this shouldn't look like that."

I chuckled. "Probably not. Frank doesn't have a spare one of those lying around by any chance?"

"His shed is full of stuff. But I'd say if he did, it'd be just as old and perished as that one."

"You can use pantyhose," I suggested. "Temporarily, to see if the motor still runs."

Aubrey stood up and smiled. "Don't think Frank'll have any of those, either."

I laughed at that. "True. I don't think Penny has any at the store, but I know who might."

"Who?"

"Mrs Whittaker. The same lady with the chicken manure. She asks for them to be donated because she uses them in her hen houses and in her veggie garden. Or, I can get you some cheap ones when I go to Stokes Bay next week."

He wiped his hands on his jeans. "Oh, I don't want to be a bother..."

"You're not a bother." I looked around. "And I do odd jobs for the Whittaker's all the time, so she won't mind us calling around."

"Are you sure it's no problem?"

"Sure I'm sure."

He brightened. "Okay then. That'd be great." He grabbed his overshirt from the counter. "I was sweating up a storm earlier, but if I don't rug up a bit, knowing my luck, it'll be sleeting in five minutes and I'll freeze to death."

"The weather here takes some getting used to." He slid the shirt on while we walked to my car, and I was a little disappointed. "But it seems to agree with you."

He looked at me over the roof of my car. "I nearly froze to death the other night watching seals."

Laughing, I got in the car and Aubrey followed suit. "Well, that was my fault. I should have told you to wear warmer clothes."

"What I was wearing is my warmer clothes."

"I meant layers," I added, then realised he probably didn't have any other clothes, considering I'd seen him wear the same ones every time I'd seen him. "Well, next time I'll bring blankets."

"Next time?"

I shrugged, trying to look outwardly calm. "If you want."

He smiled and relief coursed through me. "Sure. You still have to show me the lighthouse, yeah?"

I found myself trying not to grin. "Yes, of course. And you can bring the telescope, and I'll bring the blankets."

I drove us out of the caravan park driveway, and at the ocean intersection, I turned right. "I've never been out this way," Aubrey said, looking out at the ocean. "There's no bee in her bonnet today."

I chuckled. "No. Doesn't mean she's not cranky."

He settled into his seat, a small smile on his face, and watched as we turned away from the water and went inland, where the scenery became green farmland. "I really like it here," he said quietly, and I wondered if he meant to say it out loud.

"I'm glad you do," I replied. "I think this place suits you."

"Mmm, maybe."

I couldn't have been entirely sure, but from his peaceful smile, I think that made him happier than he let on.

We arrived at the Whittaker's and I drove slowly down the driveway, giving old Mrs Whittaker some time to peer out the window and see my car. By the time we'd pulled up and both got out of the car, Mrs Whittaker was walking out, wiping her hands on her apron. She was probably eighty, she'd kind of accrued a stoop in her posture, but her eyes were sharp, and I'd never seen her grey hair in anything but some kind of tidy swirl.

She smiled expectantly at me. "Patrick. To what do I owe the privilege?" She inspected Aubrey. "And who is this young man?"

"This is Aubrey. He's doing some work for Frank, and we were hoping you had some bags of manure for a few gardens. And an odd request for some pantyhose."

Mrs Whittaker looked at my jeaned legs. "Well, I don't know if I have any your size, and you might want to buy some proper silk ones if you don't shave your legs."

Aubrey coughed to cover his laugh.

"Ah, no. They're not for me. They're for Aubrey."

She looked at his legs. "Your size I might have."

Aubrey gave her a winning smile. "Not for me to wear. It's to use as a makeshift fan belt for one of Frank's washing machines. But thank you. If I ever do need any, I'll know who to ask."

She returned a cheeky smile. "Manure is heaped at the back of the coop, but you'll need to bag it yourselves. I'll bring the pantyhose out."

Frank was right about one thing, Aubrey sure was a

worker. He never even hesitated, just picked up the shovel and went straight to work. I held the old feed bags open and he filled them. The muscles in his forearms stretched and bulged, and he was clearly stronger than he looked. His short brown hair was spiky and rough cut, and I wondered if that was the in thing these days or if he hacked into it himself. I wasn't any fashion guru, but I was pretty sure it was the latter. Any which way, it suited him.

He finished shovelling all we needed, then because one of Mrs Whittaker's chicken coop posts had a bit of lean, he righted it and propped it up with a smaller post. No one asked him to, he just saw that it needed doing, so he did it.

I liked that.

It showed character and ethics, that underneath the mystery that was Aubrey Hobbs, he was a good person. He did a good deed not expecting anything in return.

Mrs Whittaker gave us the pantyhose and, as per Hadley's unwritten law, she told us her shed door was sticking and suggested when we had some time, we might come back and have a look at it for her. You know, as good-will for the manure and pantyhose.

As we drove away, Aubrey grinned at me. "So that's what you mean by the bartering system in this town."

I smiled right back at him. "Yep. You don't have to come back out with me. I'll fix her shed door and turn her garden beds over for her, and there'll no doubt be a box of veggies and eggs in it for me."

He was still smiling. "I don't mind. I'd like to help, actually."

I'd like it if he came with me too. "Okay."

And just like that, we had another date.

Date.

When did I start thinking of these as dates? When did my heart think that was okay?

"The boot of your car is gonna stink like chicken shit," he said, distracting me from my sullen thoughts.

"Nah, this isn't too bad. You should smell it in summer."

He scrunched his nose up. "Today was bad enough." Then he laughed. "Frank's gonna love it."

———

BACK AT THE CARAVAN PARK, Aubrey dumped all the bags of manure, except the two for me, and held up the pantyhose. "Well, let's see if your theory works," he said, walking into the laundry.

For him to get to the bottom edge of the machine where the belt ran, he had to kneel at the back and stick both hands into the guts of it. I knelt beside him and held the top of the machine, tilting it a little to give him a better angle while he shoved and pushed and grunted to get it into place. Our sides touched, from knee to hip, as we both knelt, and while he was leaning down so he could look up and under where the new belt was supposed to go, I couldn't help but admire his form. The way he stretched, how his shoulders and arms moved, how strong his thighs were. I didn't mean to. I didn't purposely do this so I could cop an eyeful while he was distracted. But something inside me, something I'd thought asleep forever, had woken up.

Something wonderful and terrifying. Something I wasn't ready for.

And before guilt could drag me under, someone at the door spoke. "There you are."

It was loud and unexpected, and it scared the crap out of me.

But Aubrey's reaction was the kind of fear that made my blood run cold. He almost turned himself inside out. He pushed back and pulled his legs up and threw his hands out, and his face... his face. My God, I'll never forget the look on his face.

And I thought I'd seen fear before.

This wasn't a startled fear. This was a scared-for-my-life kind of fear.

Instinctively, I put myself between him and the person who spoke. Just positioned myself ever so slightly, but it didn't go unnoticed.

Because it was Collin at the door—Sergeant Collin O'Hare—and he didn't miss a thing. "Jesus," I said, trying to play it up a bit. "You scared the life out of us."

Collin was frowning now, trying to look around me to see Aubrey. "Everything okay in here?"

"It was," I said. "Until two seconds ago when you *scared the life out of us*." I looked behind me then and gave Aubrey a smile. "You okay?"

He nodded weakly, and he'd grown pale. I swore I could hear his heart hammering, and then I noticed he'd cut his knuckle. "You're bleeding."

He stared at his hand. "Oh."

I shot Collin a look and got to my feet. "We're trying to fix Frank's washing machine. Is there anything I can do for you?"

He still hadn't taken his eyes off Aubrey. "I just thought I'd check on our newest resident, see how he was settling in."

Aubrey was still kneeling behind the machine, inspecting the cut on his hand.

"He's fine," I answered for him. "He's doing some work

for Frank, and he's been with me out to the Whittaker's place."

Collin met my gaze then. He straightened and puffed his chest out a little, making his police uniform stretch deliberately. I didn't need to be a detective to see he didn't like this development between Aubrey and me.

Aubrey stood then, and I took his cut hand. Blood dripped down his fingers. "Need me to look at that?"

He spoke quietly and wouldn't look at me. "It's not too bad. I banged it when I was startled. I'm fine."

Jesus. He really wasn't fine at all.

"We better get this cleaned up and disinfected," I said, more to Collin than to Aubrey. "The back of that machine is covered in twenty years of dust and God knows what." I let go of his hand then and pretended not to notice how it shook. I shot Collin a look. "Right then, if you need anything else...?"

Collin shook his head slowly, looking between us warily. "No, it's all good. Sorry for startling you."

I led Aubrey to his van and opened the door for him. I waited for him to go inside, then I followed, and when I looked back, Collin was watching us. I met his gaze as I pulled the door closed behind me.

I wasn't quite prepared for the inside of the van. It was old and very brown. Brown veneer cabinets, brown cushions, brown lino, brown carpet, telling me it dated back to the early eighties at least. A small bed up one end, a small stove and sink, a tiny cupboard, one drawer, and a fridge I doubted still worked, and a built-in table and surround seat that doubled as a second small bed. It was tidy though, and Aubrey obviously kept it clean, but it had that inescapable dank odour that old vans had.

Aubrey ran his hand under the sink for a second, then

sat on the corner of the seat, as though he was trying to make himself as small as possible.

"Sorry," he whispered quickly. "I didn't mean to react like that."

"Please don't apologise," I murmured. "You've nothing to be sorry for."

"I wasn't expecting anyone to..."

"Me either. He startled me too." I looked around the van. "So, do you have a first aid kit?"

He shook his head.

"Disinfectant?"

"Um." He swallowed hard, then shivered.

"How about a cup of tea?"

He looked at me then with haunted eyes that made my heart squeeze. "I can make it for you."

I put my hand up and he reflexively flinched, like I was about to strike him.

Oh my God.

"I'll get it," I whispered, trying to be as inoffensive as possible. Space was tight and I didn't want to crowd him, so I stepped around him the best I could to stand in front of the sink. There was an old kettle, so I filled it and switched it on and searched for cups and tea bags, trying to get my mind around what I'd just discovered about Aubrey.

That panic in his eyes, that bone-chilling recoil for fear of being hit could only be the result of one thing; he'd lived with abuse of some kind.

I found some mugs and tea bags, ignoring the cheap, no-label brand. There was no sugar, no milk, and in the pantry, the only food I found was some two-minute noodles, half a loaf of bread, and a tin of peaches.

I'd been so curious about his story, wanting to know

what led him to Hadley, and now I wasn't sure I wanted to know.

I did find some paper towel, so I took two squares of it and pumped the old-style kitchen sink like he'd done a few seconds before. So I wasn't bearing over him, I knelt in front of him and took his injured hand and gently dabbed at the cut on his knuckle.

"It's not so bad," he murmured. "Just bled a lot. Sorry."

"It's no problem." He let me hold his hand as I wiped the blood off, and thankfully he'd stopped shaking. The kettle started to whistle, obviously one that needed to be turned off manually. "I'll make you that tea."

I sat our teas on the table and slid in opposite him. The table was small enough that I could lean across and take his hand again. Our teas were too hot to drink straight away, so it gave me more time to clean his hand properly. I didn't want him to think he owed me any kind of explanation, so I was quite happy to sit in silence. I just wanted him to be comfortable; I certainly wasn't going to push him.

But then he said, "I didn't mean to freak out." It was just a whisper and he spoke to our hands, and when I looked at his eyes, he blinked a lot and wouldn't look at me. He let out a slow and unsteady breath. "I left... I couldn't... he used to..." He couldn't even finish his sentence.

"It's okay," I said softly. "You don't need to explain anything."

His eyes became glassy, as though he might cry, but he shook it off, and when he sipped his tea, he made a face. I sipped mine, and yeah, it wasn't great.

"Sorry," he mumbled. "The tea's kinda crap."

"The tea's fine," I lied.

"No, it's crap, and you're a terrible liar."

I smiled, and eventually, finally, he did too. Though

there was that depth of sadness in his eyes that I now recognised for what it was. No matter what he'd gone through, or because of it, I didn't want him to be alone with his demons tonight.

I wanted to take him home and keep him safe, feed him, and make sure he was looked after, but I also wanted him to know that the new life he was trying to build here was okay too.

"So," I started, "how does fish and salad for dinner sound? I can call Cassy to order it, then run across to the takeaway shop and grab it." I looked out the window. The winter sun was low in the sky. "It's getting late, and I don't have anything cooked at home, so I was going to get something anyway."

"You're a terrible liar." He was trying for funny but didn't quite pull it off.

I looked right at him. "I don't want you to be alone right now. But I'll understand if you want me to go."

"I don't want you to go." His eyes brimmed with tears. "I don't know why I trust you, but I do. I haven't trusted anyone in a long time... It's been so hard. Everything has been so hard up until I came here and met you. I'm not making much sense, and I'm sorry. There's so much I can't tell you."

I reached over and covered his hand with mine. He didn't pull away or flinch, so I considered it a win. "Thank you for trusting me. And you don't have to tell me anything. Someone hurt you, I can see that." He nodded and a tear tumbled down his cheek. I squeezed his hand. "Until you're ready to tell me, you don't have to. I don't need to know details. I just want you to know you're okay here."

He wiped his cheek with his sore hand. "It's not that I

don't want to tell you," he mumbled. "Legally, I can't. I won't implicate you."

Implicate? Right, then. So it was complicated. "That's okay, Aubrey. Like I said, I won't ever push you." Now he squeezed my fingers as if my promise meant more than I understood. "So? Fish for dinner sound okay?"

He let out a teary laugh. "You're always feeding me."

"I know it seems that way, sorry." I chuckled. "No pressure; I don't want anything in return. I just want to know you're okay."

He stared at me for a long, quiet moment. "Fish sounds really good."

"I'll order it and run and grab it. Or we can eat it at the shop. What would you prefer?"

Aubrey shrugged. "I'm not really up for people staring at me, so can we just eat it here? If that's okay?"

"Of course it is."

I quickly dialled the takeout store and gave my order to Cassy, telling her I'd be there in twenty minutes to pick it up. When I slid my phone onto the table, Aubrey was chewing on his bottom lip, a worried line at his brow.

"What's wrong?" I asked him.

"The policeman," he replied. That deep sorrow was back in his eyes. "Sergeant O'Hare. Do you reckon he'll be back? Was he just here to check up on me, or do you think it was something else?"

"He said he was just here to see how you were getting on. He's nosy and likes people to think he runs a tidy town. Don't worry about him. I can tell him to mind his own business if you want."

"No," he answered quickly. "Don't poke the beehive. It's fine. I'll just keep my head down and it'll be okay."

I realised then that I was still holding his hand, and I

reluctantly let it go. "Aubrey, to be honest, I don't think he was checking up on you so much. I think he probably saw my car and wondered what I was doing here. If I was seeing Frank or you. He..." I wasn't sure if I should say anything, but I was pretty sure Aubrey needed the truth. "He kind of made his interest in me known, but I turned him down."

Those big brown eyes pierced right through me. "Will it ever be the right time?"

"For him and me? No."

"For anyone else?"

Oh Jesus. "Three weeks ago, I would have said no, not ever." My stomach twisted and my heart just about galloped out of my chest. "But now I'm not so sure."

CHAPTER SEVEN

AUBREY

SOMETHING WAS HAPPENING between me and Patrick. I didn't know what it was exactly, and I didn't know how far I wanted it to go. I trusted him. More than I'd trusted anyone in a long time... since my pop was alive. There was an ocean of warmth in him, of protection and safety, that shone like a lighthouse beacon.

Like *his* lighthouse beacon.

I was excited for him to show me the lighthouse and to sit up on the top walkway with my telescope and watch the stars. But I was more excited to spend time with him. He said there'd be food and blankets and star-watching, and that right there sounded like heaven to me.

There was also the part of me that warned against getting close to anyone, but I pushed it down. I didn't realise just how much I wanted company, even just friendship, until Patrick. He had his own past to contend with, demons that warred in his eyes every time he looked at me.

After dinner last night, he offered to come by and pick me up, but I told him I could walk. It was literally a ten or fifteen-minute walk and it was a clear night; the wind was cold but not unbearable, and given we intended to spend most of the night outside, I told him it'd help me acclimate. He didn't look even mildly convinced, but he'd conceded easily enough.

That was the thing with Patrick. He knew when to push and he knew when not to, when to take care of me and when to give me space.

After my freak out yesterday when Sergeant O'Hare scared me, Patrick didn't run a mile. Just the opposite, in fact. He'd moved in front of me, protecting me. Then he removed me from what was an uncomfortable situation and took me to my van. He had to know I'd feel better there, in my space, where there was no noise, no people. Just him.

And he could have insisted I go to his house, where there was more room and he'd have been more comfortable. But he didn't. He insisted we stay in my van and have dinner there; it took a special kind of person to know when little things like that made all the difference.

I hated that he'd seen my few possessions and the very lack of food and heating, but he didn't seem to mind at all.

When I'd insisted on walking to his place, he'd just shrugged and agreed. He wasn't so overprotective to insist he come get me or to imply I wasn't capable of making my own decisions. He wasn't overbearing, insistent, or controlling.

He wasn't like Anton.

Not one bit.

So, with that reassurance in mind, I pulled on my coat, gloves, and beanie, grabbed my grandad's telescope, and set off for Patrick's house. It wasn't exactly hard to miss; the twenty-five-metre lighthouse was a dead giveaway.

I followed the road around the cove and found myself smiling as his house came into view. It was small, as far as houses went, but it was a warm, earthy home. The sandstone stood against the harsh winds, and the stooping shrubs surrounding it gave it a cottage feel, and there couldn't be a house better designed for Patrick.

I knocked on the door and was met by Patrick with a tea towel in one hand and a smile that made my insides curl in a wonderful way I hadn't felt in years.

"Come in," he said, stepping aside. He was wearing dark jeans and a blue flannelette shirt. "How was the walk over? Not too blustery, I hope."

"No, it was fine." I peeled off my gloves, then my beanie, and found myself smiling at him. I took my coat off and draped it over the edge of the sofa. "It's nice and warm in here though."

"I have to keep the house warm for Her Royal Highness," he said, gesturing to the cat in front of the fire. He walked into the kitchen. "Dinner tonight is sausage casserole and mashed potatoes. That sound okay?"

"Sounds perfect. Smells divine."

He smiled happily and turned back to the sink. "It's five minutes away. Make yourself at home. Can I get you a drink?"

"No, I'm fine, thanks." I was drawn to Tabby who sprawled out when I knelt down beside her. I scratched her belly and was rewarded with a purr, then apparently I was worthy of her to get up so she could nudge me and curl herself around me. I picked her up and stood, and she purred louder. "I thought you said Tabby didn't like anyone."

Patrick stuck his head out, stared, then shrugged. "Well, she clearly likes you."

She settled in my arms and gave Patrick a smug glare,

making me laugh. "She's not snobby at all. She's a great judge of character."

Something on Patrick's face changed then, like I'd said the wrong thing. Or maybe something that struck a chord, but he turned back to the sink without saying a word. I was left standing there, not in an uncomfortable silence, but there was nothing for me to do but look around his living room.

The photos on the mantel drew me in. I'd seen them before but hadn't paid too much attention to the details. There was a family photo with a much younger Patrick and a couple who I assumed were his parents. They looked happy and decidedly normal. The second frame was a candid shot of a blond man who looked maybe early thirties, wearing yellow fisherman waders and a short-sleeve shirt. He was on a boat, holding the rope to what looked like a crab pot. He was looking at the camera, and he was laughing in the sunshine.

He was gorgeous and happy and vibrant.

"Um, dinner," Patrick said. He was holding a plate, and very clearly, my looking at that photo was the reason for the frown on his face. I gently put Tabby back in her spot in front of the fire and took my seat at the table. I wasn't sure what to say, but I certainly wasn't going to upset him any further.

"This looks amazing," I said, looking at our plates. "You're the king of hearty, warm food."

He almost smiled. "I like homecooked meals. And this was my mum's recipe."

"Well, I'm honoured you've asked me to share it with you. Thank you."

And finally a proper smile. "You're welcome." We

began to eat—and it really was amazing—and he asked me how I got on with the garden and the washing machine.

"Garden is thoroughly manured, and the washing machine still doesn't work."

"Oh, that's a shame."

"Yeah, I'll need to pull the motor apart and see if I can find if anything's amiss." Not that I really knew what to look for.

"I can help you if you like?" He sipped his water. "Even just to help lift it or something. It was heavy as hell."

"I'd like that."

I'd really, really like that.

We finished our meals, both of us smiling more genuinely, talking about our days. Patrick had been busy doing his lighthouse checks and maintenance, which was endlessly fascinating to me. I couldn't hide my excitement. "I can't wait to see it."

He grinned. "Wanna go up now?"

I looked at our empty plates and the unwashed oven dish and saucepan. "Shouldn't we clean up first?"

"Absolutely not." Patrick took our plates to the sink but turned around to face me. "We should absolutely climb the lighthouse and look at all the stars. Washing dishes can wait."

His boyish smile and the shine in his eyes made me chuckle. "Then yes, I really do want to go up now."

He disappeared for a few seconds and came back out with two pillows and a folded blanket. "I've really been looking forward to this," he said, putting the bedding on the sofa so he could pull on a coat and beanie. "I don't know much about astronomy, so you'll have to teach me."

I slipped into my coat and fixed my beanie onto my

head, then grabbed my grandad's telescope. "Fingers crossed, the clouds stay away."

"I've been tracking the weather all day. We should have a clear night."

He really was excited, which made me happier than I could remember being in a long time. "And I've been looking forward to hearing all about the lighthouse, given you are its keeper."

"I might disappoint you," he said, opening the door. "It's not that exciting."

"I'll be the judge of that."

He grinned, picked up the pillows and blankets, and we set off for the lighthouse. It was a dark night, given the new moon, but the lighthouse was pretty hard to miss. He stopped at the steps leading up to the door. "Okay, so here she is. Made of sandstone back in 1821, and it took eight men three years to build. The red-and-white spiral paintwork is called Barber's Pole, for obvious reasons and has no other function but visibility, because this area is so prone to fog and very high seas."

"It looks like a barber's pole."

His smile widened. "It does." He unlocked the door and pushed it open, then hit some switch to light up the inside. "The lighting isn't good, so watch your step."

"Isn't that ironic? That the lighthouse has poor lighting."

He snorted. "Internal lighting. There's only two light bulbs; one at ground level, one halfway up. Not including the pretty big light bulb at the top." He grinned at his own joke.

"Is that a lighthouse keeper joke?"

Patrick chuckled. "I don't get to make many. I have to take them when I can."

"What do you mean? It's one of the biggest phallic shaped things in the southern hemisphere. There has to be better jokes than that."

He let his head fall back as he laughed and the sound echoed up the lighthouse. Then he looked up the spiral staircase that snaked its way up to the top. "Well, your leg and arse muscles are in for a workout," he said, then shot me a horrified look when he realised how that sounded.

I blinked.

He shook his head, his eyes wide. "Oh, no, um..."

Then I cracked up laughing, probably more at his expression, but a little to cover the blush on my cheeks. "See? There are so many jokes to be made."

"Sorry," he mumbled before turning back to the stairs. "I meant there's a lot of steps, so you might feel that. A hundred and two steps, to be exact." He stood on the first one. "You ready?"

I nodded and he started to climb, then stopped. "Hold onto the rail. It can get a little dizzying. How are you with heights? I should have asked you that first, sorry."

"I'm all good with heights."

"It's only twenty-five metres," he said, as he started to climb. "That doesn't sound like much, but it's pretty high once you're up there."

I quickly followed, our feet clanking loudly on the metal staircase. It was narrow and steep, and my face wasn't far from Patrick's arse.

"The view is spectacular though," he added.

"The view's pretty good from here too," I said. He stopped and turned to look down at me, gave me a pointed smirk, at which I grinned. He started again and I could see what he meant about the climb. "I see what you mean about getting dizzy."

He stopped again. "Are you okay?" He sounded alarmed. "Just keep hold of the rail and keep your back or shoulder to the outside wall."

I looked up at his face and his genuine concern made me smile. "I'm fine. I was just commenting, that's all."

Just a dozen or so more steps and we reached the top, and Patrick shoved all the bedding under one arm and put his free hand on my shoulder. "You feel okay?"

"Yeah, I'm fine. But yes, it's been a long time since my legs and arse were on an elliptical. How many times do you have to climb this thing?"

"Three times a week, minimum. But I like to check it every day." Then Patrick stood back and waved at the huge light. "What do you want to know?"

"Everything."

He took a deep breath and gestured to all the parts, panels, switches, and boxes. "Well. It's got a 300 mm lantern, 190 mm rotating beacon, which is a high-current Lampchanger, high-current flasher. It flashes every nine seconds and has a ninety-five-metre focal plane. There's an ACMS remote unit, ACMS transfer unit, audiovisual controller, sensor modules and panel, flash controller, engine-generator, environmental control unit, fuel oil Daytank battery charger, 12-volt nickel-cadmium storage battery, 24-volt nickel-cadmium storage battery, 12-volt battery charger, 24-volt sound signal, videograph fog detector, solar charge controller, solar distribution box, multi-array controller..."

I slow blinked and he stopped talking. Then he added, "Sorry, I get carried away. No one ever really asks."

"It's just a lot of information to take in," I amended. "Tech-speaking to a non-tech-speaking person."

He smiled kindly. "It's just a really big light."

I chuckled. "That surprisingly pumps out some heat."

"It does."

"How far does the light shine out to sea?"

He looked seaward. "They can see this up to ninety-five metres."

Oh. I'm pretty sure he just said that in that tech-spiel. "Wow."

Patrick was quiet for a second before facing me again. "We'll go out to the walkway through this door."

I followed him again, to the back of the lantern room out onto the external catwalk. "Do we not go to the front?"

He stopped and dropped the pillows and stared at me. "Did you want to burn your retinas out of your head?"

Oh. "Of course," I said with a laugh. "That was silly, sorry."

"It wasn't silly. Nothing you say is silly." He fixed the pillows, which I realised now were our seats. He sat, pressing his back to the lighthouse, and patted the pillow next to him. "Are you warm enough?"

"I am. Those steps got my blood pumping." I sat down beside him, our shoulders touching. "But I'm thinking that'll wear off soon."

Patrick held up the blanket and threw it over us, then he looked up at the sky. "Is there too much light pollution to see them?"

I undid the telescope case and extended it fully and put it to my eye. A second later, I handed it to him. "Have a look."

He looked through the telescope and panned an arc at the sky. "Wow."

"The lighthouse projects outward, so looking in the opposite direction and upward doesn't affect it too much."

"Oh my God," Patrick murmured. "That's incredible."

He handed the telescope back to me. "Tell me what I'm looking at."

I studied the stars for a few seconds. "Well, on this side of the lighthouse, we're facing northeast, but we are on the southern end of Australia in winter, so Aquila, Cygnus, Sagittarius, Scorpius."

"Really?"

I chuckled. "Yes, really." I looked back up high in the clear sky and found what I was after. Keeping the telescope trained on the constellation, I leaned right into Patrick and put the eyepiece to his eye. "See that cluster of stars, kind of shaped like an S tipped over a bit."

"Um, I don't know what I'm looking at," he replied.

"There's a bright red star."

"Oh! I see that! And the S. I can see it."

I chuckled. "That's Scorpius."

Stars forgotten, he looked at me. "No."

It made me laugh. "Yes."

He looked back through the telescope. "It really is red! I had no idea stars were different colours."

"The bright red one in Scorpius is called Antares. But yeah, the colour differences are real. Stars are like a fire, the hot coals glow red, but the hottest coals glow white. The colour of a star depends on its temperature. Red stars are coolest. They have a temperature of four- or five-thousand degrees at their surface."

"Really?"

I nodded. "Yellow-white stars like our sun are hotter... about six- to ten-thousand degrees. And blue stars are the hottest of all, with surface temperatures of fifteen- to twenty-thousand degrees."

"How do you know all this?"

"My grandad taught me."

Patrick gave me a warm smile, then went back to star-watching. "It's amazing."

I could talk about astronomy all day long. It was a comfort to me, taking me back to fond memories of summer nights spent camping out with my grandfather when life was nothing but carefree campfires and constellations.

"Blue stars are massive. Like five or ten times the size of our own sun. Massive stars burn hottest, so they're blue. White and yellow stars are young to middle-aged middleweights. Most of the red stars, like the one you're looking at, were once massive blue stars that are nearing the end of their lives."

Patrick looked at me again. "Oh. That's kind of sad."

I nodded. "It is a bit. To think they've been around for aeons and how that has to come to an end."

"When will it die?"

I could have thought he was joking, but he was dead serious. His voice was quiet and his eyes guarded, sad even. I patted his thigh. "Not in our lifetime. Maybe another million years."

"Oh." He chuckled. "So, really soon then?" I laughed and he bumped my shoulder with his. "Tell me more."

"About what?"

"Everything you know about stars."

I barked out a laugh. "We could be a while."

His smile was so pure before he put the telescope back to his eye. "I don't mind."

So, for the first time in forever, I let my guard down and I talked about the stars. I spoke about nebulas and super-novas, helium and hydrogen, and the planets, of course. He listened intently, and I showed him Jupiter, which could be seen in winter, though barely.

He was intrigued and amazed, and it was genuine. Not

like Anton, who would listen for a minute then roll his eyes. He'd never understood it, he never even tried to. But Patrick did.

But the weather turned colder and a gale chose that exact time to whip around us. "Holy Jesus, that's cold," I said, pulling the blanket up.

"Come on, let's go down and get out of this wind." He jumped up to his feet and held his hand out to me. "We can do this another night if you like?"

Patrick pulled me to my feet, bringing me close, our chests almost touching. I looked up at him, so close, so perfect. He was everything I needed: strength, warmth, and all man. It had been so long since I'd felt anything, since another man had touched me, wanted me, since I'd felt safe in strong arms. And I needed it. I needed to erase the bad with something good. So without thinking, without thinking at all, I leaned up on my toes and kissed him.

His beard tickled my upper lip, making me smile, and it took a stupid-long second to occur to me that he wasn't kissing me back.

He pulled away with a shocked look on his face. "Aubrey, I can't..."

Oh God.

Hot shame and blistering rejection burned through me as I realised what I'd done. I just ruined the best thing in my life, the only good thing in my life. I took a step back, my heart screaming at me to turn and run.

It just took a second for my body to catch up.

"Aubrey," he said, stepping forward, and he reached out to grab my arm, but I pulled it out of reach and turned and ran.

I yanked open the door, and taking hold of the hand railing, I ran down the stairs as fast as I could.

"Aubrey, wait!" Patrick called out after me. His voice echoed loudly down the lighthouse, but I couldn't stop. I needed to run. I shouldn't have allowed myself to get so close to anyone. I shouldn't have let myself care. I needed to leave, and as much as I wanted to stay in Hadley, I knew my time here was done.

The spiral staircase was steep and I missed a step, but my hold on the handrail stopped me from falling. But then I heard Patrick on the stairs above me, chasing me, and a familiar panic slithered through me.

The way Anton used to chase me before I learned that it only made everything worse.

Fear turned my legs to wood and jelly in the way only fear could, and I missed the last few steps. The handrail slipped out of my hand and my left foot caught the last step as I fell, my head missed the wall by an inch, but my ankle twisted as I hit the ground, and a stomach-curdling pain shot up my leg.

CHAPTER EIGHT

PATRICK

"AUBREY, WAIT!" I started after him, trying to stop him. I wasn't expecting him to kiss me. He'd thrown me for a six, and I panicked.

I'd told him no.

The look on his face would never leave me.

I didn't want to hurt him. I was just caught unprepared. I needed to tell him it wasn't a hard no. It was more of an I'm-so-confused kind of no.

I needed him to just stop running.

Then a shrill cry cut the air in the lighthouse and I looked over the railing to the very bottom and found Aubrey sprawled on the ground.

Oh no.

I took the stairs two at a time. I'd ascended and descended these stairs countless times, and I was familiar with each and every tread and the dizzying curl of the staircase. I got to the bottom and stopped cold.

Aubrey was sitting up, pushed against the wall, one knee brought up, one leg straight out in front of him, his arms up protectively, and an unholy fear on his face.

Not just fear, but sheer terror.

"Whoa," I whispered. "Aubrey, are you okay?"

His chest heaved and he blinked a few times like he'd just returned from somewhere extremely unpleasant. He sagged and sucked back air, but kept one hand up in a stop motion. "You chased me," he mumbled, then shook his head. "Please don't chase me like that."

I sat down slowly on the bottom step. "I'm sorry. I just wanted to talk to you."

"I shouldn't have kissed you. I apologise. I'll just be going." He tried to push up the wall, but he yelped as soon as he put weight on his foot and fell back to the floor.

I stood up and put my hands out like he was an unbroken pony, wild and scared. "Aubrey," I said gently. "I won't hurt you. I promise. I'll never hurt you." I moved a slow step closer, not wanting to scare him any further. "I want to have a look at your leg." I crouched down slowly and gently touched his shin. "Can you tell me where it hurts?"

"My ankle." His chin wobbled and his eyes brimmed with tears. "I'm sorry."

"Hey," I said soothingly. "You did nothing to apologise for."

Jesus, whatever had happened to him left him shaking.

"Aubrey, can I help you walk to my house? It's warm there, and you'll be safe. I promise. I want to take a look at your ankle. Then if you want, I'll drive you back to your van."

He nodded quickly and a single tear ran down his cheek. He swiped it away, and so God help me, I wanted to pull him into my arms and hold him... but I didn't dare touch him. Not like that.

"I'm just going to put my arm under yours and help you up, okay?"

He nodded, so I helped him up, and together we hobbled out of the lighthouse, only to stop at the top of the few steps outside. Even the ground between the lighthouse and my place wasn't exactly flat, not to mention how dark it was.

"Aubrey," I said. "Will you be able to—"

"I'll be fine."

I got the feeling that was his standard response to everything. But we only got down two of the three steps and he bit back another yelp.

"Okay, I'm going to carry you," I said. "Is that okay?" He didn't object, so I assumed it was. "Put your arm around my shoulder." He did, and I scooped him up bridal style. He was heavier than I expected, even if I did think he was too thin, but I could carry him easily.

"This is humiliating," he murmured.

"Don't be embarrassed." I got to my door and gently put him on his one good foot, and once inside, I helped him to the couch. "Pop your foot up. You'll need to keep it elevated."

He winced as he took his boot off, but then lay down with his foot up, his head resting on the arm of the sofa. "I think it's just a sprain."

"I can drive you to see a doctor," I said. "We can be at the hospital at Penneshaw in an hour."

"No doctors!" he replied sharply. He frowned at his ankle. "I can't see a doctor."

"Okay," I answered slowly, warily. "No doctors." That was odd. It sounded more than just a fear of doctors or hospitals. I peeled his sock down to reveal an already puffy ankle.

He could wriggle his toes and there was no pain anywhere else, so I was satisfied it was just a sprain. I wrapped a bag of frozen peas in a tea towel and strapped it to his ankle with another tea towel. I sat on the floor by his legs so he didn't feel crowded in. "I'm sorry," I said gently. "About before."

"I shouldn't have kissed you. It was uninvited and foolish."

"No, it wasn't," I offered. "I was just surprised, that's all."

He was silent for a while, still frowning. "I don't want to have to leave Hadley."

"Leave? Why?"

"Because I ruined this." He looked at me then, his eyes a deep, haunted brown. "You're my first friend in forever, and I ruined it. Tonight was the best night of my life, and I was so happy. It's been so long since I've had anything good in my life, and it sounds crazy, but I wanted to feel something more. I wish I could take it back. I'm sorry."

His lip trembled again, and I wanted to touch him, some part of him, to reassure and to mollify. I wanted to comfort him, hold him. But I settled for taking his hand instead. I slowly slid my fingers over his knee, giving him all the time to rebuke me if he felt pressured. But he didn't. In fact, he covered my hand with his, and as soon our hands touched, his grip was a little tight.

"I'm not sorry, and I wouldn't take it back," I admitted. "Watching those stars with you was pretty incredible for me too. And when you kissed me, I wish I'd reacted better. I wish you hadn't hurt your ankle. But please don't leave."

Neither of us spoke for another few long moments, but we still held hands, then he said, "I'm sorry I freaked out. When you chased me... I panicked. Sorry."

"Don't apologise. I should be the one who apologises." I gently squeezed his hand. "I didn't mean to frighten you."

He swallowed hard and his bottom lip trembled again. "I was... there was a guy... he used to..." A tear rolled down his cheek and he quickly wiped it away with his free hand, then shook his head. "I'm sorry I freaked out."

I shuffled up a bit so I was closer to his face, and leaning against the sofa, almost leaning against his thigh, I stared into his eyes. "I won't ever hurt you."

He nodded, ever so slightly, and his eyes welled with tears again. "Thank you."

"I am sorry I reacted that way when you kissed me," I murmured. "Maybe one day you'll let me try again."

"You said you weren't ready."

I closed my eyes and sighed. "I want to be. I didn't think I ever would be again." I looked at him then. "Until you came along." He didn't reply, he just squeezed my hand and waited, somehow knowing I had a story to tell. And I wanted to tell him the truth. I wanted to tell him where I was at, why I was such a mess over whatever was happening between us. "My partner died," I whispered. I still hated saying it out loud. Like it made it real all over again, old wounds ripped open. "It was four years ago. We lived here. He got up and left for work, like any other day, and he didn't come home."

"Oh, Patrick," Aubrey said, putting his free hand to my face.

Just then, Tabby jumped up behind Aubrey's head and walked down his shoulder to sit on his chest. I barked out a teary laugh. "I swear she's trying to tell me something."

He waited until she'd done her nesting circle and plonked herself down. He gave her a scratch under the ear. "Why's that?"

"She was Scott's cat." I took a breath and let it out slowly, willing myself not to cry. "She only loved him. She hated me, then when he disappeared, it was as if she blamed me. She couldn't bear to be in the same room as me sometimes. She kind of came around over the years, but I've never been her favourite person. She loves you though."

Tabby purred and closed her eyes into his touch. "She does."

"The other night after you left, when she'd been all over you, I asked her if she was trying to tell me something."

Aubrey put his hand to my hair, and I leaned into his touch, just as Tabby had done. "It's confusing for you," he said.

I nodded, then said out loud something I could barely admit to myself. "I feel like I'm cheating on him."

Aubrey traced his fingers through my hair above my ear. "Guilt is so unfair."

"It is."

His eyebrows furrowed. "What did you mean when you said he disappeared. You said Scott disappeared."

"He was a crab fisherman. There was a terrible storm... Three men on the boat were never found."

He frowned, a knowing sadness in his eyes, and he put his hand to my face. "I'm sorry. I'm sorry you went through that."

I swallowed hard and tried not to be drawn down the familiar path of emotional hell. "I am too."

Neither of us spoke for a long time. We just sat there— me on the floor, him still lying on the sofa—holding hands, and eventually I moved a bit closer and put my head back on his arm. The fire crackled, the cat purred, the wind howled outside.

"Oh shit," Aubrey said. "My telescope. I left it up in the lighthouse."

"I'll get it," I said, getting to my feet. "You stay here and keep your foot up. I'll just be a sec." I got to the door and stopped, barely able to look at him, too scared of what he might see in my eyes. "Please be here when I get back."

"I will. I promise."

With a nod, I opened the door and ran for the light-house. By the time I got to the top, my legs were burning; I hadn't done the stairs three times in one day in a while. I collected the pillows and blanket and his telescope, of course, locked the doors, and went downstairs. I had my hands full, so I took my time. The last thing I needed was to fall and injure myself while Aubrey was already injured.

I tried not to think about finding him gone. He said he'd stay, and I hoped he would.

He promised.

I held my breath and opened the front door, and there he was, now sitting up a little with Tabby still perched on his lap. Relief put a smile on my face.

Aubrey clearly was very adept at reading people. "You thought I'd leave."

I put the pillows and blanket on the edge of the sofa and handed him his telescope. "I did. A reflection of me, not you."

"Tabby wouldn't have let me leave anyway," he replied. Then he tried to move and grimaced at his ankle and bit back a cry. I was pretty sure it hurt more than he let on.

I knelt before him and gently lifted his foot to rest on my thigh. I unwrapped the tea towel and took the frozen peas away to reveal a swollen, already purplish ankle. "Oh, Aubrey, this looks really painful."

He wiggled his toes. "It kinda really hurts."

"You'll need to keep it elevated and strapped," I said. "It's getting late, and I'll drive you home if you want, but—and this is only if you want—I'd prefer you to stay here." I held my breath.

He shot me a look but didn't say an immediate no, so I struck while the iron was hot. "The bed in your van is a bit on the small side, and I'd hate for you to bump your ankle in your sleep or need to use the bathroom at three in the morning and need to walk to the amenities block. If you stay here, you'll be comfortable, and I can help you if you need." He was still staring at me, so I added, "Or I'll drive you home right now if you want. No pressure."

He blinked and spoke slowly. "You want me to stay?"

"Yes. Why do you sound so surprised?"

"Because I threw myself at you. Then I turned and ran and..." He gestured to his foot. "And couldn't even do that right."

"I wasn't lying when I said I wished I'd reacted better and that maybe one day you'll let me try again." I could feel my cheeks heat and let out an embarrassed laugh. "Not tonight, but one day."

When he didn't say anything, I risked looking up at him. Even Tabby now sat up on his thighs, giving me a judgemental scowl, like how dare I put Aubrey on the spot like that. But Aubrey's gaze was imploring, gentle and even a little scared. He nodded. "I'll stay."

I finally smiled and lowered his foot to the floor. "You can have my bed," I said. "I'll take the couch."

"No." He shook his head. "Thanks anyway, but I'll take the couch." Then he gave Tabby a scratch under her ear. "But I do need to use the bathroom, so you're gonna have to hop off me, Miss Tabby."

"Here, let me. I'll be the big meanie. She hates me

anyway," I said, picking her up and putting her beside him. Then I held my hands out to Aubrey. "And I can help you to the bathroom."

He took my hands and I pulled him up to standing. He kept his left foot off the ground and hopped a little to get his balance. I put my arm around him and he did the same, using me as a crutch, and together we got to the bathroom door. The room itself was small and he could easily lean on the vanity countertop. I quickly stood back and pulled the door closed so he had privacy. "Want a hot chocolate before bed?"

"Um. Sure."

I left him to it, and the few minutes spent stirring milk on the stove gave me some time to try and put things into perspective. It had been an interesting night, that's for sure. He'd kissed me and I'd said no, I wasn't ready. And I wasn't. I didn't think. My head was telling me I was, but my heart wasn't so sure...

Because then I'd told him I hoped he'd try it again some-day. To kiss me, that is. I wanted him to kiss me. And I'd told him about Scott and how I missed him, and it felt good to talk about him in a positive way, as hard as it was, as sad as it was.

How was I supposed to move on after his death?

By living your life. I could have sworn Scott's voice whispered in my mind. *By letting yourself be happy.*

You're allowed to be happy, Patrick.

I poured the warmed milk into two cups just as I heard the bathroom door open, and the awkward shuffle-hop of Aubrey trying to walk. I quickly went to him and slid my arm around his waist so he could lean on me again. We walked to the couch, and he turned in my arms, not pressed up against me, but close enough for me to feel his body warmth. It wasn't a platonic distance; it was a promising kind of distance. It was a heart-skipping closeness, a butter-flies-in-my-belly closeness.

It was an I-want-this kind of thing.

He smiled all shy-like and I had the mental image of gripping his face and kissing him, which was followed by a cold slap of guilt. I helped him sit down and get comfortable and walked back to the hot chocolates I was making. I stood at the sink and took a deep, calming breath before taking him his cup, which he took with a smile.

"You okay?" he asked, sipping his drink.

I sat opposite him in the single seater. "Yeah, I am. Tonight's been... eventful."

He snorted quietly. "That's one way to put it."

"Can I be honest with you, Aubrey?"

He paled a little and he looked away before nodding. "Yes, of course," he whispered.

"Tonight's been confusing."

His gaze shot to mine. He clearly hadn't expected me to say that. "I'm sorry I rushed you."

I smiled gently at him. "You didn't rush me. You're just making me want things I wasn't expecting to ever want again."

"Oh." He blushed again and looked up at me through his lashes. "Should I be sorry for that?"

Jesus, that boyish playfulness had trouble written all over it. I shook my head slowly. "No." I smiled ruefully at myself. "I should probably be thanking you. I guess. I'm not sure yet. I don't..." I finished with a sigh.

"You're confused."

I nodded.

"That's okay. Actually, that's probably to be expected. I don't know what I'm doing either, if that's any consolation. I um... I have a lot of unresolved issues too." He frowned at his hot chocolate. "Can I be honest with you?"

"Yes, of course."

"There's a lot of things I can't tell you. It's not because I don't want to. I can't tell you things because I don't want to implicate you."

"You said that before, that it was for legal reasons," I added. "Did you have to sign an NDA or something?"

He almost laughed. "Ah, no. Nothing that easy."

Easy? Nondisclosure agreements were hardly easy. "I get it though, Aubrey. You came from a bad relationship, horrible even. You don't need to tell me anything more than that."

"I just don't want you to think I'm being dishonest or lying to you. Because I'm not. Or, I don't mean to. It's not lying, and I'm not being deliberately deceitful. When I said you were my first friend in ages, that's not a lie. And when I said tonight has been one of the best nights I can remember, that's the God-honest truth."

"I believe you."

"Being at the top of the lighthouse stargazing with you was... well, it'll be right up there with some of the best nights of my life. If I can just pretend the kissing you and spraining my ankle part didn't happen. But talking to you and clearing the air means a lot, and this hot chocolate is pretty damn good."

I chuckled, and my smile lingered. "If I ask you something, will you be completely honest with me?"

He made a face. "If I can..."

"On a scale of one to ten, how bad does your ankle hurt?"

He let out a relieved laugh. "About a six. Maybe a seven."

"Would you like a Panadol or Advil?"

He nodded. "Please."

I pulled out my first aid kit and got the tablets and a glass of water for him. "Here you go. I should have offered them sooner, sorry."

He shrugged and swallowed down the tablets. "I've had worse. It's been a while, but I can kind of compartmentalise the pain."

I blinked, and I was sure the alarm on my face said everything words couldn't, at what he was implying, at what he'd been through. "Oh, Aubrey."

He tried to smile. "Like I said, it's been a while."

"You deserve to be treated so much better than that."

"I know. That's why I left."

"I'm glad you did."

He nodded, then stifled a yawn. "Sorry. I'm more tired than I realised."

I took out the bandage from the first aid kit. "We should strap your ankle. Can I do that for you now, real quick?"

Aubrey gave me a small nod and smile, the kind that told me getting looked after was a nice change. I slowly pulled his jeans leg up. "Would you rather sleep in your briefs?" I asked. "I can help you get your jeans off if you like?"

He smirked, then whispered, "I think I should keep them on."

Oh.

I hadn't realised how that came across. "I just thought you might be more comfortable..."

He grinned at me. "Blush suits you."

I rolled my eyes and proceeded to wrap his ankle. He winced a bit and gritted his teeth, but didn't complain. I grabbed one of the pillows we'd taken to the lighthouse and put it at one end of the couch, then opened out the blanket. "Will this be enough?"

"More than enough. It's a helluva lot warmer than my van, that's for sure." Then he kind of realised he'd just admitted that his van was cold. He made a face at confessing things weren't as great as he'd let on. "The blanket and the fire are perfect, thank you."

He got settled and I put the blanket over him. "Can I get you anything else?"

He smiled at me, all sleepy and cute. "No. I'm fine, thank you."

Tabby jumped up on him again, finding a suitable spot and quickly curling up to sleep. It made me chuckle. "She's definitely trying to tell me something."

Aubrey gave me a tired smile as he stroked her fur. "Goodnight Patrick."

"Night."

I left him then, made a quick stop to the bathroom, then stripped and crawled into bed. I knew sleep wouldn't come easy. My mind was turning in circles, confusing circles of Aubrey, brown eyes and pink lips, boyish looks, ragged hair. I wish I could remember what his lips felt like, but it was a blur of fear and not being able to think.

I wish I could remember. I touched my lips, but there was no remnant of him there. I wanted to kiss him, and that terrified me.

I hadn't wanted anything physical since Scott.

I hadn't wanted anything at all since Scott.

But something was changing inside me. A shift. An awakening. A small, flickering flame I thought long extinguished. Along with it came a swirl of guilt, and I lay there most of the night trying to determine if that swirl of guilt was trying to extinguish the flame or make it burn brighter.

———

I WOKE up to the sound of mumbling and clanging, so I pulled on some jeans and went out to the kitchen to find Aubrey at the sink, left foot lifted off the ground, talking to Tabby as he washed up the dishes from last night. Tabby was sitting on the kitchen counter like she knew she wasn't allowed to, and they seemed to be having a great conversation about her spending the day snoozing in front of the fire.

"Morning," I said, still not quite awake.

"Oh, hey," he replied, shuffling around on his good foot. His smile was brighter than the sunrise coming in through the window. "I woke up early and realised we didn't clean up after dinner last night."

"I can do that," I said, waving at the sink. "How's your ankle?"

He looked down at it. "Sore, but I'll live. Tabby here was just telling me you need to put wood on the fire, but there was no wood inside."

I smiled. "Want coffee?"

"Would love some. I was going to boil the kettle but didn't want to wake you."

I picked Tabby up and held her to my chest. "And you, Miss Tabby, know you're not supposed to sit on the kitchen bench."

Aubrey fought a smile as he continued to wash up. "I asked her and she told me she could totally sit up there."

"I'm sure she did." I flicked the kettle on with a laugh. "I'll just grab some wood from outside, then I'll dry up your hard work here. Then I'll make you breakfast. How does that sound?"

"It sounds really good."

I put a very disgruntled cat on the sofa and quickly

grabbed some wood from the pile at the side of the house. I came back in, my breath a billow of puff. "Holy crap, it's fresh out there." I stoked up the fire, dried the dishes with Aubrey, then made us some coffee.

He hobbled to my small dining table, and I pulled out my chair. "Put your foot up while I'm cooking. Scrambled eggs on toast sound okay?"

"Sounds like heaven." He sipped his coffee and smiled at me.

I liked that he was so happy in the morning. "Did you sleep okay?"

"I did, thanks. My ankle woke me a few times, probably when I rolled over or moved it, but your couch is really comfortable."

"I've fallen asleep on it many times. But it does my back no favours." I whisked some eggs with some cream, then popped some bread in the toaster. By the time the toast was done and buttered, the scrambled eggs were done, and I put the two plates on the table and took my seat.

"This looks amazing," Aubrey said. "You know you're cooking skills are incredible, right?"

"I've been told that, yes."

He smiled and tasted his first forkful, and his groan was obscene. I shifted in my seat and smiled at how oblivious he was. The eggs were good though, and it was easy for me to forget that Aubrey didn't get to eat breakfasts like this very often.

Half his plate was gone before he spoke. "Patrick," he whispered. "This is really good."

"Thank you."

He stared at me. "No, I don't think you understand. This is *really* good."

I laughed. "I'm glad you're enjoying it. I enjoy cooking,

and I like feeding you." I stopped. "That sounded so wrong."

He laughed. "I know what you mean." Then he made a face. "I think."

"I just like making sure people are looked after," I explained. "I'm not creepy, I promise."

He put his hand over mine and squeezed. "I know that." He let go of my hand to pick up his coffee, and I wished he hadn't. I wished I had the courage to reach out and take his hand, but I didn't.

"What's your plan of attack for today?" I asked as we finished our breakfast.

"I have a washing machine to fix."

"Even with your ankle?"

He made a face, which ended in a frown. "I need to keep working so it doesn't cost me anything. Frank said I could stay for free as long as I was fixing up his place."

"I can help you," I offered. "I have to get a few things done here first, but then I can drive you and we can take a look at it together. It might also help to outnumber Frank a bit if there's two of us."

"Are you sure?"

"Yes, of course." I put the plates in the sink. "I'll just have a real quick shower, then while I'm outside getting a few things done, you can take as much time as you need to shower."

He chewed on his bottom lip. "Thank you. You could have kicked me out last night, but you've been nothing but kind."

I sat back beside him, took a deep breath and a leap of faith. "Well, I enjoy your company. And like I said last night, I hope you'll give me another chance to maybe react better and not be so scared."

"Scared?"

"Terrified." I let out a surprised laugh at how easy that just came out of my mouth without thinking.

His face softened, and again, he slid his hand over mine. "For what it's worth, I'm kind of scared too."

I interlocked our fingers, and we just sat there and smiled at each other long enough for my heart to notice and pick up speed. "I better go get my day started." I took a quick shower and headed straight for the lighthouse. I got through the logbook entries and everything was working perfectly, but I couldn't slack on my job just because I wanted to spend time with Aubrey. Thankfully the weather was clear and cool, the swells weren't anything to be concerned about, and soon enough, I went back inside.

In the few hours I was gone, Aubrey had showered and re-strapped his ankle, cleaned up the kitchen—again—and folded the blanket he'd used and straightened the lounge room. He was also struggling to walk.

"You poor thing," I said. "Come on, I'll buy us a coffee from Penny's on the way to the caravan park."

"Oh, you don't have to do that," he said quickly.

"Well, if I don't call in for my morning coffee and paper, Penny'll send out a search party. I'm already late."

He chuckled. "Right. Don't want the good sergeant calling around?"

"No." I sidled up next to him and put his arm around my shoulder. "To the car with you."

With one boot on, one boot off, we got him to the car, and when we got to the store, he sighed. "I just don't think I can walk that far. Do you mind if I don't come in with you? It'll be quicker if I stay here."

"That's fine. I won't be long." I got out and darted into the store.

"Oh, hello darling," Penny greeted me from behind the counter. "I was wondering if you'd be in. A little late today," she hinted.

"Ah, yes." I tried not to blush and failed.

"Want your usual?" she asked.

"Uh no, actually. Can I please have two?"

Penny stared at me, then her eyes darted over my shoulder. I turned to find Collin standing not too far away, and he'd clearly heard what I'd said.

I cleared my throat and repeated my order. "Ah yes, two coffees today, thanks."

"For anyone in particular?" Penny prodded.

"Hadley's newest resident, Mr Hobbs," Collin said, not overly pleased. "I saw him in your car."

I cleared my throat. "Yes, Aubrey." I gave Penny a pleading look. "Coffees to go, thanks."

She nodded sympathetically as she made the coffees. "Well, not that it's anyone else's business," she said, aimed directly at Collin. "But I think it's lovely. And about time."

And just like that, with a reminder of time and what I was trying to live through, I took my two coffees with a dash of guilt and left.

CHAPTER NINE

AUBREY

I DIDN'T KNOW what was said to Patrick in the store, but he came out an awful lot quieter than when he went in. I saw the cop; he'd stopped and stared at me in Patrick's car as if he couldn't believe his eyes, then went inside.

Patrick handed me the cups and didn't say a word as he drove us to the caravan park.

"Everything okay?" I asked.

He gave me a smile he couldn't quite make work. "Yep. It's all good."

But it wasn't. It very clearly wasn't.

He pulled to a stop in the caravan car park, took the coffees, and put them on the roof of his car, then helped me hobble to the amenities block. We were almost there when Frank came out. "Was wondering what happened to ya," he said, looking me up and down, frowned at Patrick, then stared at how I was holding my foot off the ground. "You hurt or something?"

"It's just a sprain, but I can still work." I had to keep working so I had somewhere to live. "It's no big deal."

He grumbled something inaudible before waving us off.

He was pretty clearly not happy. "Great," I mumbled. "Last thing I need is to be kicked out."

"You'll be all right," Patrick said. "Frank's always pissy about something. He'll get over it."

I had my arm around his shoulder and he had his arm around my waist so I could put as little weight on my foot as possible. Even though I was sure my ankle was only sprained, it really did hurt. But his strength was divine, his body all hard planes and tender skin. And he smelled so damn good, it took every ounce of willpower not to lean in and inhale.

"Where did you want to go?" he asked as we got to the amenities block.

"To the washing machine. I'll keep working on it today."

"I'm pretty sure there's no point in telling you to try and rest, is there?" he said with a smile.

"Nope."

He helped me sit at the back of the machine, and I had to admit, it took more out of me than I thought possible. Stupid ankle. I touched the bandage and saw that my toes were pink from the cold. I was still inspecting it when Patrick came back in with the coffees. "They're cooled down enough to drink now," he said with a smile. Then he looked at my foot. "You need a sock for that foot."

"Yeah, you're probably right."

He handed me the coffee and looked around the laundry room and at all the tools stacked up near me. "Have you got everything you need? Do you need me to grab anything?"

I looked at all of Frank's old tools. "No, I think I'm good for now."

"Okay, I'm just going to duck over the road. Won't be long, then I'll come back and help you... if you need me to."

I smiled up at him. "Sure."

He gave a nod, smiling more genuinely now, and disappeared out the door. I sipped the coffee he'd bought me— real, proper coffee like I used to take for granted—and hummed at the taste. No memories followed it, and I smiled at the progress I'd made. No memories of Anton pummelled me like they used to. Like he used to.

I was better than that. I was better than him.

I deserved this new life. And I deserved a chance at love. Proper love, happy love. Not controlling, possessive love, but the kind that encouraged growth and dreams.

I wanted that.

And I knew it was fast and crazy, but so help me, I wanted it with Patrick.

I didn't want the riches and fame that Anton sought and sold his soul for. I just wanted to be happy.

And I wanted that with Patrick.

I had to hope he'd want it with me too. There was something growing between us, and when he'd rejected my kiss, I'd been horrified. And mortified. But then he'd told me why; he told me about Scott, his boyfriend who had died.

No, not died. Disappeared.

Like I'd disappeared.

Patrick had lived through what everyone in my old life had lived through. What I'd put them through. I'd faked my death.

I was sure Patrick would kill for the chance to know what really happened to Scott, to know for sure. There had to be something about not knowing that must eat at him. It would have kept him awake at night for years...

Would he hold it against me for doing the same thing that had turned his life upside down?

Probably.

Or maybe he'd understand. He was reasonable and kind. And he'd told me he was glad I'd escaped. So maybe, just maybe, he'd understand.

I got busy trying to fix the washing machine, trying to keep my mind on track. And when I leaned right down and looked up at the top of the motor, I could see a wire socket was dislodged. I reached up, squeezing and bending my hand and arm like a contortionist, stretching as far as I could. I could touch it, only just, but if I wiggled up further...

I tried to push the socket in, going by feel alone. It jiggled and I couldn't see what I was doing, and with a final push...

I had the now-broken wire in my hand.

"Bloody hell."

I heard a shuffling of feet and deliberate muttering, and I realised Patrick was making noise so his appearance didn't startle me like the sergeant had done the other day. "What's wrong?" he asked, his footsteps getting closer.

I held up the small wire with a socket from where I sat on the ground. "This... is not supposed to be detachable."

"Oh, bummer."

Then I noticed that he was holding a metal crutch. He held it up like it was an Olympic torch and grinned like he'd won gold. "Look what I found!"

I laughed. "You found it?"

"Well, not exactly. Cassy's brother broke his leg two years back, and I wondered if he still had it lying around."

"You went and tracked it down for me?" I used the washing machine to pull myself up, keeping the weight off my foot. "You didn't have to go to any trouble."

"It was really no problem." Patrick's blush disappeared

under his beard. It was endearing. "They live just behind the takeaway shop. And it's just across the road."

"Well, thank you. That's very kind." Then I thought of something. "Do I owe them anything?"

"Nope. Just gotta give it back when you're better." He held it out to me, and I took the crutch and I gave him the wires I was holding.

I slipped my hand through the arm support and tried it for size. "Was Cassy's brother twelve when he broke his leg?"

Patrick laughed. "Yeah, it's a bit short. We just need to adjust the height." He studied the wires in his hand. "This looks like a connector, and you can see the wire here is broken."

"Yeah, which isn't good."

"Well, not necessarily. I think they have these at the auto shop in Penneshaw."

"Oh cool." I shrugged. "Can we send them a picture or something to see if they can send something?"

He kept his eyes on the wires. "We could go one day if you want?"

"To Penneshaw?"

"Well, yeah... you don't have to. I try to go once a week or maybe once a fortnight. Mostly for groceries. Sometimes I'll go and see if Mr MacPherson on Starboard Street needs anything. He can't drive anymore."

I found myself smiling at him. "You're one of the good ones, Patrick."

He smiled all shy-like. "Not really."

"Yes, you are. And yes, I'll go to Penneshaw with you."

His smile made my stomach swoop. "Want me to fix your crutch?"

I blinked. "My what?"

He burst out laughing. "Your crutch. Not your crotch."

I snorted. "I thought we went from waiting to dating in point-oh-two seconds."

He laughed, long and loud, then lifted the end of my crutch and readjusted the height to fit me better. "Waiting to dating, huh?"

Now it was me who blushed. "I didn't exactly mean dating..."

He shrugged. "It's not off the table, Aubrey. Just need to mentally get through the waiting part."

I slid my hand over his. "Me too. You're not alone in that."

He nodded and smiled kindly. "Thank you." Then he said, "Oh! I almost forgot." He pulled a fluffy thing out of his back pocket. It was bright pink and woolly, and it took me a second to realise it was a sock. "Cassy said her grandma knitted them but she would never wear them because, well..." He held the sock up as though it was exhibit A.

"It looks like a Muppet was sacrificed," I said. It was hot fuchsia pink, fluffy, and hideous. "I love them!"

Patrick chuckled. "I didn't think you'd be too opposed to it."

"You assumed I'd like to wear something soft and pink and fluffy?" I asked with a raised eyebrow and a smile.

"Well, not exactly. I just..." He sighed. "I just thought it might be something you'd wear." Then he made a face and frowned. "God, that sounds really wrong. I meant for your foot."

I used the crutch to step in a bit closer and I leaned in slowly to kiss his cheek, making his blush deepen. "Thank you. And you're right. I do like to wear soft things. I don't care too much about the colour, but pink is nice."

"Muppet-sacrifice jokes aside."

I laughed. "Yes."

He tapped his hand on the top of the washing machine. "Sit up here and I'll put it on for you."

I was pretty damn sure I could put my own sock on, but if he wanted to do it, I wasn't going to say no. I heaved myself up onto the old machine and Patrick gently took my foot. "Jeez, your toes are frozen." He looked alarmed. "How's your ankle feel?"

"Sore."

He frowned, then inspected the bandage. "Well, you strapped it well enough." He stretched open the sock and put it on my foot so tenderly, I almost didn't feel it at all. He smiled at me. "Need a hand to get down?"

I chuckled. "Need? Or want?"

He rolled his eyes and handed me the crutch. I was obviously getting down by myself. "Yeah, I better go tell Frank the good news."

"That he needs to pay for a new wire connector?"

"Well, that. And that I can't do the work I originally said I would. I thought I might be able to suffer along, but I can't be shovelling gardens or fixing panelling with my ankle like it is."

Patrick made a face but didn't say anything and walked with me to Frank's door. I knocked and could hear him shuffling to the door before he opened it. He looked me up and down again. "What's up?"

"I think I found what was wrong with the washer." I held up the offending connector. "Patrick thinks they might have new ones at the auto shop in Penneshaw."

Frank grunted. "And?"

"And I can probably go with him sometime this week if you give me the green light."

He narrowed his eyes. "And the money to buy it, I presume?"

"Well, yeah."

"It'll be five bucks, Frank," Patrick said from where he stood behind me.

Frank rolled his eyes but nodded. "Yeah, whatever. Guess you're trying to save me money in the long run."

I smiled at him. "And I hurt my ankle last night but I can still work if you were worried about me not upholding my end of the bargain. I just might be a bit slower than I'd hoped."

Frank gave me a hard glare. "I ain't about to kick you out, boy. I can see the work you been doing." He nodded to the amenities block and the tidied garden. "Just get yourself mended, and don't be slack about it."

I smiled at his gruff exterior. The truth was, he was giving me a place to live for free while I couldn't work, so he was hardly a mean man. "I won't be slack about it. I promise."

"Good. Now rack off and leave me alone. I'm missing the afternoon movie." The door closed in my face and I turned around and found Patrick trying not to smile.

"He's a cranky bastard, but he's a good guy," he mumbled.

I laughed. "Yeah." I walked toward him, using the crutch. "Thanks again for this," I said, nodding toward it. "Not sure how I'd get around otherwise."

He smiled at me for a long second. "You're welcome. So, about going to Penneshaw... What day suits you?"

I looked around and scoffed. "Let me check my schedule."

He rolled his eyes. "Okay then, smartarse, what about tomorrow?"

I smiled right back at him. "Tomorrow would be perfect." Neither of us spoke for a bit, not too sure what to say, but not wanting to say goodbye. He had no reason to still be here but obviously didn't want to leave. "What's the time?" I asked.

He checked his watch. "Ten to three."

"Okay well, I better pack up my mess in the laundry," I said. "Before it gets too cold."

It looked like Patrick wanted to say he'd stay and help or maybe just even stay. He glanced between the laundry and my van, twisting his hands until he realised what he was doing. Then he shoved his hands into his pockets and rocked back on his heels. "Okay then, well, I guess I'll see you tomorrow?"

I bit my bottom lip to stop from smiling too big. "That sounds good."

"Okay then. I better let you get back to it." He made no attempt to move.

"Yeah, okay," I replied, not moving either.

"Before it gets too cold," he added, still being all shy and making no attempt to leave.

"Um." I pointed my thumb toward my van. "Did you want to stay for a cuppa or something?"

He let out a long slow breath. "I do, but I won't." He took a step back and made a frustrated sound. "I'm trying to go."

I chuckled. "I can see that."

He groaned and ran his hand through his hair. "I should go."

"Okay," I said, grinning. "Thanks again for the crutch. And the sock. I'll need to think of something to do with the other one."

He barked out a laugh and walked to his car. "I don't want to know."

I winked at him. "Yes, you do."

His nostrils flared and he opened his car door. "Goodbye, Aubrey."

"Goodnight, Patrick." I made a show of lifting the hem of my shirt to wipe my face, giving him a good eyeful of my belly and chest. When I looked back at him, he was staring, lips parted. I gave him another grin and turned and walked, or hobbled really, back to the laundry.

It took him a while to start the engine of his car, and I looked over my shoulder and laughed as I walked inside. God, I'd forgotten how much fun it was to flirt. How much fun it was to feel alive and have fun.

It was a warm blanket against the chill of the fading afternoon. And for the first time in a long, long time, I was looking forward to tomorrow.

———

PATRICK PICKED me up just after twelve and we headed out of town toward Penneshaw. The thing about Kangaroo Island is, that no matter which direction you went, you ended up in the right place sooner or later. The island wasn't very big, and there were really only four biggish towns on it. Penneshaw was the biggest, so if anyone from Hadley needed anything specific, they either had to go into Penneshaw or buy it online.

My God, I missed online shopping.

I missed having a credit card or even an ATM card, for that matter. I missed having a bank account. I missed having ID. It was silly how such small things to everyone else were huge for me.

I felt like I'd almost been erased. It was my own doing, I understood that. Didn't make the fact that I didn't exist on paper any easier.

"You okay?" Patrick asked me. We were about fifty k's into the trip and I guessed I'd been quiet.

"Yeah, just thinking."

"About?"

"Ugh, nothing much," I lied. Then I changed the subject and put the spotlight directly on him. "You look really good today."

"Oh." He blanched. "Um, thanks?"

I laughed at his reaction. "I'm pretty sure you know that grey jacket matches the flecks of silver in your beard, and that shirt brings out the blue in your eyes."

He looked at me, then at the road, then at me, then at the road. The atmosphere in the car could possibly have its own barometric pressure, cranking down a notch or three, warming us both.

It probably wasn't fair for me to throw him in the deep end so much, but it wasn't like I was lying. "And you perfectly match the sky outside. Blues and dark greys. It's sexy AF."

"AF?"

"Sexy as fuck."

He barked out a laugh. "Is that what the cool kids are saying these days?"

"Apparently." I shrugged. "Or they were six months ago when I had access to the internet and television."

He looked at me again, though something on his face had changed. "You've coped okay?"

I liked how he phrased it. He didn't say something negative like 'must be tough' or 'that must have been hard'. He turned it into a positive, saying I'd survived. "Yeah, I coped okay. You'd be surprised how much you don't miss it."

"I rarely watch much TV," he admitted. "And I don't care about social media at all. But sometimes it feels good to be connected to the world."

I nodded. "Yeah. I remember feeling like that." I looked out the window at the passing greenery. "Now I want no part of it."

He was quiet, and when I looked over at him, his brow was pinched. "You left everything behind, didn't you?" he asked quietly.

I nodded. "Every single thing."

He reached over and took my hand, threading our fingers and resting our hands on his thigh. "Sometimes we have to do whatever it takes."

I nodded slowly, though he had no idea what it had taken to walk away. He had no idea of what I'd done. I wanted to tell him. I really did. I wanted to give him honesty. But I couldn't involve him, and I most certainly didn't ever want to hurt him.

———

WE WENT to the auto place first, and like Patrick had said, they had exactly what I was after. I'd shown them the broken one, they produced a brand new one, and I handed over Frank's tenner.

As I put his change and the receipt in my wallet, Patrick saw how empty my wallet was. He saw it and glanced away quickly, but he'd seen it. I knew he had. The look on his face confirmed it.

He didn't just see how empty it was of money—I did have my own ten-dollar note—but how there were no cards, no licence, no Medicare card. Just one old Melbourne tram card, and nothing else. Hell, even the wallet was second-hand.

I snapped my wallet shut and pretended nothing was wrong. "Where to now?" I asked brightly. I took the new connector piece, which the sales guy had called an accelerator connector, carefully turned, and used the crutch to walk to the door.

"Um, have you eaten?" he asked as we got outside. "I haven't had lunch yet, and it's now past one. I'm starving. How about you?"

I was pretty sure he'd eaten before he picked me up, and this was so he could make sure I had something to eat. And the truth was, I was hungry. "I could eat. What do you feel like?"

He nodded down the road. "There's a bakery down here. They have the best meat pies in Australia."

"Officially? Or is that just the Patrick Carney unofficial title?"

He grinned. "It's the official Patrick Carney title." We drove to the Best Pie Shop in Australia, and I struggled a bit to step up the tall gutter. Patrick took my elbow and made sure I was steady on my one foot and crutch. "You okay?"

"Yeah." The truth was, this much moving and getting in and out of the car had kinda sucked. My ankle and foot ached. "But I might stay out here if that's okay," I said, fishing my wallet out. I gave him my ten dollars, which he didn't want to take. "Please Patrick. Let me have a little bit of dignity, please."

His face fell and he took the note. "Sorry. I don't mean to—"

"I know. But I do have some cash." I lifted my chin. "And I'll need tomato sauce and a small Coke, thanks."

Patrick gave me an apologetic smile, took my money, and disappeared inside. I looked up the street, it wasn't busy by any means, but there were enough people for me. I told myself they were staring at me because of my one hot-pink-socked foot, but it was windy enough for me to pull the hood of my jacket on to hide my face.

I'd grown complacent from being in Hadley.

I noticed a newsagent just two shops down, so while I was waiting, I hobbled down there to look at the magazine posters advertising all the latest editions. I'd missed fashion magazines and trashy tabloids. As gaudy as they'd been and as badly written and full of lies, they'd been an escape for me once upon a time. I smiled at the poster of the latest edition of *Yorker* when a newspaper headline caught my eye.

Canberra   Bushfire   Death   Toll: Coroner's verdict.

The   Australian   Capital   Territory's Coronial inquest determines who is to blame for the deaths of 43 people in last year's tragic bushfires. Liberal MP Anton Gianoli, whose boyfriend perished in the fires, speaks out.

"There you are," Patrick said, walking toward me with bakery paper bags in his hands.

I started in his direction, probably faster than I should with my ankle, but I didn't want him to see what I was reading.

"Everything okay?" he asked, glancing back at the newsagent.

"Sure. I think I've overdone it on my ankle though," I lied.

He gave me my change. "Yeah, you're a little pale."

I nodded and kept hobbling to the car. "Do you mind if we sit down somewhere?"

"Yeah, of course." He helped me to the car, opening my door and waiting for me to get in and manoeuvre the crutch before closing my door for me. I couldn't even feel guilty, because my ankle was sore and that wasn't a lie, but my being pale had nothing to do with pain.

It had everything to do with that newspaper.

43 people.

Anton Gianoli.

God, even seeing his name in print made me shudder.

"You sure you're okay?" Patrick asked, pulling the car out onto the street.

I nodded. "Yeah. I'm sure this pie will fix me right up."

"I can grab you some Panadol or Advil from the chemist," he said. "There's one next to the park. We can eat there and I'll duck in and buy some." Then he added quickly, as though I might object, "I need some more for home anyway, so it's not a problem."

I wasn't going to argue. I let my head fall back on the headrest. "Thank you."

He stopped the car at the park. "How about we just eat in the car," he suggested, looking up at the sky through the windshield. "The wind's picked up anyway. That southerly must be fifty knots."

"Is that a lot?" I asked with a smile, grateful for the change in subject. "Star boy here, remember? The ocean is your domain."

He smiled right back at me. "Yeah, star boy. Fifty knots is pretty windy."

We ate our pies—and yes, Patrick's declaration that they were the best anywhere might very well be true—and when we were done, Patrick ran into the chemist and came back a few minutes later with a bag. He pulled out a small bottle of water and a box of tablets. "For you."

"Thank you." I really was grateful. My ankle hurt, and my head was starting to throb, wondering what else on earth was in that newspaper article. It wasn't like I could look it up online...

I wondered what they'd found. I wondered if they knew I hadn't died. I wondered what would happen to me when it all got found out. I mean, how long could I live like this? I couldn't pull this off forever. How long would it be until someone put the pieces together?

If someone in Hadley got too nosy or too close to the truth, I could simply disappear. Like always; if someone started asking all the wrong kind of questions, I'd be gone.

And even after this short a time, the idea of walking away from Patrick left me heavy and hollow. My first real connection with another living human in far too long. I liked him. Even more than like, if I was being honest with myself. What he represented to me was invaluable.

If I was adrift and lost, and I certainly felt it some days, then he was my shining beacon, my tether and guide to something good and whole.

My lighthouse.

The irony of that wasn't lost on me at all.

"I need to grab a few groceries," Patrick said. "Did you want to wait in the car?"

"I can come in," I said. "If I push the trolley, I can scoot along without putting weight on my foot."

Truth be told, it was the last thing I felt like doing, but I wanted to grab one of those newspapers. Only when we went in there, they'd sold out. I did get a loaf of bread and a small carton of milk, but I was very glad to get back in the car. I must have groaned more than I'd intended when I finally lifted my foot in.

Patrick climbed in and eyed me cautiously. "Do you think you could take a few days off to rest your ankle?"

"Nah, I'll be okay. I sat on the edge of the garden bed this morning and turned all the soil and weeded, and that wasn't too bad."

"Frank said he wasn't going to kick you out, so take a day and put your foot up. If it's still not better in a few days, would you consider seeing a doctor?"

"No. No doctors."

He drove for a while in silence, chewing on his bottom lip. Eventually it got the better of him. "Can I ask why? You don't have to tell me, but if you're scared of doctors or hospitals, and a lot of people are, it's nothing to be ashamed about. But I can go with you if you want."

"I'm not afraid," I said lamely. I felt myself getting close to dangerous waters but wanted to give some kind of truth. "You know before when you said I left everything behind?"

He nodded, concern etched at the corners of his eyes. "Yeah."

"Well, I left that behind."

"Your doctor?" He made a face. "I'm not following."

"No. My Medicare card."

Patrick frowned at the road. "You can just get one reordered, can't you?"

My mouth was suddenly dry, so I sipped the water. "No, I can't. I can't use anything traceable. Sorry, I can't tell you more than that. You deserve more, and I'm sorry."

"Is he, your ex, is he...?"

"He has ways of finding information," I replied vaguely. "And I can't... I can't let that happen, Patrick. I won't."

He reached over and took my hand again. "Okay. I'm sorry, I didn't mean to push."

"You didn't push. Believe me, I know what pushing is."

His grip tightened on my hand, in a comforting, reassuring way. He dropped me home, but I wasn't in any hurry to get out of the car. "Thank you for today. You've been a great help. Again."

"Can I come by tomorrow afternoon and help again?" he asked. "We might be able to get that old washer up and running."

"I'd like that."

"It's supposed to rain tomorrow," he said, looking out the window. "So I won't need to be doing any grounds maintenance. Just my usual systems check and reports. I can be here before lunch."

"Sounds good." I met his gaze and was almost physically drawn toward him. I could have so easily leaned across the console and kissed him. But I would wait until he was ready. And the confusing part was, his eyes said yes, but his heart said no.

I had to make myself look away.

"What're your plans for tonight?"

I sighed at the prospect of another cold and lonely night. "Not much. Rest my foot for one thing. But I might see if Frank has any old books or newspapers I can read. Helps pass the time when there's no TV or phone, or anything, really. There's only so much staring at the van walls I can do."

"Oh, Aubrey," he mumbled.

"It's not that bad," I deflected with a laugh. "And I have a deck of cards, but there's only so many times you can lose against yourself before solitaire gets old."

He almost smiled. "I have a stack of old newspapers. I

can bring them around. I get the paper every day, out of habit, I guess. I use them for the fire, and the crosswords keep me company at night," he finished quietly.

It took me a second to dissect what he said. His loneliness, his being alone, his daily ritual to stave off isolation, or because of it. But the newspapers...

"I'd like that," I answered. "It doesn't matter how new or old they are. Just something to read would be nice. And to see what's been going on in the world... though maybe I'm better off not knowing."

Patrick smiled. "I can bring them around tonight if you like?"

I studied him for a moment. As much as I'd like him to come back tonight, I was pretty sure he needed more time. "Tomorrow is fine, but thanks."

"Okay," he whispered. We did that staring thing again, where neither one of us wanted to be the one to say goodbye.

The thrill of something new beginning between us and the mere thought of endless possibilities eventually won out, and I smiled. "Thanks again for today. For taking me to get the part for the washing machine, and for lunch, and you know... for just hanging out."

"You're welcome. Thanks for keeping me company."

"I enjoy your company."

Patrick smiled in a way that made my stomach do a somersault. "I like spending time with you, too," he replied.

Just then, Frank's curtain pulled back, and he watched us for a grouchy second before letting the curtain fall back into place. "I feel like a kid again, getting busted by my grandad when Jeremy Jackson kissed me after dropping me home after school."

Patrick shot me a tender look. "Did he take it okay?"

I nodded, smiling at the memory. "Yeah. But he scared the shit out of Jeremy. Told him if he intended to date me, to get his arse out of the car and introduce himself properly like a gentleman."

Patrick chuckled. "And did he?"

"Oh, yeah, Jeremy was cool." I batted my eyelashes at Patrick. "He was my high school crush and we dated in year twelve."

"You dated guys in high school?"

I nodded. "Yep. Did you?"

He shook his head. "No. Not until college. My mum and dad... my parents didn't agree with my *life choices*."

"I'm sorry to hear that," I said, taking his hand. I threaded our fingers and frowned. "When will people learn it's not a choice?"

He sighed. "Some, never. I haven't spoken to them in a long time. Not even when Scott died. They never contacted me."

"It's their loss, Patrick. You're a good, good man. You deserve better than to be treated like that."

He gave me a sad smile. "You sound like Scott."

I squeezed his hand and smiled. "Scott sounds like he was a good man too."

"He was."

We were quiet again, though it wasn't building anticipation this time. It was melancholy. The clouds had settled in, low and dark, like they somehow sensed our sullen moods. I rubbed my thumb over the back of his hand, along his knuckles. "My grandad died just after I graduated high school," I said. "He left a huge hole in my life. My parents died when I was three. It was a car accident, and I can't even remember them. But my grandad... well, he was my entire world."

Patrick leaned the side of his head on the headrest and stared at me. "That must have been hard."

"It was. But he taught me how to love the stars. And that there is infinite space in all directions and some people think that makes us insignificant, like a speck of dust in the universe, but he always used to say that's what made us so special. So it's all about perspective, and I think of losing him much the same way. His death was horrible, but his life was a gift. Like the stars when they go supernova; they burn so bright they can't sustain it. They can either create a black hole, or they can create whole new galaxies." I shrugged. "Sounds silly, but I'd rather think of him as a galaxy, you know?"

He nodded, a little teary. "I know exactly what you mean."

I reached across with my free hand and cupped his cheek, gently stroking his beard. Then I leaned across slowly and kissed his cheek, right where my hand had been, before pulling back. "Thank you, again, for today. For everything."

He nodded, and it looked like he was struggling to speak.

"I'll see you tomorrow," I said, opening my door. Cold air swirled into the car and I jostled the bags and crutch until I got out, pulling my coat up around my ears. Patrick waved me off, and I slowly made it to Frank's door. I gave him his change and the receipt, told him I'd be fixing the machine tomorrow. He'd given me some old Reader's Digest magazines when I'd asked, and after bidding him goodnight, took my bread and milk and hobbled down to my van.

———

TO GET the new accelerator connector plugged into the old motor, I had to take the makeshift pantyhose fan belt off, then sit down on the floor and contort my arm up into the machine and, using just my fingertips, somehow manage to plug it in. I dropped it a dozen times, swore a lot, and was just about to throw the connector and the whole damn machine into the freaking Indian Ocean when I heard a familiar car pull up outside. Patrick made as much noise as he could without being too obvious, though he was completely obvious before he spoke. "Hey. Just me."

I stuck my head around the machine. God, even just seeing him made me smile. He wore navy work pants and a sweater, like he'd put a little effort into his appearance to see me. I liked that a lot. "Hey, just me. How're you going?"

His eyes, his whiskers, his smile, everything was gorgeous. He walked over and crouched down near me, looking at the back of the machine with me. "Good. How're things here? And your ankle? How's it feeling?"

"Ankle's a bit better today. I rested it this morning." Which was very true. I figured if Patrick was coming to help, I'd draw out how long he'd have to stay for as long as possible and start a little later. "But this machine is being a pain in my arse." I demonstrated how I'd been trying to reach up into the motor, almost turning myself inside out in the process.

"Here," he said. "What if I tilt it back, will it be an easier angle for your arm?"

He tilted the machine back, holding its weight while I manoeuvred my hand up into the motor. And he was right; it was easier. After just a few minutes, it was in place. "Okay, wow. So you could have turned up an hour ago."

Patrick chuckled and set the machine back down. "You

know, a washing machine tech or a small motor person could have probably fixed this machine in ten minutes."

"Yeah. But where's the fun in that?"

He grinned. "Okay, so what now?" He inspected the motor and made a face. "Should we clean it a bit first?"

I snorted. "I think the rust and the calcium build up are keeping it from falling apart. Nope, now we put the fan belt back on and see how she goes."

We did that, both of us working together while trying to keep my pink-socked foot out of the way. It was tricky, and at times we were basically pressed right against each other, but I certainly didn't mind. I nudged him with my elbow and said, "Jeez, it's hard to believe we're doing all this pushing and shoving and grunting, and we're not even naked."

He sputtered out a laugh just as the fan belt slid into place. "Yeah, I uh, haven't made noises like that in a while."

I laughed. "Me either.

"Okay then," he said, his cheeks red. "Let's see if it works."

We plugged it in. We connected the water. We turned it on. Patrick gave me the honours... I cranked the old dial to On and pulled it.

And nothing.

"Well, shit. That was anticlimactic."

Patrick laughed. "Well, what do we do now?"

I sighed and looked at the working washing machine. "We could take the back off this one and see how it's supposed to look?"

Patrick shrugged one shoulder and smiled. "Okay."

So that's what we did. For the next three hours, we worked together, side by side, sitting, standing, kneeling, laughing, and talking. We studied the working motor and compared them, found a few things that needed tweaking and tightening. But then Patrick realised the drum was slightly misaligned from the bottom pin. With more shoving and grunting, and a lot more laughing, the drum clunked back into place. Patrick helped me to my feet, he plugged it back into power and grinned at me. "I've got a good feeling," he said.

I turned the dial back to On and pulled the knob.

There was a clicking noise, a random whirr, then the old washer coughed and spluttered to life.

"Yeah!" Patrick cried.

"Woohoo!" I echoed his excitement. "We did it!"

Patrick threw his arms out and collected me in a hug, lifting me off my feet. He spun me around while I laughed, and then he slowed and the atmosphere changed, the mood turned into something else, and he let me oh-so-slowly slide down his body.

We locked gazes and he glanced at my lips, licked his own, and his arms tightened around me. His eyes, normally the colour of the sky, darkened like storm clouds just rolling in. I could see it the moment fear washed over him, at how close he'd come to kissing me.

So I buried my face in his neck instead. "I can't believe we got the old bloody machine to work."

Patrick set me down on my feet, and I quickly lifted my left foot off the ground, having landed on it awkwardly. "Ow, shit," I hissed.

"Oh my God, sorry," Patrick said quickly, fussing with his hands. "Are you okay?"

I nodded. "Just forgot about it, that's all. I'm fine." I turned to open the lid of the washing machine and the water stopped, as it should. "We should go tell Frank the good news."

Patrick handed me the crutch. "You sure you're okay?"

It's like the idea of even possibly hurting me horrified him. "I'm fine. Honestly."

It was drizzling outside and Frank was mildly impressed, but impressed nonetheless. And then, after Frank had waved us off and closed his door, as we stood out of the rain not sure what to say next, Patrick and I were back to the dilemma of leaving or staying. "Oh," he said. "I have a stack of newspapers for you in the car. I'll grab them and run them to your van."

By the time I'd hobbled to my van and got the door open, he came running over with his arms full and a wide grin like running in the rain made him happy.

I could really get used to that.

And he wasn't kidding about it being a full stack. "Oh wow. Thank you!"

He dumped them on the table. "Like I said, I use them for the fire and not much else, so you're welcome to them."

The van was so small, I didn't think either of us realised just how close we were standing. I leaned my arse on the table to get my foot off the floor, but also to let Patrick know I was comfortable in his personal space. If he wanted to kiss me, I was right there, and I was close, and I was willing.

He let out a low breath, clearly very much on the same page. But he was still warring with himself; the civil war of Patrick Carney. But I understood, and even though I craved his closeness, I wouldn't rush him.

"It's okay," I whispered. "There's no rush, Patrick."

He let out a nervous laugh. "Am I that obvious?"

I took his hand. "Yes. And that's a good thing."

But then he was breathing harder and he squeezed my hand, and he moved closer and my heart stopped. He put his free hand to my face—warm and calloused and everything I needed. "I want to kiss you," he murmured. "But..."

"But you're not ready," I whispered. "And that's okay. I won't rush you."

He closed his eyes. "I feel like I'm the one who should be saying that."

"We're on the same page," I amended.

He stared at me, those stormy eyes raging, and he leaned in and kissed my cheek.

It was so incredibly sweet and tender, it made me giddy. I was smiling like a loon.

"I should go," he said, his cheeks red and a smile tugging at his lips.

I nodded. "Okay."

"Can I see you tomorrow?" he asked.

"Yes, please."

He laughed and hesitated to let go of my hand, then hesitated again at the door. "Yes, I'm going," he said, and I laughed as he ran out into the rain.

———

I SPENT the next few hours drinking tea and reading newspapers. Out of the thirty-odd that Patrick had given me, I found two articles about the bushfire. The first was from two months ago, claiming the families of the victims were eager to hear the coroner's findings, how the fire was started deliberately by some kids smoking cigarettes in correlation with extreme heat and weather conditions, and what laws and recommendations were expected to be handed down in regard to parkland maintenance and building construction. There really wasn't any information I couldn't have already guessed.

But the second newspaper was from just yesterday, the headline I'd seen at the newsagents.

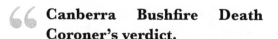

Canberra Bushfire Death Toll: Coroner's verdict.

The Australian Capital Territory's Coronial inquest determines who is to blame for the deaths of 43 people in last year's tragic bushfires. Liberal MP Anton Gianoli, whose boyfriend perished in the fires, speaks out.

My heart was beating so fast, my palms were sweaty, my stomach was in knots. I tried to read it slowly, and I was grateful Patrick wasn't here to see me.

The findings were rather simple, the expected laws and recommendations to be handed down that followed in the article were in-depth and complicated. While the fires had been deliberately lit, other factors contributed to the intensity and control of the blaze. I skimmed through the article until I saw a familiar name.

Anton.

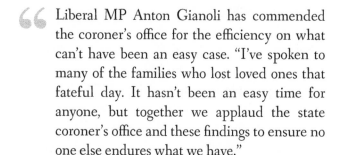

Liberal MP Anton Gianoli has commended the coroner's office for the efficiency on what can't have been an easy case. "I've spoken to many of the families who lost loved ones that fateful day. It hasn't been an easy time for anyone, but together we applaud the state coroner's office and these findings to ensure no one else endures what we have."

A cold shiver ran down my spine, and despite how my stomach rolled, I kept reading.

> Mr Gianoli downplayed his role in the expediency of the case. "I don't think my role in the political arena held any influence over the coroner's office. I did whatever anyone else would have done. I wanted to honour not just Ethan's memory, but his life, and demand the dignity he so rightfully deserved."

I clenched my jaw and tried to breathe calmly, though anger now sloshed with the bile in my stomach.

Dignity I so rightly deserved? Like the dignity he showed me? I didn't realise black eyes, split lips, and punches to the gut were what he called dignity. That threatening to kill me was the dignity I so rightly deserved.

Fuck him.

Fuck. Him.

I kept reading.

> From the total forty-three deaths, thirty-nine were confirmed and identified by the coroner's office, and four were not. Without dental evidence and with the missing persons' belongings found, the coroner's office supports the police findings that the four missing people were lost to the fire. With the bushfire heat intensity on the ground estimated to reach 1100 degrees Celsius, it was not likely coronial evidence would ever be found. The police stated, in regards to the four identities in question, there had been no

transactions on bank accounts or claims made in any legal or financial manner since the fire. These findings were given to the coroner to assist in the coronial inquest, and although it hadn't been official, it would be likely the coroner would soon sign-off on these four deaths.

It gave names and ages of three other people. Two men and one woman. And me. Ethan Hosking, 26.

"Ethan's last words to me," Anton Gianoli went on to say, "were that he'd been evacuated, that he'd see me soon, and that he loved me. I'm grateful I had the chance to tell him the same. Many people didn't get that chance, and I count myself as lucky."

"Liar. Liar!" I yelled at the newspaper, scrunching it up in a rage. I wanted to scream! I wanted to yell and scream and punch the shit out of something.

But my rage became full-fledged nausea and I vomited in the sink instead.

———

AFTERWARDS, I lay down on my bed and tried not to think about what I'd read. I hadn't even realised the rain had stopped until there was a knock at my door. "Aubrey, it's Patrick." He sounded very excited, like a kid almost. I opened the door and he bounded in. His abruptness and barging inside might have scared me if it weren't for the huge grin and the fact he was almost vibrating. "Do you trust me?" he asked.

"Um…" I was stunned, not sure what the hell was going on, but his excitement was contagious. "Yes. I do trust you."

And that right there was a monumental step for me. I *did* trust him. No matter what he was about to ask, I trusted him not to hurt me.

He laughed, his face so full of life and bright. "Then close your eyes, and come with me."

CHAPTER TEN

PATRICK

I'D LEFT Aubrey and gone straight home, busying myself inside with chores and making dinner, trying to not think about how close I came to taking his face in my hands and kissing him.

He'd stared at me with want and patience in his eyes, and I'd wanted to. I'd *really* wanted to.

I didn't know what stopped me. A whisper of guilt that it wasn't Scott... Or was it just fear? Because getting involved with someone also meant the risk of losing someone, and if I fell in love again and lost him, I was absolutely certain my heart wouldn't take it.

I'd thrown the last log onto the fire and stood up, coming face-to-face with the photo of Scott; his grinning face, his shining eyes. I could almost hear the echo of his laughter every time I looked at it. I could just imagine what he'd say to me if he were here right now.

He'd tell me to stop being so damn afraid. *Quit bein' a 'fraidy-cat,* he'd say. *Let yourself be happy, Patrick. Jesus, didn't my dyin' teach you nothing? Life's too damn short, Patrick. Don't waste a minute.*

I sighed. "It's not that easy," I replied to his photo.

It's exactly that easy.

With a shake of my head, I went outside with the intent to get more firewood. But I'd only got one step out the door when I saw it.

The aurora australis.

The southern lights.

The horizon was awash in greens and reds, the most amazing array of shimmering lights, dancing in the sky.

My very first thought was *Aubrey*.

I raced back inside, grabbed my keys and coat, and ran to my car. I drove right up close to his van and knocked on his door. I didn't want to scare him, but I didn't want him to miss this. "Aubrey, it's Patrick." He opened the door and I took the steps into his van in one stride. He was a little wide-eyed, so I put my hands on his arms. "Do you trust me?"

"Um." He swallowed hard. "Yes, I do trust you."

"Good. Then close your eyes and come with me."

"What?"

"Come on, hurry! Put your coat on, grab your beanie and your telescope," I urged. I found his beanie on the table near the newspapers, so I picked it up and fitted it to his head.

He snorted out a laugh. "Okay, but I can't hurry too much." He used the table as a crutch as he walked to his robe to grab his coat.

Oh dammit. His ankle...

He still had the pink sock on, which was a bonus. He slid his coat on and shoved the telescope in his pocket. "Any clues as to where we're going?"

"Nope." I picked up the crutch and handed it to him. "I

want you to close your eyes, and keep them closed until I tell you to open them. Can you do that?"

He blinked but gave a small nod. "Patrick..."

I put a hand on his arm. "It's okay. We'll walk slow and it's not too far, but you have to keep your eyes closed. Is that okay?"

His eyes tightened at the corners like he was testing his resolve. "Yep." Then he squinted his eyes shut and pulled his beanie down so he couldn't see even if he did open his eyes.

I took his hand, moving in close so he could feel me. "I'll help you walk, okay?"

He nodded, and true to his word, he kept his eyes shut as we got out of his van, one slow step and limp at a time. But as soon we were on the grass and I directed him, telling him how he was going and I kept my arm around him. "Not far now."

"The wind's died down," he said.

"Yeah, the sky's really clear."

He smiled then, like he might have had some clue what I was going to show him. I had asked him to bring his telescope after all. But this was incredible.

We walked past my car. "Almost there." We neared the entrance to the caravan park, and I wanted him to see this from the street. This road led right to the ocean intersection and the view was unimpeded. A few other people were down near the railing to the ocean, but we were pretty much alone.

"I can hear the ocean," he mused.

"Well, wait till you see this," I said. "Aubrey, it's beautiful."

"Can I look now?"

"Just a few more steps." We walked out the drive and

away from the trees. "Okay, stop. Face the sound of the ocean, and open your eyes when I count to three." He straightened up and was smiling as he pulled his beanie back, but his eyes were still closed.

"One."

I stood beside him.

"Two."

I took his hand.

"Three."

He opened his eyes and he stared at the wonder above us. Green lights danced and shimmered across the sky, with tints of red at the edges. His eyes went wide, his mouth fell open, and he slowly turned to me. His face was illuminated green; his grin was breathtaking. "Oh, Patrick."

I laughed. "I knew you'd love it."

He started to walk down toward the ocean, slow on his crutch, but he never stopped looking upward. "Are you freakin' kidding me?" he asked with a laugh. "How often does this happen here?"

"Um, maybe three times in my five years. They're visible in New Zealand and Tassie more often than here. The conditions have to be just right for us to see it."

"When electrically charged particles from solar winds enter the earth's atmosphere and interact with gases in the atmosphere," he said. "That's what conditions are required. There must be one helluva geomagnetic storm in the South Pole right now."

I found myself smiling at him, at his excitement, his absolute wonder. When we crossed the coast road and got to the guardrail, he leaned his crutch against it and took out his telescope. "Oh my God," he whispered. "I've never seen anything like it. I never thought I'd ever..." His words trailed off as his grin widened.

I didn't know which was more spectacular, the sky or the look on his face.

He scanned the sky with his grandfather's telescope, watching the southern lights dance and shimmer, watching the night sky and stars put on the show of a lifetime. He sighed and he laughed, and he shook his head in utter disbelief, but he never stopped looking.

"Pretty incredible show, huh?" a voice called out. It was Jim Baker. He waved and smiled as he and his wife, Nadia, and their three kids crossed the coast road a bit further up.

"I'll say," I replied.

Aubrey moved a little closer to me and I put my hand on his waist. Like a wary soldier, he glanced over at the other people, like he'd only just seen them, but kept his scope to his eye, never taking his gaze off the lights for more than a second. Maybe he didn't like being out at night, or maybe he didn't like the dark. I didn't know.

I rubbed his back and moved a little closer, leaving my hand on his hip.

Some of the other people were taking photos, so I took out my phone and snapped a few shots of the sky, the horizon, and the reflection of green on the ocean. Then I leaned against the railing and took a selfie, and when I was finished, Aubrey was grinning at me.

"Can I take a photo of you with the lights?" I asked.

He nodded quickly. "Sure."

So I did, then I asked, "What about a pic with the both of us?"

He turned around and leaned in close, both of us looking at the camera with the ocean and lights behind us. I snapped a few, not knowing if any were good or not. I was reluctant to move; his body felt good against mine, but he turned first, only to look back up at the sky. He gave me his telescope. "Have a look."

And wow. It really was spectacular through the telescope. "It looks ethereal."

"It really does."

I looked at Aubrey then and found him watching me. His face was lit with green refractions of light. His smile was the prettiest I'd ever seen on a man. "Oh, Patrick," he whispered. "I can't believe it. It's the most beautiful thing I've ever seen."

I was stuck staring at him. "Yes, it is. You are." I didn't know if it was the experience of witnessing the lights with him or seeing him experience the lights. But I was done fighting it. I was still scared—probably more scared than I'd ever been. But I couldn't *not* do this. I put my hand to his cheek. "The southern lights are beautiful, but they're nothing compared to you."

His smile became more serene because he knew I'd crossed whatever line my heart had drawn. He knew I was about to kiss him. I gently lifted his face and slowly pressed my lips to his. My heart was thumping like the waves on the rocks below, frightening and powerful. But it felt right.

Aubrey opened his lips, allowing me to deepen the kiss. He slid his arms around my back, melting into me while I cupped his face. I tasted his mouth, his tongue, so warm and silken, so perfect and right. I held him like he was made of glass; so gentle, so fragile. Or maybe that was me, and maybe he was holding me together.

When his tongue touched mine, I thought my blood might catch fire. It had been so long since I'd felt this, since I'd felt anything. But right there, in front of the very waters that had broken my heart, I felt alive, wanted, and I felt, for the first time in four years, that I was not alone.

Aubrey smiled into the kiss, and it slowed, languid and tender. I hummed before pulling my lips from his; I pressed my forehead to his.

"Evening, Patrick."

Aubrey jumped, startled, so I tucked him against me and turned to the familiar voice. "Penny."

"Enjoying your evening, I see," she said with a smirk and a wink. She held onto the railing and looked up at the green-lit sky. "It is very lovely."

Aubrey pulled back enough so he could peek around my shoulder but quickly ducked back again. He really wasn't good with strangers. "Um, Penny," I said. "This is Aubrey. Aubrey, Penny."

Aubrey glanced at me, then over at her. "Uh, hi."

"I know you," she replied.

Aubrey shrank back. Penny didn't seem to notice, but I sure did.

"You've come into the shop," she said brightly.

He cleared his throat. "Uh, yes."

"You're staying at the caravan park," she went on. "We notice new people around here. But I must say, Patrick's been keeping mum about you."

"Yes, well," I replied. "On that note, we'll be going." I turned to Aubrey and couldn't hide my smile. "You ready?"

He nodded. "Yes. Very."

"I didn't mean to scare you off," Penny said as we started to walk back across the street. "And for what it's worth, Patrick, I'm happy for you."

Oh God.

"I'm trying to walk as fast as I can," Aubrey said, hobbling quicker than he probably should.

I chuckled and pulled him to a stop. "Hold on to your telescope and your crutch, I'll piggyback you."

He stared at me, his face awash with green, his open mouth sliding into a smile. "Is that your best pick up line for sex? Because it could use some work."

I thought back to what I'd said... I barked out a laugh. "Uh, no. That's not what I meant at all."

He laughed right back. "I know. So, piggyback?"

"It's either that or I can carry you bridal style."

He hummed like he couldn't decide. "Bridal style, I think." He leaned in close. "That way I can see your handsome face. Though piggyback and having you between my legs is almost too good an opportunity to pass up."

I burst out laughing and looked back to see Penny watching us, smiling. Aubrey was smiling. I was smiling. "Oh, what the hell," I said, scooping him up, bridal style.

He was light enough, but I was glad I didn't have to carry him too far. "You're heavier than you look."

He laughed. "Gee, thanks. And you're more handsome close up than you look."

I carried him into the caravan park and set him down at my car. He steadied himself on one foot, then leaned back against the door and pulled my coat so I pressed against him. "If you were okay with kissing me once, do you think you might like to do it twice?"

I chuckled and settled my weight against him. I could feel his interest hardening against me, and it spurred me on. I lifted his chin and covered his mouth with mine and kissed him. Our tongues collided, and he moaned into the kiss, pulling me harder against him. Now that I'd kissed him once, I didn't want to stop. I slid my hand along his jaw, cradling his face and kissing him for all I was worth.

Eventually we had to slow down. We both needed air, but there was a good chance if I didn't pull away right now, we'd end up semi-naked and denting my car.

"Oh boy," I said, trying to catch my breath. "I should probably go. It's getting cold..."

"I hadn't noticed," he whispered, his breath a puff of steam. "If you wanted to come in for a cup of tea..."

I barked out a laugh. "Uh, I don't think tea is what you mean." I readjusted myself and grimaced, making him chuckle.

"I don't think you'd mind."

"It's not the part of my body I'm used to making decisions for me."

His gaze softened. "It's okay, Patrick." He sighed and looked up at the sky. The trees kind of hid the view, but the lights were beginning to fade. "Tonight has been one of the best of my life, so thank you."

"Oh. You're welcome." I knew it would be special, with the southern lights and all, but I didn't think it'd be *that* special.

His smile became wistful. "Down there, by the water, I could feel my grandad with me, seeing the lights for the first time too. He'd have loved this, Patrick. So thank you for coming to get me. If not for you, I would've just crawled into bed and missed the whole thing."

Oh.

"You're welcome," I whispered, fixing some hair that stuck out from under his beanie. "Can I see you tomorrow?"

"Yes, please."

I chuckled at his prompt reply. "Maybe I could kiss you again tomorrow?"

"I'll be disappointed if you don't." He curled his hand around mine. "I'll be disappointed, but I'll understand if you need time. Either is fine with me. Just being with you is fine with me."

I leaned against him, pressing him against my car, my

forehead resting on his. "Thank you." I kissed him again, with soft, closed lips this time, but somehow it felt more personal. I took a reluctant step back, my mind and heart at war with my body. "I'll see you after lunch."

I waited for him to get into his van before I drove home. I somehow remembered to grab some firewood before I went in. I fed Tabby, got ready for bed where I laid there, staring at the ceiling for hours.

I waited for guilt to slither in beside me, but it didn't. I didn't feel bad for kissing Aubrey. In fact, it felt really good. He was smaller than the guys I'd have thought were my type. Scott was my type: broad and burly. Aubrey was shorter and more slender, still strong but younger than I'd have pictured myself being attracted to. And I *was* attracted to him. I couldn't deny it; my dick had certainly shown an interest, and that was the first time since Scott. Sure, I'd taken care of myself since then, jerking off when the physical need arose. But this was different. My body was awake to Aubrey. My mind too. And now my heart was stirring... but there, lying in bed after kissing him, there was no guilt.

And then, because guilt shifted into whatever shape it wanted, I felt bad for not feeling bad.

I doubted this was a war I'd ever win.

———

I KNEW COLLECTING my morning coffee and papers was going to be akin to interrogation routines I'd seen in movies. Penny was either going to hold my coffee hostage, or my dignity, until I gave her answers. It didn't stop me from smiling as I walked in. In fact, I hadn't stopped smiling since I woke up. I'd finally fallen asleep sometime around one and woke around six feeling happier than I'd been in far too long.

Penny spotted me as I walked in and her grin was wide and a little smug. "Well, good morning, Patrick. Nice evening last night? The southern lights weren't the only thing on display..."

"Uh." I looked around the thankfully empty store.

"There's no one else here," she said. "That's why I'm yanking your chain. All jokes aside, Patrick, I'm happy for you."

"Um, thanks. It's still only new and nothing serious."

"But it's good," she said gently. "And it's about time."

"Is it?" I asked, not meaning to sound so biting. "I mean, is there ever a perfect timeframe? A milestone we have to pass that says it's okay to move on?"

Penny studied me for a second and sighed. "I reckon there is, yes. The distance is different for everyone, but I reckon when your heart starts to look for someone else, then that's your milestone marker."

"Mm, maybe," I conceded. "I don't know if my heart went looking... He just kind of turned up."

She started to make my coffee but gave me a nudge with her eyes in a not-so-subtle pry for information. "All mysterious-like, too."

"He's not that mysterious, Penny. He's a nice guy."

"So, where's he from?" she asked.

"The mainland," I replied.

Penny rolled her eyes and smiled. "I gathered that much. But if you're not telling, then I won't ask. Just as long as you're happy, Patrick. That's all that matters."

The truth was, I didn't know the answer to where he came from. I didn't know much about him at all, only snippets of details. Personal details, like about his grandfather and the ex who'd treated him horribly, how he left with nothing, and that his ex had ways of finding information. That was all I knew.

But I knew how he made me feel—young, alive, and happy—and that was enough. "Yes, I'm happy. But like I said, it's new and nothing serious, so I'd appreciate it if the whole town didn't know." She made a face, so I added, "If they don't already."

"I might have mentioned something to Cassy this morning, but she already told me you got the crutch for him, so we'd assumed you were friendly..."

Well, between Cassy and Penny, there was little doubt. All of Hadley Cove knew by now.

"I haven't seen Collin this morning," she whispered, putting my coffee and paper on the counter. "But I suspect he already knows. He told me you had Aubrey in your car the other day."

"He sprained his ankle," I admitted. "Walking around isn't much good for it, so I drove him." I paid for my coffee and newspaper and waited for her to give me my change. "I don't mind being gossip fodder. I guess it means they're leaving someone else alone, but I can't imagine Aubrey will like it too much. He's a private person, for good reason."

Penny's face softened. "People in this town like you, Patrick. They want you to be happy. We can't help it if us romance-starved women talk about hearts and flowers."

"There's no hearts and flowers, Penny. We're not there yet."

She reacted like I'd shot her in the heart. "Oh, you wound me! All new hot and steamy romances need hearts and flowers. Yours'll be the first new relationship this town has seen in years. You have to give us something to dream about."

I tried not to smile and failed. "I don't know if relationship is the right word."

"You were looking pretty relationship-like last night, laughing and kissing under the southern lights, then you carrying him off up the road." She swooned dramatically. "A girl can dream, Patrick. Even a fifty-two-year-old, grey-haired, eternally single girl like me."

I snorted. "Okay, well, if it gets to the hearts and flowers stage, I'll be sure to let you know. But as for now, we're just... we're just taking it slow." I felt ridiculous even admitting this to myself, let alone to someone else.

"Well, let me ask you this," Penny said. "Do you want it to get to the hearts and flowers relationship stage?"

I couldn't answer that—not out loud, anyway—and maybe that was answer enough. Penny nodded like it was. I took my coffee and papers and walked out into the rare sunshine. I considered walking across the road to see Aubrey and check how his ankle was this morning but made myself go home instead. I'd be seeing him in a few hours anyway, and I was trying not to get ahead of myself.

Were we at the hearts and flowers stage? Was it even a relationship? Would we ever be? I wasn't sure. But like Penny had pointed out, did I want it to be those things was the question I should be asking myself.

Because the answer for me was a nerve-racking, heart-stopping, guilt-inducing yes.

I couldn't help but wonder if Aubrey was asked those very questions, what would he answer.

God, coffee swirled bitterly in my stomach, and I was pretty sure I could add vomit-inducing to the list.

CHAPTER ELEVEN

I WASN'T LYING when I told Patrick it was the best night of my life. The southern lights were absolutely incredible. I'd dreamed of seeing them ever since my grandpa told me about them, and I truly did feel him there with me. Like how we'd camped out and lain about the fire and talked about dreams and laughed until the last star met the sunrise.

He'd have loved Patrick.

And when Patrick kissed me? That made an already perfect night even better.

I knew he'd struggled with how he felt about me. He was very honest with me, which I was grateful for, but he was also an open book. Whatever he felt showed in his eyes. And when he'd kissed me... he meant it. There wasn't any doubt. He'd crossed some mental line last night when he'd decided to kiss me; whatever had been holding him back—his memories, his grief, his guilt—was gone.

I also wasn't lying when I offered for him to come back to my van. Did I want to do more than kiss? Hell yes. Would it go as far as sex? I hoped so. I wanted it. I wanted him. I wanted to feel his strength and warmth. I wanted him to take me, have me, in all the ways he wished to have me.

Not only did he cross some line last night, but I did too.

I trusted him. When he'd barged into my van all excited and asking me to go with him, he'd asked me point-blank if I trusted him. And I answered instinctively, unequivocally, yes. I trusted him not to hurt me, not to do anything he knew I wouldn't like.

So last night was kind of a big deal for both of us, and I hoped, hoped, hoped he wouldn't wake up this morning and freak out. I said I'd give him time if he needed, and I would. And by the time lunch rolled around, I'd almost convinced myself he wouldn't show up, or if he did, it would be to say we were over. I was resigned to it. I expected it.

But when he turned up and was wearing a shy smile and blush on his cheeks, I held onto the hope that maybe, maybe he'd be okay. I was painting the handrail that lined the walkway when he walked over, and then he stepped in real close, slid a hand around my waist and greeted me with a soft kiss. "Hello."

"Hi," I replied, surprised, and very happy. "I'm glad you're here."

"Did you think I wouldn't be?"

I shrugged. "I wondered if you woke up this morning with a severe case of *What have I done?*."

He let out a nervous breath. "Truth is, I wondered that too. But I woke up this morning happy, actually. And a bit excited, if I'm being honest."

"Excited? What for?"

"For seeing you today." His lips twisted into a smiley pout, but his eyes were guarded. "Were you not... excited? Or nervous? Or did you go to sleep last night without a worry in the world?"

"No, last night, I went to bed with your kiss and your body on my mind, and one hand on my..." I winked. "If you know what I mean. This morning I woke up worried that you were going to bail."

Patrick chuckled and scraped his teeth over his bottom lip. "Just one hand?"

I laughed, and our gazes lingered. "I'm glad you didn't freak out and bail."

"Me too. And I'm glad you're okay with me... not freaking out and bailing." He eyed my foot and the crutch. "Painting while standing on one good foot, is that a skill?"

"I have many."

His laughter caught the sunlight, the flecks of silver in his beard, the smile in his eyes. "Did any of those skills include a lunch break?"

I laid the paintbrush on top of the paint can. "No it did not, and I'm starving. What do you have in mind? I can make us some toasted sandwiches. Not very exciting, but—"

"Toasted sandwiches sound perfect."

I only had some home-brand sliced cheese on two-day-old bread, but I toasted them up in the old frying pan, and Patrick sat at my table and ate with me like I'd served him some fancy five-star meal.

"You know, this is really good," he said.

"Well, it's not hand-dived scallops paired with mountain kabu turnips, or Sommerlad chicken breast with brioche cream."

He chuckled as he swallowed his last bite. "I don't even know what that is, but I take it you do."

I smiled fondly at him. "You'd think I'd miss the fancy food, but nope."

"What do you miss the most?"

I let out a long sigh. "You know, I've thought about that

a lot. There isn't much, to be honest. I thought I'd miss my wardrobe or coffees that cost six bucks, but I don't. It's pretty amazing what you don't actually need to survive. All the material things don't mean much at the end of the day. Though I had a pair of blue suede boots that I loved. I wouldn't mind having them back, even if I could sell them for enough money to buy food for a few months."

Patrick's eyes narrowed at his plate before he gave me a harrowed look. "That can't have been easy. Not leaving the boots behind, but everything. The whole ordeal." He reached over and took my hand.

"It's not. But I'm happier now. Even living in a van that's older than me." I squeezed his hand. "I do miss having a bank account. That kind of sucks. But I don't miss the internet or being glued to my phone."

He smiled. Kind of. "You don't have a bank account? I mean, you said you left it all behind..."

"I left everything. I can't open a bank account because I have no ID."

I could see all the questions he wanted to ask swim in his eyes, but he left them unsaid. In the end, he settled for, "And you can't get ID?"

I shook my head slowly. "Not right now."

"Do you think...?" He swallowed hard and held my hand a little bit tighter. "Do you think he... your ex, will find you?"

"It's... complicated. It's more complicated than just him wanting to track me down. It's been over a year, so I'm pretty sure even if he did know I was still... if he knew where I was, I don't think he'd expect me to go back to him. I'm out of that hold now, I guess. But going back opens up a lot of other questions and..."

He frowned. "And?"

"And it's complicated."

He considered that for a while, probably chewing over all the slivers of information I'd just given him. "Can I ask you something? You can say no comment if you don't want to answer."

Oh God, here it is. I wasn't ready for the hard questions I couldn't answer. But I also wasn't ready to say goodbye to the only good thing in my life. "Okay."

"Where are you even from?" He shook his head like it was ridiculous to even ask. Which it was. I mean, it was crazy that he didn't even know the very basics about me. "Penny asked me and I couldn't answer because I don't know."

"Penny asked?"

"She saw us last night, remember? And this morning when I got my coffee and paper, she tried to interrogate me. I told her you were a private person." He shrugged again. "But, Aubrey, the thing is, Cassy knows too because I borrowed the crutch from her for you and she pretty much guessed. And between her and Penny, it'll be all over the Hadley grapevine by now."

I threaded our fingers and rubbed the back of his hand. "I'm okay with that. As long as you are. This is your town, and they're probably worried about you."

He smiled. "Maybe. Their concern is probably forty per cent worry, sixty per cent for their daily gossiping. Don't be too alarmed if your ears burn for a while."

I chuckled and studied our joined hands for a while. "I was born in Wagga Wagga, New South Wales. My parents were killed in a car accident when I was three. I don't remember them. I went to live with my grandpa after that. He raised me like his own." I looked up at Patrick then, who was watching me so intently, so warmly, I could almost feel his arms around me from his stare alone. "Grandad died when I was nineteen. I was at uni. He went to the super-market and sat down on the bench seats out the front. He sat there so long a staff member came out to ask if he was okay, but he couldn't speak. They called an ambulance, of course, and took him to hospital, but he died before they got there. He had a massive stroke. Fit and healthy, watched what he ate, never smoked or drank, and in the end, it didn't matter."

"That's so unfair," Patrick whispered.

"It really is. He was a good man." I huffed out a sigh. "Losing the one and only person you've got isn't easy."

Patrick's hold on my hand tightened and I knew my words had struck a chord. "No, it's not."

"He'd have liked you," I admitted.

Patrick gave me a small smile. "And I'm sure I'd have liked him."

"Oh, he'd have probably driven you insane with the million questions about ocean navigation and charting."

Just then, Patrick's phone rang. "Sorry," he mumbled before answering. "Hello, Mrs Whittaker... Yes, fine, thanks, how are you?... Of course I can." He paused. "Can you give me a second?" He held his phone to his chest and smiled at me. "Are you busy this afternoon?"

"No. I need to give that handrail a day to dry."

"Want to help me fix a chicken coop and a veggie patch?"

I grinned at him. "Sure." Then I stuck out my pink-socked foot. "But I'm not sure how helpful I'll be."

He didn't seem to care. He just grinned and spoke into the phone. "We'll be there in half an hour."

And half an hour later, after calling into Patrick's place to pick up some tools and some bottles of water, we drove into Mrs Whittaker's place. She met us at the back door and watched curiously as I hobbled out of the car with Patrick.

"Mrs Whittaker, you remember Aubrey?"

She looked at my pink sock and walking crutch, then finally my face. "Oh yes. You borrowed the pantyhose. I imagine they'd go well with that sock."

Most people would probably find her abrupt or rude even, but not me. I laughed. "Pantyhose and socks together? No self-respecting man would ever wear his pantyhose with socks."

Her eyes were hard, but she fought a smile. "And I should think not. The static electricity could charge Patrick's lighthouse." She gave a wink. "If it doesn't already."

I laughed again, and Mrs Whittaker did too. Patrick looked between us, a little shocked and a lot amused. "Pardon?"

She ignored him and trudged down toward the chicken coop. "That damn feral dog is putting a lean on the wire. He ain't got in yet, but I don't reckon it's got another night in it as it is. My girls haven't laid in two days because he's scared them half to death." She stopped walking in front of the chicken coop which, yes, had a rather wary lean to the wiring. Then she waved her gnarled and wrinkled hand at her vegetable garden. "And the damn birds and bats are having a feast on my cabbages. The spinach is all but ruined."

"Leave it to us. We'll fix it right up," Patrick reassured her.

"Come on up to the house before you go," she said and left us alone.

So, for the next few hours, we worked on fixing the wire on the chick coop, making the frame stronger with some palings we found alongside the old shed. Then we did the same with the netting and hessian over the garden. The hessian was for protection from frosts, the netting from birds and bats, but together we got it all upright and secure. Patrick did most of the hard work, and I hobbled along and helped where I could. He was always patient, and while I was sure he could have done it quicker by himself, he waited for me to get my footing right and never got angry or frustrated with me.

I had to say, I really liked working with my hands and helping people out. And I really liked doing it with Patrick. The afternoon was warm, which was a nice change, but as soon as the sun got low and the wind picked up, the temperature dropped.

I regretted not bringing my beanie and coat, and I was kinda pissed at myself because it meant my time with Patrick would be cut short because, no doubt, he'd want to take me home so I didn't freeze to death.

We carried Patrick's tools to the boot of his car and he opened my car door. "I'll just run in and see Mrs Whittaker. Won't be long."

I fell into the seat, not even attempting to hide the wince at lifting my foot into the car. I'd probably overdone it again. It was getting better, but spending most of the day on it certainly wasn't doing me any favours.

Patrick came back out just half a minute later with an open box in his hands and a grin on his face. He walked around to my side of the car and plonked the box on my lap. Inside was an array of vegetables: potatoes, tomatoes, zucchini, eggplant, carrots, parsnips... Patrick got in behind the wheel, still smiling. "Payment for our trouble."

I laughed. "I really do like the whole bartering way of life here."

"So, we can halve it, or we can go back to my place and I'll cook up the best pasta and casserole you've ever tasted."

That wasn't even a contest. "Do you really have to ask?"

Patrick laughed and drove us straight to his house, where he carried the box in and waited for me to amble inside. He put the box on the table and turned and cupped my face. "I've been waiting all day to do this," he whispered before lifting my face to his and pressing his lips to mine.

I quickly fell into the kiss, opening my lips for him and letting him devour my mouth. He wrapped me up in his arms and sighed when I melted into him. We stood there and kissed, all lips and tongue, languid and tender, until he made a pained sound and pulled away. "Was it worth the wait?" I asked, all kiss-drunk and heart-thumping, body thrumming.

He licked his lips and his eyes were a shade or two darker. "Very. But I should start dinner. Or at least try and think coherently somewhere that's not this close to you."

I chuckled. "Or not. I don't mind."

He bit out a frustrated sound that was more whine than growl. "Dinner. Yes, dinner." He took the box from the table and slid it onto the kitchen counter. "Can I get you anything to drink?"

"Actually, I'm a bit of a mess." I motioned down to my dirty jeans and sweater. "Would you mind if I grabbed a quick shower?"

His nostrils flared and he tried to laugh. "You're trying to torture me, aren't you?"

I barked out a laugh. "No, I thought you might appreciate the space. But if you'd rather picture me naked and wet just a few metres away..."

He gripped the kitchen counter and groaned, then took in a long, deep breath and let it out with a painful smile.

"I'll grab you some clean clothes. We can wash and dry yours while we cook and eat dinner." He smirked at me as he walked past, and I was pretty sure he adjusted his dick as he disappeared down the hall. He came back out a few seconds later with a swathe of grey sweats and handed them to me. "For you."

I took them gratefully. "Thank you." Our gazes locked, and for a heart-stopping moment, neither one of us moved. Something was going to happen between us tonight. I could feel it in the heat of his gaze. "I won't be long," I said.

I brushed past him, our bodies touching, and the heat in the room soared. Yep. Something was definitely going to happen tonight.

I left the crutch at the bathroom door and put the toilet lid down so I could sit to unwrap my ankle. It was sore; I had overdone it, but my body was singing with anticipation. I didn't want to push Patrick too hard, too fast. The very last thing I wanted to do was scare him off. His body reacted to me and that probably scared him enough, but I wanted him to know it was okay. I wasn't playing him, I wasn't teasing.

I wanted him. And I wanted him to want me.

I allowed myself to enjoy the hot water, giving my dick a few slow pulls. I didn't want to jerk off to completion. I didn't want to waste it when it would be so much better with Patrick's hand... and I hoped that would happen tonight. I scrubbed myself clean and even washed my hair, then dried off and dressed in Patrick's clothes. They were far too big but incredibly soft, and they smelled of him: of warmth, and soap and the ocean. It made me smile.

I took my bundled-up dirty clothes and the bandage, collected the crutch at the door and held it with my clothes, then hopped into the living room. When I all but fell into the sofa, I realised Patrick was watching me from the kitchen. "You know, I don't think a crutch should be used like that. It only works if you use it to help you walk."

I snorted. "I know, but I needed both my hands. One for the dirty clothes, the other to hold your tracksuit pants up so they didn't fall around my feet and twist my other ankle."

Patrick came over to me, smiling, as he wiped his hands on a tea towel. "Here, let me help," he said, taking my balled-up dirty clothes. "I'll go put this load on now." He disappeared before I could argue and came back just as I'd finished straightening out the bandage to re-strap my ankle. "Want me to do that for you?"

"I don't want to be a bother. You're halfway through making dinner."

"I've finished. It's all chopped and set to simmer. I don't need to cook the pasta for about an hour yet," he said, sitting on the sofa with me, and patted his knee. "Put your ankle up here."

I scooted back against the armrest facing him and tucked my good foot under his arse to keep it warm. He raised an eyebrow, and with a smile, I slowly lifted my bad ankle onto his thigh.

He inspected the bruising and swelling with a frown and wrapped my ankle firmly, slowly. His fingers were expertly gentle. I couldn't help but think what they'd be like all over my body. When my ankle was wrapped, he ran his hand over my shin and took a slow breath before he looked at me.

I was almost lying down. If he turned just so, he'd be between my legs. We both knew it, that this was it. Anticipation unfurled in my blood, my belly tightened, the desire in his gaze, the heat... the fear. He needed me to guide him, to reassure him. "Do you want to kiss me, Patrick?" I asked, my voice rough.

He nodded and exhaled slowly.

"Do you want to lie over me, press me into the sofa?"

His nostrils flared, and he nodded. "Very much."

"I want you," I murmured. "We can take it as slow as you like. But I'd really like to feel your weight on me right now. If you want to, that is."

He swallowed hard and lifted my leg as he moved, and then like heaven and earth aligned, he knelt between my thighs and lowered himself onto me. Our mouths met, hot and wet, tongues colliding. Our hips met. Desire set the room on fire.

There was nothing else. Just me and him, desperate mouths, rolling hips. I clawed at his back and down over his arse, pulling him harder against me. He slid one hand underneath my arse, the other holding my face, caressing, pushing my hair back, thumbing my jaw.

He was so turned on, his rigid cock rubbing hot and hard against mine, and he shuddered and pulled back before gasping for breath. His eyes were dark, his pupils blown, his lips swollen and red. "God, Aubrey, I'm about to embarrass myself." He shuddered, and I could see the self-control battle with the need for release.

"I want you to come," I murmured, gripping his arse and arching into him. "Don't be embarrassed. I want to see how beautiful you are when you come."

He closed his eyes slowly, and a shudder rolled through him. He thrust his hips, and I opened my legs wider and lifted my arse the best I could. He crushed his lips back to mine, plundering my mouth with his tongue. He gripped the top of my head and my arse, and with an almighty groan, he came.

I'd never seen anything so stunning.

Or hot.

Waves of aftershocks rocked through him as he collapsed on top of me. I held him tight, teetering on the brink of my own release, so close... so close... I bucked my hips. "God, Patrick."

He leaned back, and I shoved my hand down my pants to grip my cock and pulled my shirt up just in time before I shot come on my belly. My orgasm hit hard and fast, pulling pleasure from my bones. My back arched and my cock surged in my fist. Spent, I collapsed on the sofa and Patrick was holding his weight off me, his eyes wide. "Holy shit, that was hot," he whispered. "God, I thought I hurt you."

I barked out a laugh. "Never."

He finally smiled, blush staining his cheeks. I realised then I still had my dick in my hand and he could see it. I couldn't even be embarrassed. "I should get you cleaned up," he mumbled. "Give me a second." He peeled himself away, a noticeable dark patch in the crotch of his jeans, but he grabbed a clean tea towel and handed it to me. "I'll just go and have a quick shower," he said, backing out of the room.

He looked a little panicky, but figuring he needed some space, I let him go. I cleaned myself up, thankful I'd had the presence of mind to lift the shirt he'd loaned me before I came all over it.

I heard the water turn on in the bathroom and decided to at least get the water boiling for the pasta. I inspected the pot of simmering veggies, which smelt amazing, gave it a stir, and Tabby kept me company while I waited for the water to boil.

She wasn't the only one we'd scared from having sex on the couch. She looked at me with wide, judgemental eyes but gave me an approving nudge and purr, so I figured we were okay.

Patrick was another story altogether.

He was a little edgy when he got out of the shower. Quiet, distant, and any attempt at a smile was all wrong. We ate dinner in relative silence, and I couldn't let it end like this.

It wasn't supposed to end like this.

Very clearly, he felt guilty for what we'd done. And I hated that I was the reason he felt bad about anything. In the absence of desire, all that remained was guilt. I didn't want him to feel bad. And God, I didn't want him to tell me goodbye.

I pushed the last of my dinner around my plate. As delicious as it was, my appetite was gone. Patrick frowned and put his fork down. "Aubrey..."

"I'm sorry if I pushed you into something you weren't ready for," I said before he could start the goodbye speech I so desperately didn't want to hear.

"It's not that," he replied quietly.

"Then what is it? Because what we have is good, yeah? You make me happy and I'm pretty sure I make you happy, but if you want to slow things down, I'll completely understand."

He shook his head. "I'm not sure what I'm ready for. I want to be ready. I really do. But that means I have to say goodbye to Scott and I don't think I can do that."

I reached out and grabbed his hand. "What? No, Patrick, that doesn't mean that at all."

"I can't expect you to hang around knowing I'm still in love with him. Because I am. I still love him. And I have conflicting feelings for you, which isn't fair on you. I'm sorry."

"Don't apologise." I stood up, still holding his hand. "Come with me." I led him to the couch and limped over, then sat down. I took his hand in both of mine. "Tell me about him. How you met and fell in love."

Patrick stared at the photograph on the mantelpiece. He took a while to gather his thoughts, and I waited. "He lived in Vivonne Bay. And when I moved here for this job, it didn't take long for word to get around. You know, that I was gay and single. He worked the fishing boats and came by to ask about tidal charts as an excuse to meet me. He was two years younger than me, charming, and very funny. He was always laughing about something. He was so easy to be around." Patrick's smile turned pensive. "We were inseparable for two years. He moved in here with me after just a few weeks. People thought we were crazy, but it was like the universe knew we didn't have long..."

I shuffled a bit closer and squeezed his hand.

"I hated his job. Fishing the Southern Ocean is just crazy. But he'd never known anything else. He started on his uncle's boat when he was fifteen, and he couldn't even contemplate doing anything different. He swore he'd be fine, even in the wildest storms. The wilder the better. He used to call the ocean his beast to ride, and he wasn't wrong." Patrick let out a long sigh. "The night before he died, the storm that rolled in was huge. There were coastal warnings, but he said they were going out anyway. They always did. The wind and rain hammered the coast, and we —" He made a face.

"Did you fight?"

He gave me half a smile and shook his head. "No. We made love, for hours. It was... magical. And when he left at three in the morning, he told me he loved me, just like always. Sorry, this isn't fair to you. I don't even know why I'm telling you this."

I leaned in and kissed his cheek. "He died knowing how much you loved him."

Patrick nodded, his eyes glassy. "He did. It doesn't sound like much, but it's a comfort to know that he knew I loved him."

"You'll always love him. You don't have to let him go. Don't ever let him go, no matter what happens between us. He's a part of you, of who you are. We should embrace that. Hell, Patrick, if he were here right now, I'd hug him and thank him. I won't ever expect you to act as if he never existed. That's not fair on you, or him, or me. If you catch yourself smiling at a memory of him, then I want you to tell me all about it; what he said, how he made you laugh. I don't want you to think I'll get jealous or sad or something, because it's just the opposite. I want you to share the joy. Celebrate his life, ya know? I can't have you in separate pieces, Patrick. The you that loved Scott is the same you that maybe wants to be with me. I want both versions of you, all of you. And if you have days when even thinking about him rips your heart out, then tell me. We'll go down to the rocks and you can scream at the ocean for stealing him away."

"He'd like you," he said blinking back tears.

I rolled my eyes. "Of course he would."

Patrick looked at me for a long, silent moment. "Thank you. You're more gracious than I deserve. I'm supposed to be the older, more mature one out of the two of us, and you're the one with your head screwed on while I freaked out."

"You didn't freak out, Patrick. You had a genuine, emotional reaction and were completely honest when I asked you about it." I kissed his knuckles, then turned his hand over and kissed his palm. "And you are the older, more mature one, I'll have you know. You have grey in your beard to prove it."

He laughed, which was the reaction I was going for. "Some would call it distinguished."

"Some would call it hot as fuck."

He leaned back and sighed, then put his other hand over mine. "You're kind of great, you know that? And you said the same me that loves Scott is the same me that maybe wants to be with you. There's no maybe about it. I do want to be with you." He let out a tired breath and gave me a crooked smile.

"But?"

Now he squeezed my hand. "There's no but. Only that I have baggage."

I leaned my head against the back of the sofa and smiled at him. "So do I." We did that just-staring thing for a while. "Can I tell you something?"

"Sure."

"You're the best thing to happen to me in a long time."

Patrick leaned his head back and smiled with kind eyes. "You're the best thing to happen to me in a long time too."

"And I mean what I said. Don't think you need to hide any part of you."

It was rich of me to say that, given I was hiding so much and we both knew it. He had every right to call me on it, or to point it out, at least. But he didn't. Instead, he pulled my bandaged ankle up onto his lap and rubbed my shin, and he studied my face for another long moment. Then he said something that I wasn't expecting, something that changed us.

"Stay."

CHAPTER TWELVE

PATRICK

I DIDN'T KNOW what I was doing. I was in uncharted waters, completely out of my depth. But I was doing what felt right, and asking Aubrey to stay, asking him to sleep in my bed, felt right.

I pulled the covers back on his side of the bed... *Did I really just think of the side I didn't sleep on as his?* He stood in the doorway, his left foot lifted so only his toes were on the floor. "Are you sure? I can take the couch."

I patted the bed. "This is much more comfy. But I'll understand if you don't want to... I mean, we don't have to do anything. That's not what I meant when I offered."

He walked over to me, his crutch clunking on the wooden floor, and stood right in front of me. "I know." He leaned up and kissed me, soft and sweet, then he leaned his crutch against the bedside table and sat on the bed, smiling up at me. "I could say something completely provocative with your suggestion of doing or not doing *anything* but I won't. I'll just say thank you."

He didn't give me time to reply, which was probably just as well, because I wasn't sure what to say to that. He lifted both feet up, being cautious with his ankle, and lay back, slowly, as if revering the experience. "Oh my God," he murmured. "This is divine."

I turned the light off, went to my side of the bed, and switched on my reading lamp. Ignoring the butterflies in my belly, I climbed in and settled on my side, facing him. "It's comfortable, yes?"

He smiled at me. "I can actually lie out straight, and this mattress is so much better than mine."

"You can't lie out straight in your bed?"

He rolled to face me and folded his arm under his head. He looked serene. "Only if I lie diagonal. I never was much good at doing anything straight."

I chuckled, then pulled up the blankets, mindful of his foot. When I settled back down, Aubrey slid over a little and put his hand on my chest, like he was testing the waters, before sidling in closer and finally resting his head in the crook of my arm.

I wasn't expecting that. I thought maybe he'd want to make out or maybe even get off again, but the delicate intimacy of him lying on me took me by surprise. I wrapped my arm around his shoulder and he relaxed with a long sigh. "You can't ask me to share your bed and have such an amazing chest and strong arms and not expect me to curl up on you."

I kissed the top of his head. "Amazing chest, huh?"

"Absolutely." He ran his hand over my shirt, his touch skimming over my nipple, warming my blood and zinging a jolt of pleasure southward. "And strong arms."

I gave him a bit of a squeeze, and he nestled in, so I rolled onto my side so I could hold him closer. His face was against my chest, and when I kissed the top of his head again, he let out a comforted sigh. I realised then that I was smiling. And very sleepy. Happy and even a little contented as I welcomed peace and slumber. We fell asleep in each other's arms and we woke up much the same. Except we'd been joined by Tabby, who decided Aubrey was her personal hot water bottle and curled up behind his knees. His hair stuck out at all angles, and when his still-sleepy gaze met mine, his smile was lopsided and lazy and utterly breathtaking.

"Morning," he croaked.

"Morning. Sleep okay?"

"Best night's sleep ever."

I was still smiling at him. "I'm glad. How does coffee and breakfast sound?"

"Like heaven."

"If Tabby's annoying you, just move her."

He looked mildly offended. "She's no trouble. I actually like the weight of her." Then he yawned into the pillow and mumbled, "Feel like I could sleep all day."

"You stay in bed. I'll get breakfast started." I got out of bed and stopped at the door. "You know what? You should stay in bed all day. I don't think anyone will argue that you deserve a day off."

He rolled over and gave a disgruntled Tabby an apologetic scratch behind the ear. "I have to finish painting that handrail today. Then start prepping the next one."

Then, right on cue, thunder clapped and rumbled right above us, followed by the sprinkling sound of rain. I smiled at him. "Well, that sounds a lot like staying-in-bed weather."

Aubrey's smile was slow, his eyebrow raised in suggestion. "Will you be joining me at some stage? Or is it a solo venture?"

I chuckled, but his invitation made my chest tight in all the right ways. "I have some things to do in the lighthouse, records and system checks. Won't take me long. Then I can make you breakfast and we can spend the day doing whatever you want."

"Promise?"

I wanted so much to crawl back in beside him. "Go back to sleep. Enjoy the sleep-in."

He gave me a peaceful, sleepy smile. "Okay." And just like that, he closed his eyes and his breathing evened out.

Seeing him all snug in my bed did crazy things to me. I couldn't deny that I liked it. I liked it a whole lot. My heart beat fast and loud, squeezing and singing. My blood ran warm, and it drew down deep in my balls and my cock started to fill.

This physical reaction to him wasn't new to me. I'd experienced it once before. I mean sure, I'd been with a ton of guys and had my share of fun, but full-body experiences —mind, heart, and sex—belonged only to Scott.

And now Aubrey.

It should have scared me more than it did. But any fear and uncertainty I'd had were gone. I'd woken up this morning with a peaceful feeling, as though a section of navigation charts had simply fallen into place, and now I knew where I was going.

I made myself leave the room with one parting glance at a now-sound-asleep Aubrey in my bed. I'd leave him be and let him sleep for now. He did deserve to have a day off. He'd spent who knew how long without a day's reprieve from worrying about food and shelter.

If I could give him this day, I would.

I'd like to give him more than just this day, but I pushed that thought aside. He wasn't my responsibility, and I was certain Aubrey would hate to think of himself as one. He'd survived this long without me, and I was sure he'd cope just fine again. But if I could make him happy for one day, I'd gladly take it.

The rain wasn't too heavy and didn't look set in by any means. After throwing on some jeans and a jumper and pulling on my boots, I ran to the lighthouse and climbed the one hundred and two steps to the top. I checked what needed checking, wrote down the readings, and signed the log book. Everything was in perfect working order, as it was every day.

I looked out at the ocean, to where blue-grey water met dark grey clouds. With no howling winds, the surface was flatter than normal, as if the rain had cooled the ocean's temper; she wasn't so angry today. We were moving out of winter, and not only did that mean warmer days and sunshine, but fewer cold fronts and smaller swells.

I was always relieved to see the back of winter.

Freezing waters and huge swells might very well be a part of life here, but I'd never not worry. Every time I saw a boat go out, a feeling of dread would lump in my stomach, and I'd say a silent prayer to any god that'd listen to watch over them.

Not that praying had helped Scott, or Theo and Damon, the two shipmates who went down with him. Wishing it hadn't happened, and wishing I could turn back time didn't help either.

I sighed, the sound loud in the round room. With a last glance out toward the unending horizon, I gave the ocean a nod and went back downstairs.

I stuck my head into the bedroom to find Aubrey still asleep, so I took a real quick shower, then stoked up the fire. And of course, Scott's photograph stopped me: his smiling face, forever young and handsome. I touched the side of the frame. "Things with Aubrey are... well, I don't know what they are. But he spent the night," I whispered, feeling the need to tell him everything. Then I had a sobering thought. If Scott was looking down on me from wherever he was, did he see me making out with Aubrey? Did he see what we did on the couch?

Oh God.

The sound of Scott's laughter echoed in my memory. *And he's still in your bed, Patrick.* His voice whispered through my mind like a warm, familiar comfort.

"I know."

Then what the ever-loving fuck are you doing out here? Get in there and give him what he's too nice to ask for.

He always did have a way with words. "Too nice...?"

He's giving you time. Because you asked for it.

"I did."

Let me tell you something, Patrick. No matter how much time you think you've got, it's never enough. Life's short. Haven't you learned that yet?

I almost laughed. That lesson was the cruellest test of my life. "I don't need a reminder."

There was only silence for a moment, and I had to wonder if I'd finally lost my shit and was hearing legitimate voices in my head or just the voice I wanted to hear.

"You'd like him, Scott," I murmured to his photo. "He understands me, about you. He gets that a part of you still lives in me, and he doesn't want to change that."

He's good for you. You need him.

That surprised me. "Need him?"

More than you know. Now get back into bed with him before he wakes up. Jesus.

I chuckled this time. Scott was never patient or one to mince words. I pulled off my sweater. "Okay, okay, I'm going."

Don't waste a day, Patrick. Not one more day.

———

I WENT into my room and found Aubrey still all snuggled in. And just thinking about getting back into bed with him had anticipation curling in my belly. I stripped out of my jeans, leaving on just socks and jocks, hoping he wouldn't be too affronted by my almost-nakedness. I wasn't assuming anything... I was just hoping.

He'd reminded me just how beautiful intimacy was, and now I craved his closeness, his touch, his warmth.

With a leap of faith and confidence I didn't feel, I slid into my side of the bed. He stirred at my presence, and I scooped him up into my arms and pulled him close. He melded against me. "You're cold," he mumbled.

"Sorry. You're all warm."

He nuzzled his face into my chest hair, then ran his hands over my hip, then stopped. "You're only wearing underpants."

"And socks," I added. "Is that okay?"

"No. I'm now very overdressed." He tried to pull his shirt off and couldn't really, so I helped him, and he quickly burrowed back into my chest. The skin-on-skin contact was... amazing. I didn't realise just how much I'd missed it. "So much better."

"Yes, it is." I sighed, feeling an earthy, warming wholeness in this contact with him. It had been so long since I'd been held like this, or even touched. It brought with it emotions, new and frightening, tangible and real.

"You okay?" he whispered. I didn't know if he picked up on my disposition or if he felt the same.

I pulled back so I could see his face. "This is good, right?

I mean, I don't want to jinx anything and I don't want to scare the hell out of you, but I'm feeling things I haven't felt in a long time, and that's as scary as it is incredible."

He put his hand to my jaw and thumbed my beard. "It is for me too."

"I've been so caught up with my own problems and I know you've had a horrible experience with trust, but I forget because you're so full of life."

"He hurt me," he replied. "For a long time. But he didn't break me. And I know you're nothing like him. I trust you. I mean, there's a lot I don't know about you, but I know I feel safe with you. And that's enough for me." He studied my face for a second. "And I know so much of my life is... well, has to be private. But I promise you, you know the important parts, the very best parts, already. I've told you things about me and my grandad that I never told... my ex."

I cupped his face and ran my fingers through his hair. To hear that he'd shared such special parts of his life with only me made me happier than it probably should have. I brushed my lips to his, but he was quick to pull back and make a face. "I haven't brushed my teeth."

I chuckled. "I'm sure I'll get over it."

"I could improvise," he said, a glint of suggestion in his eyes. He skimmed his hand down my side, gave my arse a squeeze, then ever so slowly, watching my face, my reaction, he slid his hand to my dick. Did he think I was going to stop him? There was no way I could have. I didn't want to stop him. My body wouldn't have let me stop him.

"Oh fuck," he whispered, gripping me through my underwear. "You're so big."

I groaned at the contact, hard and so incredibly turned on. No one had touched me in years. "That's so good."

Aubrey let go of me, only to slide his fingers under the

elastic, and then we were skin on skin, his hand, my cock. It was hot to the touch, and when he wrapped his fingers around me and pumped, I thought I might come.

But that wasn't enough for him. With the devil in his smirk, he slithered down under the blankets, his warm breath and soft kisses on my chest, my stomach, my navel, lower, lower... then he licked my cock from base to tip. I gripped the covers and closed my eyes to the sensation. "Holy shit."

And then he took me in his mouth, and I fought to not arch my back, to resist, to want, to need. My whole body was taut, strung tight and on the precipice.

Warm, wet, hot. Sucking, licking, devouring.

Then he groaned, and I stopped resisting. I sank into the bed and gave myself over to the sensation, to his ministrations. My orgasm teased me, just like he did. So close to the edge... so very close.

He devoured me and I let him. He gripped my shaft and pumped, sucked the head, and moaned around me. Then, so help me God, he took me into his throat and swallowed around me.

Pleasure barrelled through me, crashing me over the edge. Wave after wave of ecstasy took me under, and after the longest time drowning in pleasure, I broke the surface and gasped for air.

Aubrey swallowed with a hum, then pulled off me with a flattened tongue, only to kneel up between my legs. His lips were wet and inviting, but he had his hand down the front of his sweatpants, jerking himself off. And that just wasn't fair. "Want me to take care of that?" I asked. "Lie down."

He fell to the side of me, frantically pulling his pants down, and I rolled over and positioned myself between his legs, careful of his ankle. His cock was long and thin, hard, and flushed dark. I licked the slit—the familiar saltiness danced on my tongue—before taking him all the way in.

It had been so long since I'd done this. And even though it was familiar, it was new all over again. This wasn't Scott; this was Aubrey. This was a new direction, a new beginning. A new me, who'd begun to leave the past behind and looked forward to something else.

This wasn't just the act of sucking dick.

This was me breaking the surface and breathing for the first time in forever. This was me letting go and learning to live again.

"Oh shit, Patrick," Aubrey moaned. He writhed under me, alive to every sensation. "God, I'm gonna come."

His whole body jerked, his cock swelled, and I fisted the base and sucked the head, swallowing every drop he gave me. Tremors racked him, he convulsed and twitched, and finally he laughed, deep, throaty, sated.

"Oh my God," he mumbled, reaching blindly for me. He ran his fingers through my hair, stroking. "Come up here."

I crawled up his body, and as soon as my head hit the pillow, he snuggled right in. His face in my neck, his arms around me, trying to get closer still. I pulled him in tight and rubbed his back, he threw one leg over mine, pulled up the covers and we dozed.

It was intimate, our near nakedness, our closeness, his heartbeat against my own. We'd definitely crossed a line, and I was pretty sure there was no going back. He'd told me he had feelings for me, and I could tell; it was in the way he held me and clung to me. I'd told him I felt things for him that scared me and thrilled me in equal measure, and I hoped he could tell by the gentle circles I drew on his back or by the way I kissed the top of his head.

He nuzzled into my chest. "Is it wrong I find your hairy chest comforting?"

I snorted. "Um..."

"I'm trying to decide if it's a weird daddy kink that a shrink might say is directly related to the death of my father and being raised by an older man who I loved and also lost. Or if it's just hot as fuck for no other reason than it's hot as fuck."

I chuckled and kissed his forehead. "And there I was, trying to decide what to cook us for breakfast."

He hummed a happy sound and kissed my jaw. "I need a shower. If that's okay?"

"Of course it is."

"I should probably go home, though, and grab my toiletries. Razor, toothbrush, that kind of thing."

I frowned. "I have a spare toothbrush in the bathroom cabinet. It's unopened. You can have that. And just use my razor and shaving cream. I rarely use it so it's not a bother."

He leaned up to look at my face. "You sure?"

"Positive." The truth was, I didn't want him to go home. I wanted him to spend the day here and another night. Maybe even tomorrow too. I wanted to curl up with him on the couch and watch some crap movie on TV. I wanted...

Aubrey threw back the covers and rolled out of bed. "Ow, crap," he said, hopping on his good foot. He leaned hands on the bed, still with his foot off the ground, and looked at me, smiling. "I forgot about my ankle."

"Is it okay?" I asked, rolling onto my side toward him.

"Yeah, it's okay. I just put it down without thinking." He grabbed his crutch. "I'll just go shower," he said, hobbling out of the room.

I got up and got dressed, then padded out to the kitchen to make us some breakfast, even though it would be more of a brunch. I settled on poached eggs and fried tomato and toast and had just plated it up when Aubrey came out. He was dressed in his clean jeans and shirt, hair smartly brushed, looking all kinds of handsome.

"Something smells incredible," he said, smiling as he used his crutch to walk to the table.

I pulled out his seat and took a quick look at his ankle. It wasn't as swollen, though the bruising had gone from purple to a pasty green and yellow. "Still sore?"

"Only when I forget about it. I can put some weight on it, but it doesn't like to bend much though."

"Fair enough," I replied, sitting in my seat. I nodded to his plate. "Eggs and tomato okay?"

"Are you kidding? This is the most perfect breakfast ever."

We ate, and he talked about what he still had to do at the caravan park once the rain cleared up. And all I could think was I'd never been so glad for gloomy skies and rain splattered windows. My thoughts went back to how we could spend the day if he didn't leave just yet, and my heart squeezed with the realisation that I didn't just want him to stay. I longed for it.

He reached over and took my hand. "Patrick? You okay?"

"Stay," I replied without thought. "Stay here today, with me. And tonight if you want. We don't have to do anything sexual if you don't want, but I just really enjoy having you here and never realised how lonely I was."

Holy shit. Where did that come from?

Aubrey slid his chair back and hopped around to my side. He sat on my lap like it was the most natural thing in the world, put his arms around my neck, and rested his forehead on mine. "I really enjoy being here," he murmured, lifting my chin for a soft kiss. "I'm sorry you were lonely, but I'm really glad I'm here with you now. I'll stay today, and maybe tonight if you're not sick of me by then."

I smiled up at him. "I don't think that'll happen."

He smirked. "And just so you know, if we don't do anything sexual, it won't be because I don't want to. Because after yesterday and this morning, I'm pretty sure I won't ever want to stop."

I felt blood pool in my cheeks, in my groin. Maybe it was his words, maybe it was how he whispered them so seductively, or maybe it was the look in his eyes. I wrapped my arms around him and pulled him in just that little bit more. But then I teased, "So my idea of us just lazing about watching TV and playing cards isn't going to cut it, huh?"

He chuckled and kissed me again. "If you met someone who was dying of thirst, you wouldn't offer him two little sips of water and deny him anymore, would you?"

I laughed and gave him a squeeze. "Are you that thirsty man, and is sex the water you crave?"

He seemed to ponder that for a second, a playful gleam in his eye. "I'd never say no to water. I'm pretty sure doctors recommend two litres a day."

I barked out a laugh. "Is that right?"

"Yep. Though if you've abstained for a while, I'd suggest lots of little sips to begin with."

I chuckled at that. "I'm all for lots of little sips."

"Then I better stay here all day to make sure you get them." He kissed me again, deeper this time, lightly tracing his tongue against mine. And just when it was getting really good, he pulled back. "Should we clean up after breakfast, or should I swing my leg around and straddle you and make sure you stay hydrated? Because sitting on you like this is sexy as hell and it's good for my ankle."

"I think hydration is important," I began to say, and he crushed his mouth to mine and swung his leg over so he was straddling me. Once he was settled, he kissed me properly, his arms around my neck, grinding against me.

I pulled him in tight, desperate for any friction I could find. He rocked down on me, moaning at the contact, and I rubbed his back and squeezed his arse. My jeans were uncomfortably tight and I could feel the bulge in his, so I picked him up and carried him to the couch. Mindful of his ankle, I laid him down and pressed my weight on his. We made out like horny teenagers, laughing breathily and groaning every time our groins met at the right angle and pressure.

He did stay all day. We stayed on the couch or on the floor, just lying tangled up in each other like we couldn't bear to not touch. There was much *hydration* all day long, and by the time we fell into bed that night, we were both too exhausted to do much more than cuddle.

He really was a very good snuggly cuddler. And he fit against me so well; our hills and valleys aligned perfectly. I was much broader than him in the shoulders and hips, and his smaller frame tucked against me like he was made just for me. When we'd brought each other to climax the last time, he'd knelt over me in bed, pumping me, and I couldn't help but imagine, visualise, and fantasise being inside him. The thought of having my cock inside his little tight arse had made me come.

But it was more than a physical reaction or a fantasy. It crossed another line. An emotional line, a complication line. Maybe not for a lot of people, but it did in my heart and head, anyway.

"Can I ask you something?" he said into my chest.

"Sure."

"If I asked you to have sex with me, would you?"

I froze, shocked at how outright he asked. "Um." I laughed.

He leaned up. "What's so funny?"

"Haven't we been having sex?" I asked, trying to dance around the question.

He rolled his eyes. "You know what I mean. Anal sex. You, in me."

I sighed, long and loud. There was no avoiding having to answer. "I was just thinking about that," I started honestly. "About how maybe..."

"Maybe, what?"

"About how maybe you might want that, but I wasn't sure how to ask."

Now he laughed and settled back down with his face on my chest. "I want that. One day soon, maybe. It doesn't have to be right away." Then he sighed and ran his fingers through my chest hair. "I mean, it does complicate things a little, and for me, it's always been about connection rather than sex, so there's no pressure. I don't have any condoms, and I'm assuming you don't either, so we'll need to wait anyway."

I lifted his face and planted a soft kiss on his lips. "You just said everything I wanted to say. Thank you." I didn't know how it was possible that we were already on the same page.

He slow blinked and lazy smiled. "Maybe when you go into town next week, we could take a trip to the chemist and get some supplies. We don't have to use them straight away, but just to have them. Know what I mean?"

I nodded and returned his smile. His hair was kinda

sticking up, his lashes were incredibly long, and he looked sleepy and gorgeous. "Thank you for staying today."

He dropped his head back to my chest. "It's me who should be thanking you. Your cooking is amazing, I don't have to walk out in the cold every time I need to pee, your house is nice and warm, and I get to have cuddles with Tabby. It's kind of perfect, really."

I snorted. "So you're only staying with me for the food, the in-house toilet, the fire, and the cat?"

Aubrey laughed and squeezed me, snuggling in that little bit more. "You're forgetting one very important thing," he murmured.

"Yeah? What's that?" I asked, fully expecting some smartarse remark.

But he didn't joke at all. His reply was quiet and made my heart bloom. "You. I'm only here because of you."

He fell asleep in my arms and I stared at the ceiling for a long time, listening to him breathe and to the voice of reason in my head.

Tell him to stay another day, Patrick.

It was strange how the voice of reason sounded a lot like Scott.

Tell him to stay forever.

CHAPTER THIRTEEN

AUBREY

PATRICK and I both stared up at the clear blue sky outside his house, at the lack of wind, the perfect railing-painting weather.

"What would it take to convince you to stay another day?" Patrick asked, looking from the sky to me with one eye squinted shut against the glare.

"Not sick of me yet?" I asked.

He shook his head. "Nope."

"My breakfast cooking skills weren't *that* good," I said. While Patrick got up early to do his work, I fixed us a breakfast of mushrooms, eggs, and toast, with coffee. He'd devoured it in no time flat and rewarded me with a big face-holding, heart-stopping kiss.

"They were pretty damn good," he countered. "I mean, if you really want, I'll drive you back. I'll even help you paint the hand railing if you want. But I was thinking it looks like the perfect picnic weather. We could go and see if the sea lions are back?"

"You want to eat food with that disgusting smell?"

He chuckled. "Okay, so maybe not."

"I really don't want to let Frank down," I admitted. "He's been kind to me."

Patrick's face fell. Though he tried to hide his disappointment, I could see it in his eyes. "I can drive you back."

I could have very well walked, even with a shoddy ankle. It was, at most, a fifteen-minute hobble to the caravan park. "No, you can drive me back, help me paint the handrails, then we'll be done in time for a picnic up in the lighthouse tonight, where I will take my telescope —and very possibly make out with you a little—and I promise I will not sprain my other ankle on the way down."

From the way he chewed on his bottom lip, I thought he was trying not to smile too big. "Okay. But then tomorrow, I'll need to do the grounds, and that usually takes a whole day."

"Well, if we get all the handrails painted today, I can stay here tomorrow and help you and make you lunch. BLTs and BJs are on the menu. How does that sound?"

He laughed. "Pretty damn good."

———

TWENTY MINUTES later we drove into town and Patrick pulled up out front of the shop. "Won't be long. I didn't go yesterday, and I'm surprised Penny hasn't called a town meeting to go find me. Coffee?"

"Sure."

He came back out a few minutes later, grinning, with two coffees and a newspaper tucked under his arm. I reached over and opened his door, and he was still smiling when he climbed in. "I survived the Spanish Inquisition."

"Wow. Nobody expects the Spanish Inquisition."

Patrick laughed and handed me one coffee and the

newspaper, then started the car. "Penny said to say hi, by the way."

I found myself smiling, almost disbelieving that I'd found myself being accepted, welcomed even.

Until I turned the newspaper over and saw the subheading at the bottom of the front page.

> Canberra Bushfires, and How It Changed the Law

And my lungs froze and my brain wouldn't work. *What laws? What did they know?*

I tried to read the words, though they didn't make much sense.

> The construction industry can expect massive changes to state and national building standards even without the coronial inquest recommendations. Forty-three people lost their lives in what the findings believe may have been preventable...

Oh. It was about construction laws.

It wasn't about me.

"Not sure what difference it'll make," Patrick said, nodding to what I was reading. I looked up at him to see we were already at the caravan park. "They can make building homes in the middle of a forest harder, more expensive, with more restrictions and conditions. More steel, more cleared zones, but people are still gonna build there. And what's to ensure that those standards are maintained five or ten or twenty years down the track when it's all overgrown again." He sighed. "It's horrible that all those people died, don't get me wrong. But with a wall of fire a hundred metres high and a thousand degrees Celsius, it won't matter what your fire bunker is made out of when there's no oxygen. Much like it didn't matter when they changed the laws on boat safety and fishing laws. Standards on floatation devices can improve all they like, but in some cases, it just won't matter. Will an improved floatation device save a who that falls in on a calm summer lake? Sure it will. But they're not real practical for fishermen in the Southern Ocean when the swells are fifteen metres and the water's freezing cold."

His words came to a sharp stop like he caught himself from ranting.

He'd gone from fire to ocean on a dime and I didn't have to guess what his bugbear was about. "It's like closing the gate once the horse has bolted," I added. "Too little too late for those left behind." I held out my hand and he took it, and we sat there for a while in the quiet warmth of the car, letting our fear and fury dissipate and swirl away with the leaves outside the car.

And for the strangest reason, I wanted to tell him.

I wanted to tell him who I was and why I had nothing, and why I had no ID, and why I felt safe with him. I wanted to tell him about Anton and how he treated me and how he was a two-faced politician who hammed-up for the cameras, being the voice for LGBT Australia, when really, he didn't give a shit about matters of the LGBT community; he spoke loudest for whichever cause would give him the most fame and money. That he was just an abusive, controlling arsehole who would throw the whole LGBT equal rights movement under the bus if it meant he secured a better retirement pension deal for himself.

I wanted to tell Patrick I was sorry.

Before I could get a word out, Patrick opened the door. I

was so lost in my thoughts, in my memories, he startled me. "You okay?"

"Oh yeah, sure. You okay too? We both kind of got lost in our heads there for a bit."

He gave me a half smile. "Yeah, I'm good. Come on, though, we should get started on these handrails if we want to get them done today. I have a picnic and a make-out session atop the lighthouse with a really cute guy tonight. Don't wanna be late."

That made me smile. "Anyone I know?"

Patrick laughed as he got out, and I followed suit. I used the crutch to walk to my van, unlocked it, and went in. Patrick stayed at the door; given the tiny space and the pile of newspapers I was still going through, there wasn't a great deal of room. I gently pulled my boot onto my left foot, testing my ankle. It was still a bit swollen, and getting the boot on wasn't great, but once it was on, it felt okay.

"How does it feel?"

I stood up and tested it, though still not with my full weight. "Pretty good. It actually feels a bit more supported. If it starts to hurt though, I'll take it off and go back to the sexy pink sock."

He smiled up at me, squinting in the sun. And I'd thought he looked good in the rain. He looked even better in the sunshine. "You ready to get painting?"

"Yep."

We collected the paint and brushes from Frank's shed and spent the next few hours cleaning, stripping, and painting handrails. Sometimes we were quiet, sometimes we talked, but it was completely comfortable and we were both smiling. I told him how I took art in high school, though I was never good at it. But it got me out of two weeks of classes so we could paint the backdrop settings for the drama class. He told me he grew up in Adelaide and how his childhood dream was to be a fireman, though in hindsight, now he could see it was probably more of an early fascination with men. I joked about getting a fireman's outfit and sliding down poles, and he laughed. His cheeks and the tips of his ears grew pink.

I liked the way he laughed. It was a deep, rumbly sound that warmed my insides. And the way his eyes would crease at the corners and sparkle with humour.

We told stories from our childhoods. Of happier times when life was far less complicated, and standing in the warmth of the sun, with the ocean breeze and the possibility of spring just around the corner, it was easy to forget about the web of trouble I'd found myself in. It was easy to think— no, to dream—that this could be my life now.

When the rails were done, we started on the trims, window frames, and anything else that needed a touch-up. I was pretty impressed by how much we got done. "I think we just did me out of a week of free rent," I said, as we cleaned up. "Too efficient for my own good."

Patrick frowned. "I didn't mean to be that helpful. Sorry." He cleaned the paintbrush some more, frowning at it. "Will he really?"

"I can't stay here for free forever," I replied. "I'll run out of work to do, eventually. I'm kinda getting to the end of the line as it is."

Patrick frowned some more, but he let the matter drop. We got all the gear squared away, and he nodded towards my foot. "How's the ankle?"

"It's okay. Nothing a picnic in a lighthouse won't fix."

He smiled at that, then looked at his watch. "Perfect timing."

Back in my van, I threw a few things into my backpack:

deodorant, toothbrush, razor, change of clothes, and I bundled up my small supply of cash to bring with me. Well, to not just leave it in the van. Oh, and my telescope, of course. A month ago, I'd have been stoked with this caravan for somewhere to stay, but after spending a few nights at Patrick's house, I could see the van for what it was. Tiny, decrepit, and full of draughts, and I couldn't ignore the dankness that came with its age.

I know that Patrick saw the van and all its faults for what they were, yet he never made me feel bad. Like to him it made no difference to him if he picked me up from a fancy house or a shitty caravan. I liked that about Patrick; there were no pretences, no façades.

If Anton ever saw my van, he'd have turned his nose up and refused to set foot inside it. He'd be horrified and disgusted because he'd think he was so much better than that.

Than me.

Though Patrick never batted an eyelid. He simply smiled, held out his hand to take my backpack, and waited for me to lock the van. "Get everything?"

"Yep."

He drove me back to his house and waited for me to get out of the car. I tried not to let it show, but my ankle was kind of aching. "I shouldn't have sat down," I joked, trying to manoeuvre my backpack and the crutch while trying to close the door.

Patrick leaned in and gave me a soft kiss and took my backpack from me. "Come inside and put your foot up. I'll start on our picnic." He held the front door open for me and waited with a patient smile for me to hobble in. "Have you given any thought to how you'll get up those lighthouse stairs?" he asked, putting my backpack beside me on the sofa. "We can have a picnic in here if you want?"

"While that's a very kind offer," I replied, "I can't see the stars from your living room."

Patrick looked at the ceiling above his head. "Good point."

"I'll make it up the stairs. I promise." I pulled my boot off, fighting back a grimace and a groan, then kept my foot elevated on the sofa. "Thank you for helping me today. Between the two of us, we knocked that over in no time."

Patrick came back with a bag of frozen peas and knelt at my ankle. "It was no problem. Though I do feel kind of bad if Frank decides you've done all you can do for free. What will you do if he needs to charge you rent?"

"I don't know." I sighed. "I'm sure I can get work somewhere."

He put the peas to my ankle. "Maybe I can help with that."

"Don't worry about it," I replied. I didn't want him to feel bad or guilty or responsible for me. "I'll worry about that when it happens."

His brow pinched, and he stared at my ankle for a while. "Does that hurt?"

"Nope. The peas actually feel really good. I hope you don't wanna eat them after they've been on my smelly foot."

Patrick gave me a small smile. When his gaze met mine, he didn't look away.

I curled my finger in a come-here motion. His smile got a little bigger, and he shuffled a bit closer on his knees. "Closer," I said, curling my finger again. He moved up so he was kneeling right near my face. I crooked my finger again, down near my lips this time. "Closer."

He leaned down until his lips brushed mine. "This close?"

"Closer."

He kissed me then, properly. Deeply. I slid my fingers into his hair as we kissed. His tongue felt divine against mine, his beard scratchy in all the right ways. He pulled away far too soon. "If I don't stop," he murmured.

"I won't complain."

"You'll miss the stars."

"I'm sure you'll make me see them. Behind my eyelids when you have your way with me."

He sat back on his haunches and laughed. "Tempting." Just then, Tabby jumped up onto my lap, stood there, and glared at Patrick. He rolled his eyes. "Yeah, point taken," he said and got to his feet. "I was going to clean out the fire first. If that's okay."

I gave Tabby a scratch under the jaw. "What do you think, Miss Tabby? Can we watch your daddy while he cleans out the fire?" Then I looked at Patrick. "She said it's fine. As long as you bend over a lot and show off your magnificent arse."

Patrick laughed as he walked out the front door, and by the time Tabby had done her nesting circles on me and found a suitable position to curl up in, Patrick came back inside with a shovel and a metal bin and raised an eyebrow at us both lying on the lounge. I smiled at him. "She chose me. I'm not responsible."

"I know she did." He rolled his eyes happily, then started to shovel out the cold embers of the fire. Even without a fire going, his house was still a hundred times warmer than my van. His sofa was longer than my bed... hell, his sofa was almost longer than my van. So yes, it was a billion times nicer and more comfortable, but watching

Patrick shovel, bending over, showing off his thighs and arse, his arms, his strength... well, it was rather delicious. A warmth settled low in my belly, a buzz of anticipation, a thrill of knowing his body under those clothes, knowing his naked form, what he tasted like, and knowing I would very likely taste him again tonight, made me warm all over.

"I don't think we need a fire," I said. "I'm about to combust just watching you."

Patrick barked out a laugh and picked up the now-full bin and, with a blinding smile, walked out the door. I gave Tabby a gentle scratch on her head, earning a louder purr for my efforts. "Your daddy's hot as hell. Did you know that? Sexy. As. Fuck."

Patrick came back in, still smiling as he bent over me and planted a kiss on my lips. "I'm going to shower. I'm covered in ash and soot." And with a quick pat for Tabby with his soot-covered hand, he disappeared down the small hall.

I thought about joining him, but I figured if I did, we would definitely miss our picnic and the perfect view of the stars. We didn't get clear nights here very often, and I didn't want to pass up Patrick's offer of the lighthouse viewing.

And I kind of liked the way my body hummed with sexual tension. Waiting was a lot more fun when I could see the finish line. Just a few more hours and I knew, without a doubt, Patrick would make it worth my while. And that buzz in my belly crept a little lower and my dick responded in kind.

It was a heady feeling.

Knowing I wasn't broken. That I could enjoy myself after being in a bad relationship. That I was still desirable, and that my mind still allowed me to enjoy intimacy and touch, even after all the horrible things Anton did to me, and that my body was on the same page.

I had half expected to cringe in fear when Patrick first touched me, but instead, I'd wanted it. I'd fucking loved it. Though I knew it in my bones Patrick would never hurt me. He was all comfort and safety, and I craved it.

When Patrick came out, smelling all clean and lovely, he held up a picnic basket victoriously. "Found it." Then he grabbed a bunch of stuff out of the fridge and held up a bottle of wine with a questioning eyebrow. "Want a drink tonight?"

"Sure. Just how safe is hopping down a spiral lighthouse staircase while drunk?"

He added two wine glasses to the basket. "I'll carry you."

"Okay. Just how safe is piggybacking someone down a spiral lighthouse staircase while drunk? Asking for a friend."

He laughed. "We'll be fine."

Tabby hopped off me and sauntered into the kitchen, no doubt, given Patrick was rummaging through the fridge, in the hopes of food. So I sat up and took a look at my ankle. It felt better already, even after only resting it for just an hour or so, so I stood up and hopped over to the fridge. I handed Patrick back his peas. "They're completely thawed."

He made a face. "Well, that makes my decision easier. Soup and bread it is."

"What? You're just gonna whip that up right now? From scratch?"

He laughed and took my face in both hands so he could kiss me. "Yes, right now, from scratch. Won't take long."

"Want me to start the fire?" He'd cleaned it out but

hadn't started it again, and I wasn't overly fond of sitting around doing nothing. "I've rested my ankle enough."

"Sure!" He kissed me and opened the fridge, pulling out a bunch of veggies and a bag of what looked like steak. "This'll be the quickest Irish stew ever made. It's supposed to take hours to get the flavours right. My nan would be horrified."

I parked my arse in front of the fireplace, with my left leg stuck out straight to save my ankle any further grief. "Is your family Irish?"

"Yep. Well, my great-grandmother was born there and raised her kids as stout Irish Catholics, so my nan was raised as such. She had thirteen brothers and sisters, apparently." He told me a little about his family history while he chopped and seared, and my God, it smelled amazing. And I scrunched up newspaper and made a teepee of kindling, crisscrossing upward the way my grandad had shown me to start a campfire.

Patrick told me how he moved to Kangaroo Island when he was twenty-three to work in Penneshaw at the marina as a dockhand. He'd been on the island ever since, eventually scoring a job with the maritime, then moved to the west side when the job at the lighthouse came up. "I was lucky to nab a government job," he said.

He stirred the soup for a while, and I had the fire going nicely by then. "What about you?" he pressed. "I know there are things you can't tell me..."

God, I wanted to tell him everything.

"I moved to Canberra when Grandad died. Most people I knew had already moved to Sydney or Melbourne, but..." I swallowed hard. "The university course I wanted to do was at Canberra."

"Really? What was that?" he asked, checking something

in the oven.

"Political science."

Patrick stood up, turned mechanically, and stared at me. "Political science?"

His reaction kind of startled me. "Um, yeah. I did two years. I started later than my old school friends. I stayed in Wagga Wagga to get things squared away after the funeral. It took longer than I thought it would."

He came out from the kitchen, tea towel in hand. Whatever was on the stove was now forgotten. "Why two years at uni? Why didn't you finish?"

"I met... him. My ex." I stared at the fire. "He... lured me in, hook, line and sinker. I didn't need school, or work, or friends."

Patrick frowned. "Did you want to finish? I could help you get enrolled or something."

I shook my head slowly. "I don't want anything to do with politics."

And just like that, I'd said far, far too much.

I smiled up at him and held out my hand. "Help me up."

He pulled me to my feet and slid his arms around me, holding me tight and nuzzling the side of my head. He didn't say anything. He didn't need to. If he had any questions, or a thousand of them most likely, they went unasked.

"Dinner smells amazing," I mumbled into his shirt. "You smell amazing too."

He rubbed my back and kissed my forehead as he pulled away. "Help me pack it all up." He dished out a huge bowl of soup, fitted a lid, sliced up a damper-like lump of bread, and put it all in the basket. "You ready?"

"Yep. Want me to grab pillows and a blanket?" I asked, already hopping to his bedroom. I came back out to find him holding the basket and my crutch. "Thanks," I said, shoving the bedding under one arm and taking the crutch, and we made our way to the lighthouse.

The night was clear, and even the wind had stopped. Despite being a little cool, it was lovely. Patrick led the way inside, switched on the lights, and started on the stairs. I looked up at the mountain in front of me. Well, it might as well have been a mountain. I leaned the crutch against the wall, held the handrail instead, and took the first step.

One hundred and one to go.

Jesus.

"You okay?" Patrick had stopped a dozen steps up and turned to look at me. "We can set up a picnic near the rocks down near where the penguins come in if you want."

"No. I want to go up. I just might take a while."

He forged on up ahead, and by the time I'd made it up twenty-odd steps, Patrick came back down, smiled perfectly, and took the blanket and pillow. "I'll get everything set up," he said as he climbed the stairs, again, easily. *Jesus! Had he been up and back down already?*

Now that I could use both hands, one on the handrail, the other on the wall, I could lever myself up much easier. It was still hard going, and I probably used my ankle way more than I should have, but I was determined.

And when I finally made it into the control tower, I was a panting and sweaty mess. Patrick gave me a sad smile, crossed the small room, and slipped his arm around my back and helped me the last few steps. He'd arranged the blanket and pillows out on the gallery and had our picnic dinner already set out. Soup and bread, cheese and wine.

"Oh wow."

He smiled proudly, excited and nervous. "You like it?"

"Are you kidding? It's perfect. You're such a romantic. I

love it."

"Romantic?" He seemed honestly stunned. "Don't think so."

"Uh. Picnic at the top of a lighthouse with homemade soup and bread, with wine and cheese, so I can look at the stars? It doesn't get any more romantic than that."

"It's not just for you," he said with the start of a smile. "I like to watch you when you look at the stars, and you did say there might possibly be making out later on, so it's kind of for me too."

"Oh, there will definitely be making out later on. So much more than making out."

He took my hand and urged me to sit with him. We leaned our backs against the lighthouse wall and shared the soup and bread while it was still warm. "This is the most amazing thing ever," I said around a mouthful of food. "Oh my God, so good."

He smirked at me. "If you keep groaning like that, we might not get to finish dinner."

I laughed and shoved another spoonful of soup in my mouth. "But seriously, this is divine. You are the king of comfort food. Everything you cook just makes me want to curl up and cuddle you."

He snorted out a laugh. "Ah, so my plan is working."

I broke off a piece of bread and handed it to him. "You don't need the subterfuge. I'd curl up and cuddle with you without the food." The truth was, everything about him spoke of comfort to me. I considered telling him this, then stopped myself, then thought *why not*. Maybe it was something I needed to say. Maybe it was something he needed to hear. I dunked the bread into the soup and said, "Everything about you means comfort to me. The way you wrap your arms around me is like a blanket. Your voice is never loud or angry, just warm and safe." I ate the bread without looking at him. I felt if he saw the vulnerability in my eyes, I'd break apart. "Kind of like I'm lost at sea and you're the lighthouse and safe harbour. I know when I'm with you, no one can hurt me."

He was still and silent for the longest moment, and I'm sure my heart stopped beating. I'd laid another piece of my soul bare to him. And I'd said the words *lost at sea*... "I keep saying too much. Sorry," I whispered.

He lifted my chin and cupped my cheek, his hand big and warm. His eyes were an honest and imploring blue. He leaned in and ghosted his lips to mine in the barest of kisses. The *almost* kind, the very best kind. "Aubrey...," he murmured. "Thank you." He kissed me again, a harder press of his lips this time but still sweet. "You don't say too much. What you said just now was perfect. It was everything."

I smiled into his hand and kissed his palm. "This is crazy, right? This thing between us? It's probably too fast and we've both got baggage and grief, but it's real, right?"

Now he took my face in both his hands and brought our foreheads together. "It's real. Yes, it's crazy and fast and complicated. But it's real. For me, at least."

I closed my eyes. My heart expanded hot and full, squeezing against my ribs. "For me, as well."

He kissed me again, this time deeper, open-mouthed and tasting of emotions and hope. When he slowed the kiss, he bit his bottom lip. "Maybe you should see what's happening in the galaxy before we get too carried away."

With a kiss-addled mind and a hammering heart, I took out the telescope and looked skyward. The night was still clear, and the blanket of sky and stars above us was phenomenally vast and glorious.

We ate cheese and drank wine as the waves crashed peacefully against the rocks not too far away, setting a soothing metronome in the background, accompanied by the wind and the buzz and hum from the lighthouse.

It was surreal, and the buzz I had from the wine made it even better.

"Can you hear that?" I asked quietly, looking to Patrick before searching the stars again with the telescope. "How the ocean and the wind speak to the lighthouse. It's like a quiet symphony; an ode to the stars," I said, almost as a joke.

He touched my hair and ran his thumb down the side of my face. "Or an ode to you. You're so beautiful." When I put the telescope down and looked at him, he didn't look away. With his thumb, he traced my cheek, my eyebrow, taking in every line, every angle of my face, like he couldn't believe his eyes. "When you look at the stars, what do you see?"

"Impossible possibilities," I answered in a whisper. "Movement and stillness, incomprehensible vastness. Infinity."

Something flashed in his eyes, something that might have been wonder, and he held my face like I was the most precious thing in the world. "That's what you become when you look at them. You find peace up there."

"Yes." I barely made a sound when I spoke, but he heard me. Or felt it in the moment between us. I nodded slowly. "No one has ever understood that, but you."

He kissed me again, and the wine was sweet on his tongue. But it wasn't enough. I needed to be closer. I needed to feel him against me in all the right places. I needed more.

So, without breaking the kiss, I leaned up, and between the basket and the wine, I managed to manoeuvre myself so

I could straddle him. He was sitting with his back against the wall, and I loved that he had to look up and strain to kiss me. I bore down on him, my hips, my mouth, kissing him hard and grinding on his dick.

Something lit up in me like fireworks.

Something caught fire; a flame snuffed out long ago burst into life.

I broke for air and kissed down his neck while he gripped my hips and rubbed me up and down his erection. "I wish we were naked," I said, whispering in his ear. "I wish we bought those condoms already."

He thrust up and shuddered. "Jesus, Aubrey." He was panting, breathless.

"I bet you'd feel amazing inside me."

And he froze.

I pulled back, thinking I'd said something horribly wrong, but no. His eyes were dark fire, galaxies all on their own. "Saying things like that to me will bring me undone."

I might have smirked when I kissed him, teased him. "Then maybe we should take this downstairs." I pulled his lip between mine. "To your bedroom."

In less than half a minute, Patrick had lifted me off him and had the picnic packed up and was waiting for me to get to my feet. I laughed at his eagerness. No sooner had I stood up, then he'd bundled up the blanket and pillows and looked at the basket, then at my favoured ankle.

I could see the question on his face. How the hell am I going to get all this downstairs in the least amount of time possible?

He went into the control room and stood at the railing, looking down to the bottom. I got to the door to see him standing there, deliberating. "What are you doing?"

He stared, then extended the bundle of blanket and

pillows, and dropped it down the middle of the spiral staircase. He turned and grinned at the look of shock on my face. "It was the most economical way to get them down," he said, brushing past me to get the basket.

"Ah, Patrick…"

But he didn't launch that over the railing, thankfully. He put it inside, against the wall and out of the way. "I'll get it in the morning." He shut and locked the door to the gallery, then came to me. He turned around and crouched down. "Hop on. I'll piggyback you down."

I snorted out a disbelieving laugh. "You don't have to piggyback me down the stairs."

"Well, it's safer. My centre of gravity will be better with you on my back than if I carry you bridal style."

"I can't decide which sounds more fun," I joked. "Piggyback or bridal. Both sound like they could be a lot of dirty fun."

He straightened and turned, sliding his hand along my jaw. "I know it hurt to get up those stairs. You won't admit it, and that's okay, but please let me do this. I don't want you to put yourself at risk of further injury."

I lightly scratched the beard at the side of his chin and met his gaze. "And if you fall? I don't want to be the reason you get hurt."

"It's too late," he murmured. "I've already fallen."

He wasn't talking about tumbling down those steps. *Holy shit.*

I put my hand to his chest, feeling his heartbeat under my palm. I slid it up his throat to his jaw and pulled him in for a kiss. "Patrick," I whispered.

"Do you trust me?"

I nodded. "Yes."

He turned around and crouched down, and this time I

jumped onto his back, and he grabbed my legs before standing up to his full height. I held onto his shoulders, sliding one arm around to his chest, and he shuffled me a little until he was more comfortable carrying my weight. "Feel okay?"

"Very," I replied into the back of his neck. I followed it with a kiss.

"Can I suggest you don't do that on the way down? Because I don't fancy my knees buckling with fifty steps to go."

I chuckled and ran my nose along his nape. "Is the back of your neck a sweet spot?"

He shivered and readjusted me on his back, then he grumbled something that sounded a lot like *sent to torture me.*

So I behaved myself as he descended, sure step after sure step, though I smiled the whole way down. And soon enough, he stepped off the bottom tread and gently lowered me to the ground. I hopped over to my crutch, Patrick picked up the blanket and pillows, but then shoved them at my chest. I grabbed them with my free hand, but before I could ask "what the hell?" he put one arm around my back, his other at the back of my knees, and scooped me up bridal style. I laughed as he jostled me like I weighed nothing.

"You said you didn't know which you'd prefer."

I looked up at him, happy to lie against his chest and in his arms. "I actually said I didn't know which would be more fun."

He laughed and carried me out. I pulled the door shut, hearing it lock, and he carried me to his house. I pointed the crutch in front of us. "Charge!"

"I'm not running," he said, panting a little.

I laughed, feeling the buzz of the wine we'd drunk, and

when he put me down on my feet at his front door, I repaid him with a kiss. He opened the door and a blur of cat tried to escape. Patrick was quick to grab her. "Oh, no you don't, missy," he said, bringing her inside.

"Is she not allowed outside?" I asked, following them in. I dumped the pillows and blanket on the sofa, then pulled the front door closed.

"Not at night," Patrick answered, letting a peeved Tabby onto the other sofa. "She's petitioning for Whiskas cat food to include baby penguins in their selection."

I burst out laughing. "Oh, right." I pointed to Tabby who was still glaring at Patrick. "Don't eat penguins, of any age." I let my crutch fall against the blankets and limped over to Patrick. "You've carried me twice. Got a third in you?"

"Not since my thirties."

I laughed again. "You're even funnier when you drink wine."

His whole face was smiling, and he truly was so very handsome. All rugged and weathered, and neat, greying beard, and blue eyes. "Where did you need to be carried to?" he asked.

I put my hands on his shoulders, then lifted my left leg to his hip, then I launched off my right foot. He caught me easily and slid his hands under my arse. "Your bed," I answered.

He looked up at me, smiling. "I think I can manage that."

I kissed him and he walked, carrying me into his room. Without stopping, he knelt on his bed before lowering me onto the mattress. I pulled him on top of me, and he came willingly. We realigned our mouths, our bodies, and I opened my legs and he settled his weight on me.

We kissed and grinded and groped and moaned until we needed air. "You need to be naked," I urged. My mind couldn't focus on anything else. I needed to feel his skin. So when he leaned back on his haunches and peeled off his sweater, I took off my top as well. But when I went for my fly, Patrick took over. He undid them and got off the bed so he could pull my jeans off more gently over my ankle. Then he took off his own, underpants included.

I ran my thumbs under the elastic of my underpants, ready to take mine down, but Patrick knelt between my legs. "Let me."

Then he kissed the ridge of my dick through my underpants. He nudged it with his nose, his breath hot. He slipped the material down, exposing just the head of my cock, and licked me.

He undressed me like he was unwrapping the best present ever. He revealed my skin, inch by inch, kissing every spot as he did. When I was finally, *finally* fully naked in front of him, he kissed the inside of my thigh, then trailed soft kisses to my balls before sucking each into his mouth, one at a time, tonguing and adoring this very delicate part of me. And only when I couldn't stand it another second, I fisted my cock, and he pulled off.

He replaced my hand with his and took my cockhead into his mouth. Warm, wet, slick, and perfect. He hummed around me, working me over and taking me deep.

I was never going to last long.

Pleasure drew up deep within me, curling tighter and tighter until I couldn't hold it a second longer. I tried to warn him. "God, Patrick. Gonna come."

So he sucked me harder, and I could see his other hand disappear between his own legs, jerking.

I turned him on. Sucking my dick turned him on. My pleasure turned him on.

"Fuck," I groaned, arching as I came.

Patrick grunted as he swallowed the first shot, but then he pulled off quickly and knelt up between my thighs, jerking himself furiously, and he let his head fall back as he came with a long moan.

My cock spilled again, my orgasm prolonging and kicking up a gear as Patrick shot his load onto my stomach.

I'd never seen anything so hot.

"Jesus."

He fell forward, our sensitive and semi-hard cocks pressing against each other as he lay on me. His full, bone-less weight, felt like heaven to me. Sweat and come smeared between us, sticking us together like glue, his rough breaths caressed my neck, and he kissed the skin there with sated and smiling lips. "I don't ever want to move," he murmured.

I rubbed circles on his back and kissed the side of his head. "Then don't."

Eventually he leaned up on his elbow, resting his head on his hand and staring into my eyes. He traced around my eyebrow, down my cheek, my bottom lip, my cheekbone, studying every inch of my face. It was such an intimate thing to do. His earlier admission of having already fallen was right there in the most tender of touches, in the softness of his gaze.

I couldn't doubt him.

"Patrick." My voice cracked as I said his name. Emotions caught me by surprise, the weight of them, their devastating impact, suffocating and lovely all at the same time.

"I know," he replied, punctuated with a soft kiss.

"We really need to buy condoms," I said, my mouth too far ahead for my mind.

Patrick chuckled. "Is what we're doing not enough? Because I think it's perfect."

"Yes! It is." I put my hand to his face, hoping he would see the sincerity in my eyes. "That's not what I meant. It's just... I want to express that with you. I want to show you, with all of me, what you mean to me."

He kissed me again, a little slower this time. "I think I already know."

I nodded, still cupping his face. "What we're doing is perfect. If this is all we ever do, it would be enough for me. I just..." I laughed at how ridiculous this sounded.

"You just, what?" he prompted, his eyes curious and a little concerned.

"It sounds a bit stupid, but there's a part of me that thinks if you have me that way, if I let you into my body, then I will belong to you. Belong with you. For as long as this thing between us lasts, I'm yours and only yours."

"Aubrey," he murmured. His eyes danced between mine and a flash of pain crossed his face. "Are you talking about being exclusive? Because I can't be anything else. I don't know how to be anything else."

"No. Yes. I mean, no that wasn't what I was talking about, but yes. I can only be exclusive too. I don't want to share. I don't want to be hurt again. I'm not making any sense, and I ruined the moment. Sorry."

"What are you trying to say?"

"That I'm falling for you too."

And there it was. Everything laid bare with nothing in between. Like the space between the ocean and the galaxies above it. Unimpeded, yet completely, unbearably impossible.

CHAPTER FOURTEEN

PATRICK

I KISSED AUBREY. I couldn't stop kissing him. I didn't want to ever stop. Even after I'd cleaned us up and snuggled back in bed with him, I kissed him again, tender mouths and languid tongues. I held him just as tight as he held me, and we kissed some more until sleep fought with want and won.

I'd made peace with not knowing certain things about him because I knew in my heart, I saw the real him. The parts of himself that he allowed me to see were the honest, genuine parts; his hopes and dreams, memories that he cherished, and the things he did tell me about were things he'd never shared with anyone.

I believed him.

And what difference did his past make? At the end of the day, he made me happy. Happier than I'd been in a long time. Hearing him say, "For as long as this thing between us lasts, I'm yours and only yours," made my heart soar.

I didn't want to quantify what we had either. If it lasted a month or for the rest of my life, he'd shown me that I could love again.

Jesus. Was I really thinking of the words *for the rest of my life* and *love* in the same sentence? About the same man?

Yes, I was.

Watching him tonight in the lighthouse, as he searched the skies above, confirmed what I thought I already knew. The look on his face, the peace it gave him, the hope... well, it locked a little piece of him in my heart forever. And seeing him underneath me in my bed as he gave in to my touch, my pleasure, and him holding me afterwards, then being all flustered and telling me he wanted me inside him because he was falling for me too? Well, that sealed the deal.

I could love again. I could live again. There was life after Scott.

And as I fell asleep in his arms, with him all tucked away and safe and breathing deep, I was pretty sure my life, my love was with Aubrey.

———

I WOKE JUST as dawn was starting to peek through the blinds to find Aubrey sound asleep on his pillow facing me, all peaceful and beautiful. So, so very beautiful: his olive complexion, long eyelashes, pink eyelids, pink lips gently parted. I gave myself a few minutes of quiet, undisturbed staring time, marvelling that this man could very well be mine.

I recalled him saying he wanted to give himself to me, requesting we buy some condoms sooner rather than later. Looking at him now, all sleep-rumpled and so utterly handsome, I had to agree.

I wanted it too.

Jesus, Patrick, just buy some damn condoms and give

this boy what he wants. You know you want it too.

"I just said that," I scolded Scott's voice in my head.

Today. Buy them today.

I rolled my eyes.

Don't waste any more time. Scott's voice was lighter now, teasing almost. *You know how time works.*

Yes, I did.

Time simply didn't stop. It trudged on while you wandered aimlessly, helplessly, with only grief and loneliness as companions. Time mocked and ridiculed, passing slowly when you were the one left behind, and at the same time flying by so damn fast, reminding you that you were stuck.

Time was a cruel beast.

Today, Patrick.

"Okay, okay," I said, causing Aubrey to stir. He mumbled something, so I kissed his forehead. "Go back to sleep," I murmured, and he smiled as he slept.

I got up and started my day.

I did my checks in the lighthouse, checked weather reports and tide charts. I brought the picnic basket down, smiling at the memory. I found Aubrey in the kitchen by then, making scrambled eggs and fried tomato and fresh coffee. He looked gloriously carefree, laughing and feeding me toast over his shoulder as I came up behind him and slid my arms around him.

He looked completely at home wearing my tracksuit pants as pyjamas, which were way too big on him, somehow making it look adorable. He fed Tabby slivers of sliced cheese that he sprinkled on top of the eggs and waited until they'd melted before he served it up. We sat at my tiny table, eating and laughing, our feet interlocked or his hand casually on my thigh until he thought of something, then spoke with both hands.

I fell a little bit more for him right there. As the sun filtered through the kitchen window, spring beckoning on the island, it was the beginning of a new season in more ways than one.

"What's got you staring at nothing and smiling?" he asked. I hadn't realised he'd stopped talking.

"You."

He blinked, then laughed, giving me a kiss as he cleared the table. "Go and do your work," he said, dismissing me with a wave of his hand. "I have plans for you this afternoon, so shoo!"

I stood up. "Actually, I had an idea for this afternoon as well..."

He turned at the sink, limping a little on his foot but not using his crutch. "What's that?"

"I thought we could drive into Vivonne Bay. They have a chemist. If you get my meaning." I cleared my throat and pretended I wasn't blushing. Talking about buying condoms when we were in bed, or at night in the dark, was so much easier.

Aubrey raised one eyebrow, then when he understood what I meant, a slow smile spread across his face. "Really?"

"Well, you said you wanted to, and that's what I want too. I'm sorry if I gave the impression I didn't want that, because I really do." I'm pretty sure my face flamed. "I mean, I'd have to be crazy not to."

He limped over to me and took my hand. "You're not crazy. We can get them, and if it feels right for both of us, then we will. But if it's not right for both of us, then we can wait."

I stepped in close and gave him a hug, letting him feel

my semi-hard dick. "I think it will feel right."

He laughed and pulled our hips together. I could feel his length against mine. "For me too." But then he was serious. "I mean it though. We won't rush it."

"Aubrey, you want it. You've told me twice. And I made a decision this morning. I don't want to wait. I don't want to waste any more time."

"I'm not going anywhere. If you're not ready, we'll wait until you are."

"I am ready," I replied, trying not to let my frustration show. "It's like I've been in a fog that cleared when I met you. At first, I felt guilty, like I was cheating on Scott or his memory at least. But—" God, could I tell him this? Would he think I was insane?

"But what?"

"But I can hear a voice in my head. Scott's voice. Or his ghost, I don't know… It sounds crazy."

There was only concern in his eyes. No disbelief, no shame, no ridicule. "It's not crazy. What does he say?"

What does he say? Like it was completely normal that Scott was talking to me. "He told me not to waste another day. He told me, and I quote, 'For God's sake, Patrick, give the boy what he wants'."

He surprised me by laughing. "I like him. I can see why you love him."

Love him.

I can see why you love him.

Those two words stopped me. I did still love him, but it was in the past. I didn't want to say I *loved* him in past tense, because that sounded like it was over and forgotten. And it wasn't. He wasn't forgotten. He never would be.

But it wasn't love like it was when he was alive. It hadn't lessened any, it just became something else. It was a permanent part of my life. Like a background hum, a comforting presence that helped me get through dark times. It was still there, and I didn't want it to disappear; I wanted that hum, that white noise that comforted me.

But there was no thrill, no excitement in my love for Scott. It was different to what I might be feeling for Aubrey. To what I *was* feeling for Aubrey.

Aubrey was present tense. He was here and alive and looking a little concerned.

"Did I say the wrong thing?"

I shook my head and gave him a kiss. "No. You said exactly the right thing." I kissed him again but he put his hand on my chest before we could get too carried away. "Yeah," I agreed. "I better get back to work."

He smiled dreamily. "Yeah, you probably should."

So, somewhat distractedly, I started on my chores for the day: lawns, gardens, general tidying of the grounds. I was done by lunchtime and went back inside to find Aubrey showered and dressed, at the table with Tabby on his lap, reading a newspaper.

"I'll just grab a quick shower," I said, walking in.

"Can I make you a cup of tea? Or coffee?"

"No, thanks. I won't be long. We can grab lunch in town if you like?"

"Sure."

I scrubbed myself in the shower, washing away the dirt and grass clippings, and the nerves, if I was being completely honest. I was suddenly hyper-aware that it had been a long time for me. A while for Aubrey too, but it'd been four years for me...

Deep breaths, Patrick. You'll be fine.

"Shut up, this was your idea."

Scott's rumbling laughter whispered through my mind.

You know what to do. You always knew what to do. He's in very good and capable hands, Patrick. Relax and enjoy it.

"Easy for you to say," I mumbled to the shower as I scrubbed myself for the second time.

Believe me, Patrick. You will make it good for him. You don't know how not to.

I shut off the water, pretending my own subconscious, or Scott's memory, wasn't making my performance anxiety any worse, towelled off, and redressed.

Oblivious to my internal chasm of self-doubt, Aubrey met me with a bright smile. "Ready?"

I took a deep breath. "As I'll ever be."

————

THE DRIVE to Vivonne Bay was a quick twenty minutes. Aubrey chatted the whole way, using his hands animatedly. He talked about the landscape we drove past, about biodiversity and climate change, and it was pretty clear he was intelligent and gave thought to his word choice. I was reminded that he'd studied political science at university, which had surprised me greatly.

I didn't know why... I hadn't seen him as someone who even attended university. He did handyman things, and generally, university graduates weren't handymen. But he hadn't graduated. His ex had seen to that, apparently, and his expression when he'd divulged this titbit about himself was one of horror awash with regret.

He hadn't meant to give that part of his life away so effortlessly.

I had to wonder what that meant. That I could possibly piece together more than he intended me to know? He'd been in Canberra, at university, studying politics. His ex was a guy with reach, access to personal data or influence. A federal cop, maybe?

That would make sense.

But it wasn't my business to know. If he wanted me to know, or needed me to know, he'd tell me. Until then, I'd respect his privacy. For now, it could sit like a pulled thread on one of Mrs Stretzki's knitted beanies. I'd resist the urge to pick at it, to unravel it into something unrecognisable.

"Patrick?" Aubrey asked. "Did you hear anything I just said, or were you as far away as you looked? You're not having second thoughts, are you? Because it's okay if you... Just forget I asked. I shouldn't have pushed any more than I already have. Condoms are more than fine with me."

I shot him a look as I drove. *Condoms are fine?* "Huh? Sorry, yeah, I was a million miles away. Sorry. What were you saying?"

He gave me a nervous smile. "It's fine, don't worry. You okay?"

His hand was on my thigh. I hadn't even realised, so I quickly held it in mine. "Yeah, yeah. I'm better than fine. Sorry, what were you saying?"

I got the feeling what he'd said hadn't been easy the first time, and asking him to repeat it wasn't fair. He made a face, took a deep breath, and spoke on the exhale. "I was just saying there are anonymous STI kits you can take home, but they're pricey. I wouldn't need to see a doctor—because I can't. I don't have a Medicare card. If you didn't want to use condoms, because having to travel out of town or buying them online is a pain, in the long term, if you know what I mean. I was just thinking... I have some money I could use, and I'm pretty sure the tests are like 99.9 per cent accurate, but I'd always be worrying, like, what if the boxes sat in the sun or something at the chemist, would that affect their accuracy and I'm not sure health is something that should be gambled on. If you know what I mean. I am, like, completely certain I don't have any STIs but I can't guarantee that."

"Breathe, Aubrey." I squeezed his hand. "You're nervous."

He laughed and shot me a 'yeah, no shit, Sherlock' look. "Sorry. I am. I can't deny it. I am."

"I am too," I replied honestly. "But I'm pretty sure we'll be fine once our clothes come off."

He nodded and let out a relieved breath. "Yeah, I'm sure."

"And about the tests... what do you think?"

"I've never had unprotected sex with anyone but An—" He stopped dead and turned to look out the window, almost as though he was trying to make himself smaller. "Fuck. I almost said his name," he whispered.

We'd arrived in town, so I pulled over and brought the car to a stop. I took his hand in both mine, said, "Look at me, Aubrey." He did, and the wariness in his eyes hurt my heart. "It's fine. Whatever you tell me stays between us, okay. You can tell me anything. I don't care about what you did before I met you. It's none of my business. You don't have to tell me anything. But you can if you want, or if you need to. I'm here, okay?"

He nodded and his eyes glistened with tears, but they didn't fall. "Thank you." He took a deep, solidifying breath. "I had unprotected sex with him. We were together for four years, and we were exclusive." Then he made a face. "Well, I was. I can't say with any certainty that he was, though, which is why I should be tested."

He looked so sad. I slid my hand along his jaw and leaned in to kiss him. "I had unprotected sex with Scott. We were exclusive, and it was right for us. And I'll admit, I like it, but I'm completely comfortable with condoms. How about we make it condoms for now and reassess once we're sure."

He nodded quickly and finally gave me a genuine smile. "Okay. Good plan."

"You okay now?"

"Yeah. You?"

"Much better." It was true. I did feel better that we'd discussed this. Sure, we'd talked about it before, but this was a plan, a responsible plan, and I was comforted to know he was thinking long term.

I did catch the beginning of his ex's name, though. He'd started to say An...

Andrew.

Anthony.

Angelo.

I stopped myself. It wasn't my business. He clearly didn't want me to know, and that was okay. So I squared it away and drove to the chemist. "Please let me buy these," he said as I pulled into a parking spot. "I'd like to contribute if I can."

I hated that he was so skint, all because of the actions of another man. Aubrey was the victim, but he was the one who paid the consequences. Though I understood his need to pay his way. "Sure. I'll pay for lunch and we'll call us even."

He rolled his eyes because we both knew I'd paid for more lunches and made more dinners than he could repay. But I didn't mind; part of me liked providing for him. Call me old-fashioned or naïve. I wasn't sure. I wouldn't make the sugar-daddy list any time soon, but I liked knowing he was looked after.

"Any preferences I should take into consideration? Extra-large?" he asked with a cheeky smile. "Water- or silicone-based lube?"

"Whichever you prefer. I'm going to make it all about you anyway, so we may as well start at the beginning."

He flushed and let out an unsteady breath. Then he palmed his dick. "Seriously, we haven't even started yet and you're making me hard."

I laughed and he got out of the car. He had his boot on his injured ankle, and he walked with a favoured limp, but it was obviously feeling better. I watched him disappear into the store and let out my own breath.

"Where are the words of wisdom and reassurance now?" I asked my subconscious or Scott's memory or his ghost. I didn't know who or what it was.

Only silence replied.

"Yeah, thanks for your help. And don't even think about starting up a conversation or input when the bedroom door is closed."

No reply. It was probably just as well.

Aubrey came back out in no time with a white paper bag. He grinned at me. "I bought two of each. You know. My grandad always said it was better to be over prepared than to be sorry. He'd be proud."

I chuckled. "I'm sure he would."

"What do you want for lunch?"

"Something with lasting energy for stamina, but it needs to be real quick because I'm not an overly patient person."

I barked out a laugh. "I know just the place."

I drove us down to the wharf, to the fish co-op. Seafood didn't get any fresher than here. They literally took it off the trawler into the co-op. Scott had introduced me to it because he knew it so well.

"It's pretty," Aubrey said as we pulled up. "The old jetty, the pylons, the barnacles, the old boats, new boats, nets. I bet this place has a story to tell."

I nodded slowly. "This is the wharf Scott worked out of. His boat used to moor over there." I nodded toward the jetty.

Aubrey's face fell. "I didn't know, sorry."

"You weren't to know. And you're right. This place does have a story to tell. As do the men who fish here." He reached for my hand and I let him thread our fingers. "Scott used to say this was the best seafood in the world. But he was biased." I smiled at that, then pointed to his mooring spot. "The photo on my mantel, of him on the boat, was taken just over there. All the boats are out at the moment, with the good weather. Come on, let's get out."

He scrambled to follow me out of the car, quickly meeting me around my side. "Are you okay with being here?"

"Yes. I've been here a lot since. When it first happened, I spent that whole week here, waiting and waiting for news until I was so exhausted I couldn't stand up. Then one of the old fishermen drove me home."

"That must have been horrible."

"It wasn't good. They found debris and belongings from the boat. Then they conducted depth soundings and imagery from near the final mayday signal, and they found her. The Southern Cross lies three kilometres out and 130 metres down. Toward the continental shelf. That storm blew them way off course. Carried them like driftwood."

"The Southern Cross?"

"That was the name of the boat," I answered. He frowned at that and made a face. "What is it, Aubrey?"

His eyes filled with tears as the sun kissed his face and

the ocean breeze rustled around us. "The Southern Cross is what brought me here. The constellation. I followed it, here, to this island. To you."

I blinked at this... what was it? A coincidence? A revelation? Fate?

"Wow."

"Crazy, huh? That it would take him from you and bring me to you." He swallowed hard. "I don't know what that means."

I put my hands to his neck and pulled him into my chest. "It means... It means you're exactly where you're supposed to be."

And just like that, he'd given another tiny sliver of himself to me. Like him, though, I didn't know what it meant, but I knew it meant something. It had to be fate or destiny or chance—but *something* led him here.

The stars, he'd said. The stars led him here. The stars he studied and adored brought him to Hadley Cove and into my life. I didn't know if it was some code of the universe, some metaphysical transaction that balanced my general ledger, but I'd like to think both Scott and Aubrey were more than a journal entry to be squared away when my life was audited.

They were both so much more than that.

I kissed Aubrey's temple. "You're right where you're supposed to be."

He sighed into my chest before he pulled away to look at the jetty, the water, the boats. "Do you think Scott sees us? Do you think my grandad knows I'm finally happy?"

Just then the wind blew around us and a kestrel hung on the air, shrilling at the breeze. I took a deep breath, and with absolute certainty, I answered. "I think Scott approves. And I think your grandad would be proud."

Aubrey's gaze shot to mine, with something like wonder and the dare to believe in his eyes. "You think?"

"Absolutely." I nodded and held out my hand. "Come on. Let's eat."

———

AN HOUR LATER, we were home. I pulled my car up to the house to save Aubrey a longer walk, and he limped a little heavier to the house. He was quick to sit at the dining table and take off his boot.

"Is it sore?"

He gently rotated his ankle, wincing a little. "It's okay. Just reminding me that it's in charge."

"Can I get you anything?" I asked, flipping the kettle on.

He shook his head slowly. "Not to drink." He pushed the white pharmacy bag on the table and a box slid out. Condoms.

And suddenly the air grew dense like the barometric pressure plummeted. Or skyrocketed. Or became a vacuum. I wasn't sure which.

He turned on his seat to face me, made a show of spreading his legs, then licked his bottom lip. I could barely breathe. How was it possible that this younger man could level me so completely? I was older, I had more experience. I was fourteen years older than him—I'd had my first kiss before he was born, for God's sake...

Oh God. I'd had my first kiss before he was born.

Yet he was in complete control. I could almost hear Scott laughing and saying "he owns you already."

He wouldn't have been wrong.

"If we go to bed now," I said, trying to gain some

control. "We won't have all night. I'd planned on taking the whole night with you."

Aubrey stood, not breaking eye contact. "You can have me now, then again, all night."

"Twice?" my voice might have squeaked.

His smile was slow and smug. "Oh, yes. Once now, then dinner, then all night."

I looked at my watch. "Dinner's three hours away..."

His smile became a grin. "I know." He picked up the paper bag of supplies, taking it and every modicum of my self-control, and walked into my bedroom.

I unplugged the kettle and followed him.

CHAPTER FIFTEEN

AUBREY

I THREW the condoms and lube onto the bed and barely had time to turn around before Patrick was there. "Let me undress you," he whispered, taking the hem of my shirt. He pulled it up and off, then threw it behind him, tracing kisses along my shoulder. He touched me like I might break, or disappear.

"I'm here," I whispered. "And I'm yours."

He crushed his mouth to mine, and I had no doubt. There was no doubt. I was his.

Not in the way that Anton proclaimed to own me. So, so different from that. I was free with Patrick, in ways I couldn't begin to explain.

He broke the kiss, only to turn me around and pull my back against his front. His erection pressed hard in the cleft of my arse, and I melted against him, into him. He kissed the back of my neck, the side of it, down to my shoulder. He ran his hands over my chest, my stomach, my cock as he sucked on my neck.

I moaned without shame, without dignity. Without care. I didn't care. I was putty in his hands, and he was moulding me as he wanted.

My hands found his hair, and I rubbed my arse against his hard-on. "God, Aubrey," he murmured. Then he undid my fly and slid his hand under my briefs, gliding them down, over my hips. He wrapped his hand around my cock, giving me long, languid strokes while his lips trailed kisses over my neck. "I want to kiss every inch of you."

"Please. Please, yes."

"Sit on the bed."

I did as he instructed and he pulled my jeans off, dropping them to the floor. He took my sore ankle and kissed it tenderly, then my knee, my thigh. "Scoot up on the bed."

I did, and he stood up straight, stripped his clothes to stand naked for me. He was glorious. Dark chest hair with flecks of grey, fit and strong, and his cock, full and hard, glistening at the tip. He let me ogle him. He smiled when I licked my lips, then he followed me onto the bed.

He kissed up my other leg, the inside of my thigh, then sucked my balls into his mouth, one at a time, lavishing me, adoring me. He pulled off and licked my shaft, tonguing the head and slit. "Can I rim you?" he asked.

I was so lost to the sensation of his mouth, his touch, it took a second for me to even register that he'd asked me something. "Um, God, yes."

He chuckled and knelt back on his haunches. He was smiling, his lips flushed and swollen, as was his cock. A bead of precome slid from the slit, making my mouth water. I sat up. "Can I taste you first?"

He rose to his knees, offering himself to me. I licked the head, tasting him, then sucked him in deep. "Oh God," he moaned. His fingers combed my hair.

I hummed my appreciation and he pulled free. He let

out an embarrassed laugh. "That's too good. I'm trying to slow down."

I grinned victoriously, licking my lips. "You taste so good."

His cocked jerked and he gave himself a squeeze before tapping my knee. "Roll over."

I did that, fixing the angle of my cock so it pressed against my belly. Huge, warm hands caressed the back of my thighs, tenderly, beautifully, and over my arse, gently spreading me.

There was hot breath at first, then gentle fingers, followed by a warm, flat tongue.

"Holy shit." I gripped the bedding and tried to keep my hips still. But my legs widened all on their own, offering him more, begging for it.

And he gave it to me. Over and over, he pushed his tongue inside me, licked the seam to my balls and adding a fingertip, and every time he pulled out, I thought I might die.

No one had ever taken me like this. Rimmed me, sure. But not worshipped me, not with such devotion to my body, to my pleasure. To me.

"I'm going to add some lube now, okay?" he said, his voice rough, husky.

A shiver ran up my spine. "Yes, please."

I heard the pop of the bottle lid and the sound sank to my balls. Then there was cool liquid and slippery fingers, rubbing and teasing, then finally, a finger slipped inside me.

"Oh my God." My thighs spread wider, and I rocked back on his finger. "Yes, Patrick. More please."

Another finger, and I thought I might die. It stretched me in that delicious-burn way it does, and I buried my face in the pillow and offered more of my arse. Patrick put his palm on my lower back, ceasing my movements, quelling my urge to rock back and fuck his fingers. He paused me, not to tease me, not to be cruel, but so he could push in even further.

I moaned long and loud; my cock was leaking. I was about to fall apart if he didn't put his cock inside me. "Patrick. I need you."

Then he curled his fingers inside me and touched me where no one had ever touched me.

I didn't need my grandfather's telescope. I didn't need to look skyward, to be outside or surrounded by night.

I saw the stars anyway.

Then he was gone from my body and I was left reeling, vacant and bereft. I'd seen an undiscovered galaxy and he took it away. I wanted to cry. I wanted to plead. But I couldn't form words. I couldn't form meanings.

Then something bigger and blunter pushed against me, inside me, and slowly, slowly, inch by inch, he corrected me.

I groaned into the pillow, fisted the bedding, all while raising my arse and urging him to sink deeper inside me. I think I swore. I think I begged. I think I cried.

Patrick massaged my back, slow circles and perfect pressure, and when he finally breathed, I knew he was fully seated in me. I was so full, so stretched, so his.

"This isn't right," he whispered.

I froze. "What?"

He pulled out. "Roll onto your back. I need to see your face, your eyes."

I wasn't sure what he meant, but I complied. Then he positioned himself between my legs and folded my knees to my chest. "Is this okay?" he asked.

I nodded.

He pressed against my hole and slid back in. He framed

my face with his hands, watching every flicker of emotion and sensation. "I needed to kiss you," he murmured. Then he did just that. His soft lips, warm mouth, and subtle tongue owned my mouth while his thick cock owned my body. He gave me both until I surrendered.

He rocked up, angling and straining, and there it was again. That galaxy of pleasure, in all its glory. "Oh God," I gasped. "Fuck yes."

He did it again and again, right there, in that perfect spot, until I soared amongst the stars. I came, shooting come between us, and he held me, cradling me as I fell apart in his arms, kissing me deeply, prolonging my orgasm and riding it out.

Only then did he buck harder, just once, twice, until I couldn't stand it. He stilled, his face contorted in a blissful silent scream as he came. I felt his cock throb, surging and filling the condom inside me, a gruff groan ripped from his chest and he collapsed on top of me.

I was almost certain that heaven had just collided with the earth. That the world outside could resort to madness and we would be oblivious to all but this moment.

I wanted to keep him inside me forever. I never wanted to move. Patrick began to pull back, probably concerned he was crushing me. I held him fast. "Stay."

He did, settling back down, his weight keeping me tethered, centred. Our breaths steadied and our heartbeats synced.

And for that moment, it was utter perfection.

All too soon, he slipped out of me, discarded of the condom, and rolled us onto our sides so he could study my face again. His fingers walked their familiar path around my eyebrow, my jaw, my bottom lip. He looked at me as if he was seeing me for the very first time.

"Do I still look the same?" I joked.

"Better." He scanned my face, my eyes. "You somehow look even better than you did before. How do you improve on gorgeous?"

I smiled. "Having you inside me, having my come smeared between us. That's how. Because I now smell like you and you find that hot."

His eyes widened in disbelief. It made me laugh, but he was quick to return to studying me again. "What's wrong, Patrick?" I asked, not smiling any more.

"Was that okay? What we just did. What I did to you?" He made a face like he couldn't get the words right. "I mean, I didn't hurt you, did I?"

Now it was my turn to put my hand to his face. "You didn't hurt me at all. What we did, what you did to me, was the best love-making of my life. And that's what it was. It wasn't just sex." How could he doubt his ability in bed? After what he let me experience. I kissed him, soft and sweet. "You took me to places I've never been. I saw stars, Patrick. Actual stars. You put my pleasure before your own. You were very, very thorough, so don't ever doubt your ability."

He blushed, closed his eyes and bit his bottom lip. So I lightly scratched his beard, and when he opened his eyes, I said, "This felt amazing on my arse. So feel free to never shave. And did I tell you I saw stars? Because, holy hell, did I ever."

Now he laughed. When his gaze met mine again, the worry was gone from his eyes. "For what it's worth, it wasn't just sex to me either."

"It was amazing. Although you could have told me you had a magic dick."

He barked out a laugh, a deep, throaty sound, and he gave me a squeeze. "Magic?"

"I saw stars, Patrick. Not just bursts of light behind my eyelids. Actual fucking stars. Galaxies, possibly nebulas. Supernova, even." Then I considered that. "Okay, well, no. Maybe not a supernova. But we can have round two after we shower, maybe take a walk, have dinner, and you can reach supernova then."

He laughed incredulously, then counted on his fingers. "Round two. Make you see stars again. Make it a supernova. Soooo, no pressure then."

"I have faith," I said, grinning. "After your first performance, I have no doubts your second performance and every subsequent performance thereafter will only get better."

He rolled his eyes. "No pressure."

I pulled back and unglued our bellies; my come had stuck us together. "Shower?"

He took my chin in between his thumb and forefinger and drew me in for a quick kiss. "Yes. Not sure we'll both fit at the same time though."

I sat up on the edge of the bed and stood on my good foot. "We'll fit."

And we did. It was a squeeze, but it was fun and flirty and wet and slippery. I tested my body for any aches and pains but felt none. He really had taken care of me, in a way that no one else had, and I felt no discomfort at all; a testament to the time he took to prepare me. And if he thought I would be too sore for round two, he needn't have worried.

I'd actually never felt this good.

We redressed and took a walk along the jagged shoreline. I forewent the crutch, only limping a little. We watched waves crash against the rocks, and like the ocean and sky were in tune with us, gone were the grey, tumbling waves and low-hanging clouds, replaced by calm tides and clear skies.

We wore only T-shirts and jeans; though the breeze was cool, the sun was warm. Patrick either held my hand or put his arm around me, and we laughed at squabbling birds and we walked to the end of the island where all that lay to the south was ocean and Antarctica, his lighthouse to the north of us. And we stood there for a stretch of time we didn't measure, he wrapped me up in his arms, and neither one of us spoke. It was a profound silence, as though he was showing the ocean he had me now, and it replied with a lick of wind and a rush of salt air.

It was a defining point for us. It felt like we'd crossed a line we couldn't return from. Didn't want to return from. We were changed from who we were just hours before, different men. Better men. Together. Oh yes, we were now very much together.

It was in the way he held me, nuzzled against my hair, and kissed the side of my head. He wore his heart on his sleeve, there was no doubt.

I looked up at him, smiling at the peace in his eyes. Was it too soon to tell him I was in love with him? We'd already declared we were each falling for the other, and even that was monumental enough. I wanted to tell him, because I certainly wouldn't be lying.

Maybe it was the only honest truth I could give him about me.

He put his hand to my face and kissed me like it was all he could do to stop himself from saying he loved me. Maybe his kiss spelled it out for me.

Maybe it did.

"You hungry?" he asked.

I nodded. "Sure."

I'd put on weight since my time here in Hadley, with all the food he'd been feeding me. I needed to. I looked better for it, felt healthier. Gone was the gaunt face I'd come here with, and I almost recognised my reflection now.

"You can piggyback me," I said, jumping onto his back. He carried me easily and we were laughing when we got back to the house. He made a minced beef vegetable stew type dish, of which every mouthful was delicious. We snuggled on the couch with Tabby for a bit to watch some mindless drivel show, and when Patrick got up to throw a log on the fire, I got up to make him a cup of tea.

I had a plan, of course.

I put his cup on the table so he'd sit on a dining chair. I used the bathroom, and when I came back out, I turned off the kitchen light and put a foil wrapper and the lube on the table. He looked up at me. "Um…"

I pulled his chair around and straddled him, sitting on his lap, facing him. I kissed him first, then said, "Round two."

"Here?"

"Right here." I writhed on his lap, rubbing us both in all the right places. "Like this."

I pulled my shirt over my head, lifting up a little so my nipples were level with his mouth. He didn't need instructions. He pulled me in closer, latching onto my nipple, sucking and nibbling, and oh my God. I was hard in no time. And I could feel him hardening too, raising his hips in search of more friction. I pulled his shirt over his head and when he leaned back again, I pushed my mouth on his, plunging my tongue inside.

I was in charge this time. It was a heady feeling, this

responsibility, this power. Knowing I turned him on, that he yearned for my touch, needed it.

"Oh God," I mumbled, writhing against his cock. My arse began to ache now, not in a painful way, but in a needy way. I wanted him inside me.

I stood up abruptly and pulled off my jeans and briefs. His eyes went to my cock, then raked up my body until he met my gaze. Heat and desire beckoned me closer, so I leaned towards him, far enough so he could lean forward and suck me.

And he did.

He sucked me so hard and fondled my balls, pumping me, and moaning around me. My God, it was good. He pulled off so he could stand and undo his jeans. I pushed them down and he sat again, so I pulled his jeans off. The sight of him naked, sitting on the chair with his cock fully erect and jutting upwards, made my mouth water.

I took the lube and turned around so he could see me apply it to myself, slipping a fingertip in, more lube, then a second finger.

"Fuck, Aubrey," he whispered.

I turned back to face him then. His cock was now purplish and glistening. *Oh yes, he liked to watch that a lot.*

"Condom," I urged.

He made short work of that, leaning back and pushing his hips up so he could roll it down easily. I made a show of drizzling lube over his cockhead, then pumping him, slicking him. Then I straddled him once more, aligning us, and slowly, inch by inch, I lowered myself onto him.

The angle was different, and I had to lean back a little and flex my hips just so... then he slid further in. I had both hands on his shoulders, my feet around the back of the chair, and let my head fall back and gave into the breach, the gift we were giving each other. He gripped my hips and thrust up into me, long and slow, while he pulled me down.

The sound that came out of my throat sounded almost animalistic; a yowl, a cry, I couldn't even describe it.

Patrick looked up at me with love and wonder in his eyes, and he slid his arms around me. I kissed him, rocked on him, rode him, owned him. He filled me, in my arse and in my mouth, he held me, he adored me.

Then he held me a little harder and thrust into me a little sharper, and I knew he was close. "I need you to come," he ground out. "You're driving me crazy."

I lifted my feet and hooked them onto the back of his chair, changing the angle completely. He had to hold me up, but I could arch my back and push him deeper inside. I fisted my cock and stroked myself. I was flying again, full of him, impaled on him and loving it. He was grunting and groaning every time I rolled my hips and the sound pushed me over the edge.

My orgasm lurched me forward, and he braced me as I came. Come spilled from me, on him, on me, and I thought the strangled cry came from me. But it didn't. It was Patrick. He bucked and went rigid, his cock swelled and pulsed inside me.

He was glorious when he came.

Rugged and strong, vulnerable and exposed, and all man.

He trembled, he shook, he twitched, and eventually he grunted out a laugh. "Holy shit." He wrapped me up tight and buried his face in my neck, and he simply just held me.

"You okay?" I kissed the side of his head and eased myself off him. I hated not having him inside me.

He pulled back, his eyes a little unfocused. "I think I found your supernova," he replied with a drunk smile.

"Holy shit, Aubrey." He held me again, breathing into my neck.

I grabbed the tea towel off the table and cleaned my come off us, then gingerly got to my feet. I was a little sore, I couldn't lie. Not just my arse, but my legs and arms, from using muscles I hadn't used in forever, but it wasn't too bad. I took his hand and pulled him to his feet. "Come on. To bed with you."

We crawled into bed, still naked, nestled into each other, and with a deep breath and slow exhale, both of us were asleep.

———

I WOKE to the sound of birds and filtered sunlight through the blinds. Patrick was gone, doing his work, no doubt, so I rolled over and stretched, feeling every delicious ache in my body. I smiled at the ceiling and gave my dick a few slow, slow tugs. *Oh yeah, that feels good.* I didn't want to jack off, not to completion anyway. Just a few lazy strokes to make myself feel good.

He'd awoken something in me or relit the fire in my belly. I felt good, I felt balanced and strong, and I felt... happy. Happy for the first time in years. Since before I met Anton. Since before my grandfather died, really.

I felt free, like I could finally look forward to the rest of my life.

And with that in mind, I rolled out of bed, took a real quick shower, put on some pants, and padded my way to the kitchen. My ankle felt much better today, and I could almost walk on it without limping. I didn't know having the best sex of my life could heal a sprained ankle, but the rest of me was limber too. I felt fluid and relaxed and danced around Patrick's kitchen while I made us both some breakfast.

Whether he could smell the coffee and toast or if it was just perfect timing, he came in just as I was plating it up. He walked right up behind me, slid his arms around me, pressing his dick against my arse, and kissed the side of my neck. His hands were warm, his nose cold, his lips soft. "Morning, beautiful."

My heart squeezed, and I relaxed into him. "Morning, handsome. I made you breakfast."

"I can see. Though it's almost lunchtime."

"Really? Did I sleep that long?"

"You slept like the dead."

"No wonder I'm hungry."

"Smells good too." He kissed my neck again, and I could feel his hardness at the cleft of my arse.

"You smell good," I countered. I was putty in his hands. My knees felt like they might give out. I could barely speak. "You feel so damn good."

"Do you know what it does to me to see you wearing nothing but jeans in my kitchen," he whispered. He kissed my neck, my shoulder. His hands raked across my chest and stomach. "Low-slung jeans, bare feet..."

I tried to turn around, but with one hand on my hip, he kept me right where he wanted me. "Patrick, if you don't kiss me right now, I will lose my mind."

He turned me around then, with a smug smile and dark eyes, and oh so slowly lifted my chin and kissed me. He kissed me until all coherent thought had left my body. And when he finally pulled away, all I could do was blink and smile.

"So? Poached eggs?"

"Huh?"

He chuckled. "For breakfast?"

"Oh right. Yes." I put my hand to my forehead. "You completely wiped my brain. Yes, here, take a plate."

He took both plates of eggs and toast to the table and I took the coffee. He sat down in the same chair he was in last night and gave me a salacious smile. "You know I will never look at my dining chairs the same ever again."

I laughed and sipped my coffee. "Good."

I had flashbacks, vivid and hot, of me in his lap, naked, with him buried inside me. And from the way he breathed out real slow and shook his head, I was pretty sure he was thinking of the same thing. "Oh boy," he murmured and shifted in his seat. We ate in silence for a while, both of us smiling, then he said, "What were your plans for this afternoon?"

"I need to go and see Frank. My ankle's a lot better, so I can get back to work soon."

"Okay," he agreed easily. "I can drive you."

"Just let me clean up here." I gestured to the mess I'd made in his kitchen. "Won't take me long."

I filled the sink with hot soapy water and set about washing everything while he dried. Which would have been fine, but apparently standing next to me while I was wearing nothing but jeans was too tempting for him.

It started with a soft caress down my spine as he reached past me, then a kiss to my shoulder, then my neck, then he pressed me up against the counter, and I reached my soapy hands up into his hair, pulling him in to kiss me harder. He spun me quickly so he could kiss my mouth, his huge hands framed my face, and when I hooked one leg over his hip, he lifted my other leg and carried me to his bed.

"Are you too sore?" he asked, lying on top of me.

"No. I've never felt this good." I bucked my hips into his

so he could feel how turned on I was. "Patrick, please have me again. I need to feel you inside me."

And that was all it took.

Needless to say, I didn't go around to see Frank. We didn't leave his house. Hell, we barely left his room.

But he took me to the astral planes again. When I was face down with him on top of me, inside me, he found my sweet spot and worked it so thoroughly, he didn't just show me a supernova.

I became one.

———

EVEN THE NEXT MORNING, neither of us were in a hurry to go anywhere. Patrick got his few jobs done early and I made us lunch, and I told him I had to go and see Frank today, and he wondered if Donna, the day-care mum-slash-hairdresser would be free to give him a haircut.

"I can cut it for you," I offered.

He laughed. "Yes, but will I be wearing a beanie for a month?"

I tickled him, and he yelped and jumped so high he scared Tabby. "No wonder she prefers me," I said, laughing. "You almost kicked her."

"I was nowhere near her, and anyway, I know she prefers you. You walk into the room and she saunters over to you like a big hussy."

I chuckled at that. "She's a good judge of character."

He smiled wistfully. "I know. All animals are. The fact she didn't hide under my bed when you first walked through the front door told me about all I needed to know."

"And what was that?"

"That you were kind. Animals, especially cats, don't

react well to people with bad intentions." He frowned. "Though that doesn't bode well for me, because she looks at me with utter disdain."

"No, she doesn't. You are the bringer of food and the maker of fire, and those are her two favourite things. She was Scott's cat, right?" I asked, and he nodded. "Maybe she was grieving too."

Patrick frowned and looked at Tabby, frowning even more. "Oh. That's horrible. Now I feel bad."

I cupped his face and pressed my lips to his. "Don't feel bad. She's perfectly fine. She's healthy, she's spoilt rotten, as much as she tries to convince me otherwise. I can see how much you love her, and so can she. She's just pissy because you don't let her on the bed."

"That's why she hates me," he added. "Because Scott used to let her do anything and everything she wanted, and I'm the meanie. I don't let her on the bed or on the kitchen bench, and I don't let her snack on baby penguins."

"Ah, the ol' good-dad, bad-dad routine," I said with a smile. "And no snacking on baby penguins. Jeez, how strict are you?"

He was smiling now. "Well, not very. But I draw the line at baby penguins."

I snorted out a laugh. "I'm glad." Then I ran my hand through my hair, ruffling it. "Come on. You can cut my hair first. Then I'll do yours."

He baulked. "You want me to cut your hair?"

"Yeah, it's not that hard. I do my own all the time. Worst-case scenario is that we both look hideous together."

We took his sharpest scissors, the water spray bottle he used for ironing, and a dining chair outside onto the front veranda in the warm sun. I took my shirt off so it wouldn't get covered in hair and sat down and let Patrick cut my hair.

The truth was, I didn't care what I looked like. If it was absolutely terrible and I looked like I'd lost an argument with a hedge trimmer, then I'd shave it. No big deal. I was used to my short hair now. Once known for my long hair—recognised by it, even—now I blended in with the crowd easier. People noticed distinct features about strangers, be it tattoos or scars or hair worthy of a shampoo ad.

Patrick sprayed my hair with water, for no other reason than that's what hairdressers did. He didn't really know what for. But he snipped and snipped and made aghast faces every now and then that made me laugh, then he urged me to keep still and snipped some more and made another horrified facial expression.

In the end, he didn't do too bad a job. I looked in the reflection of the window and ruffled the top of my head. "Looks good."

He looked at my hair, gave me a sorry shake of his head, and handed me the scissors. "Well, I hope you're better than me."

He pulled his shirt off and sat on his chair, and I went to work. He had silver hair at his temples and at the nape of his neck. It matched his beard. "Just cut the grey ones," he joked.

I leaned down and whispered in his ear. "They're sexy as fuck."

But I trimmed around his ears and tidied up the top. I'd never profess to be a stylist-extraordinaire, but I did an okay job. I stood in front of him, legs spread, and finished the top, and given I was happy with it, I sat on his lap, straddling him. Not as sexual as I did the other night, but he smirked up at me. "Aren't you too sore? I rode you pretty hard last night."

"You rode me to heaven last night," I replied, fingering strands of his hair. "You can do that to me every day."

He put his hands on my hips and pulled me a little closer to his crotch. He had mischief in his eyes and a frisky smile. "I thought you called it a supernova, and now it's just heaven? Is that a downgrade or an upgrade?"

I kissed him. "Not sure. You might need to do it again to remind me."

He laughed just as a car came around the house and stopped a few metres away. No one drove up to Patrick's house. All visitors used the car park down by the road. His driveway was private. And it wasn't just any car, but a police car.

"Shit," I mumbled, climbing off Patrick and scrambling to put my shirt on. Not that there was much reason to. Sergeant Collin O'Hare had already seen us both shirtless, seen me sitting on his lap, seen us laughing, kissing.

Patrick stood and turned, shielding me from view. I don't know if it was intentional, but I'd never been gladder for his size and stature.

"Patrick," the cop said. He tried to look around Patrick to me, but Patrick didn't move.

He pulled on his shirt, calm as anything. "Collin. What can I do for you?"

"Just checking to see if you were all right," he replied, still trying to get a look at me. "Penny said she hadn't seen you in two days. She wanted me to send out a search party, but I settled for a house call." He narrowed his eyes. "Frank hasn't seen his tenant in a few days either."

"Frank's tenant has a name," Patrick said. "Aubrey's been staying with me until his ankle heals. He can't work for Frank while he's incapacitated, so it made sense."

Collin stepped sideways, closer, and gave me a cold, hard stare. "Doesn't look too incapacitated to me."

His scrutiny, his coldness, made the blood drain from my face. I actually felt a little sick. How had I become so careless? So lazy with my identity? "My ankle," I said weakly. I couldn't even swallow, my mouth was so dry. Then I realised I was holding scissors, and he seemed to notice at the same time. His stance changed, and I very slowly put them on the ground.

Collin relaxed a little, then looked to Patrick. "Can I have a word?" He shot me a scathing glance. "It's a private matter."

I didn't wait for his reply. I just said, "I'll be inside," and went as quick as I could.

What did he have to say? Did he know who I was? Did he know my god-awful secret? I was suddenly struck by the very real possibility of being found out.

I no longer cared about Anton finding me. I no longer cared if the police charged me with fraud or identity theft or whatever the hell charges they could throw at me. What even were the charges for faking your own death? I didn't know. I didn't care.

Now, my only one real fear was losing Patrick.

This whole house of cards I'd built could come tumbling down, and I'd care for none of it, but I couldn't even bear the thought of losing him.

Or worse, hurting him.

Oh God, finding out my truth would kill him.

I felt sick. Worse than sick. I felt every bit the fraud I was.

CHAPTER SIXTEEN

PATRICK

"HOW WELL DO YOU KNOW HIM?"

I blinked at Collin. "I don't think that's any of your business."

He looked out to sea and squinted, a pained look. "That's not what I meant. Clearly you know each other... well. In that sense." He stopped, cleared his throat, and started again. "I mean, what has he told you about himself?"

"He's told me all I need to know."

"Where he's from? Why he's here?"

"Yes."

"And?"

"And if you want to know, you can ask him yourself." He clearly didn't like my wall of defence. But he'd made no attempt to hide his wish to date me and this was clearly just poorly veiled jealousy.

"I'm telling you, unofficially, I don't believe he is who he says he is," Collin said quietly. "And look, I get how this sounds. I'm not blind, Patrick. You like him, and if it works out, then I'll be happy for you. But..."

"But what?"

"But some things aren't adding up. I'm being cautious, that's all. And I'd urge you to do the same."

"Look." I sighed. "Leave him be. He has his reasons for leaving his old life and for being here. He's not doing any harm."

"What kind of reasons?" he pressed. "Because I've looked into the name Aubrey Hobbs, and I couldn't find much."

"You've looked into his name?"

"I have every right to know who comes into my town and what trouble might follow them."

"Just as he has the right to move here without police scrutiny when he's done nothing wrong." He'd made me cranky, but it wouldn't do anyone any favours if I lost my shit at Collin. "Can I make a suggestion?"

He didn't say yes, but he didn't say no either, so I forged on. "If you do any more poking around in his past, don't make waves. Apparently the asshole he left behind has a certain reach, and Aubrey has genuine fears of being found. Genuine fears, you get what I'm saying?"

Collin considered this and gave a nod. "If it's a matter for the police, he should come forward."

"And if the guy who belted the piss out of him and did God knows what to him for years is a cop? Or maybe a police prosecutor? A judge? A hitman? How do you think that will end?"

Collin began to say something but wisely chose not to speak at all.

"Just leave him be, Collin. He's finally happy. I'm finally happy, and he's not hurting anyone." I sighed. "And if you do find out his entire history, do me a favour. Don't tell me. I don't want to know. I don't need to know any more than he's already told me. I trust him."

Collin squinted at the sea again. He was silent for a while as he digested what I'd said. "I'll let you get back to your... haircuts?" He frowned at that. "And go and see Penny before she sends out her own search party."

I knew his intentions were good, if somewhat misguided, so it was hard to be mad at him. "I will. And thanks, Collin."

He left to get in his car, and I took the chair we'd used and the scissors that were, for some reason, now on the ground, and went inside. And the look on Aubrey's face stopped me where I stood.

He was pale, haunted, and scared.

I put the chair down and the scissors and went to him. "Hey," I said gently, not sure if I should touch him or if it would freak him out. But I had to. I had to soothe him somehow, the only way I knew how. I wrapped him up in my arms and held him tight. "It's okay. He's gone."

"What did he want? Does he know?"

"Does he know what?"

Aubrey froze, then wriggled out of my hold. "I mean, was he here for me?"

"He's gone," I repeated. Jesus. The look on his face... "He just wanted to check up on me. I've been so caught up in you, in us, that I forgot about Penny. I haven't been into the store in two days, and she's been worried."

He swallowed, though it didn't look comfortable. Then he nodded. "Okay. Yeah, we've been a bit self-absorbed, haven't we?"

I was going to tell him that Collin was getting nosy, but quite frankly, Aubrey looked scared enough. "How about we go for a walk to the store? We'll see Penny, then we can walk to the caravan park and see Frank."

He nodded again. "Okay. Sounds good."

He was jittery, so I figured the walk would expend some pent-up energy. "Is your ankle okay?"

"Oh, um, sure. I'll use the crutch, but the walk sounds nice."

"We can get some fish and chips for dinner. How does that sound?"

He tried to smile. "Not sick of me yet?"

I leaned in and kissed his forehead. "Not even close."

Ten minutes later, we walked into Penny's store. "Well, I'll be," she said, folding her arms. "So you haven't eloped to South America to lie on some hot beach and drink cocktails with your new man?"

I laughed at her and waited for Aubrey to walk in behind me.

"Ah, so," Penny went on to say. "You're both accounted for. Just as well." She walked out from behind the counter and gave me a hug. "I told you to let me know if you were going MIA so I didn't worry."

"Yeah, sorry," I said, officially rebuked. "We got... busy." I blushed at my own stupid self, and Aubrey laughed.

Penny nodded with a smile. "I can see that. You both look radiant. Is radiant the right word?"

"I could think of more manly descriptions, but I'm not that insecure." I gave her an apologetic smile. "Sorry for making you worry."

She pretended to be mad, but her smile gave her away. "No doubt Collin's been around."

"Oh, yes. Left not long ago."

She winced. "Sorry. But he'd asked if I'd seen you or Aubrey, and I said I hadn't. As a matter of fact, I hadn't seen you for two days. Cassy hadn't seen you in longer than that, and neither had Frank." Penny gave Aubrey a pointed glance, then me. "It was Frank who told me you'd been sniffing around the... what did Frank call you?" she asked rhetorically. "Ah, pup. That's right. He said Patrick had been sniffing around the young pup. Figured if I found one, I'd find the other."

Aubrey's shoulder's sagged when he sighed. "A pup? I'm really not that much younger than him."

I touched his back, not sure if he was up for public displays of affection but needing to touch him a little, and gave him a smile. Then I turned back to Penny. "So, what you're saying is, everyone in town knows."

She nodded brightly. "Pretty much." She straightened a box of chewing gum on the counter. "And for what it's worth, Patrick. Everyone's very happy for you."

"Oh." I pretended I wasn't embarrassed. "Um, thanks?"

"Well," she went on like I hadn't even spoken. "Except for Collin. I thought he was starting to see someone. A fella from Stokes Bay. I think he was holding out hope that you might be interested one day, but evidently not."

I sighed. "He's a nice guy, but he's not for me."

Penny gave Aubrey a not-subtle pointed nod. "Well, we can see that. I bet Collin saw it too. Hope he didn't cop an eyeful when he came knocking." I chuckled, and even Aubrey smiled. "Oh God," Penny said, her eyes going wide. "He did, didn't he?"

I put my hand up, needing to stop this before it hit the Hadley grapevine. "Not exactly. We were giving each other haircuts, without shirts."

Aubrey nodded slowly. "On Patrick's front veranda. I was sitting on Patrick's lap."

Penny laughed and clapped her hands. "Oh, I shouldn't laugh. Poor Collin."

"Anyway," I said, trying not to be embarrassed. "We're just going around to see Frank now. We should have dropped by yesterday or the day before. I *am* sorry, I didn't mean to make anyone worry. Though I'm grateful you care. Thank you."

"Yes, yes." She waved me off. "You were busy. I get it. At least someone's getting busy around here. Lord knows, it's not me."

"Okay, then," I said, ushering Aubrey to the door, trying to save him from Penny's usual tirade about the lack of single men on the island. "I'll be back in the morning for my usual."

"Good. Newspaper and one coffee, or two?"

I grinned at her from the door, probably a little smug, and held up two fingers. "Two."

She rolled her eyes dramatically. "Just don't be strangers next time, either of you."

We walked out onto the footpath and Aubrey smiled. I didn't know if it was at the blue sky and crash of the waves on the rocks across the road or if it was because Penny included him in her 'don't be a stranger' spiel.

"She's a good friend to you," he said as we headed toward the caravan park.

"She is. She's loud and says some crazy things sometimes, but she has a heart of gold." I smiled at him. "She likes you."

"Yeah, how do you know?"

"Because she said she did. She's a pretty sharp shooter, and if she doesn't like you, you know about it. But she can see you make me happy, so that makes you okay in her eyes."

He stopped on his crutch. "Do I? Make you happy?"

I thought my heart might stop, but I couldn't lie to him. I nodded. "Yes." We just stared at each other, neither one of us speaking or game to look away first. But then a car had to go around us, and I realised we'd stopped right in the middle of crossing the street. "Come on, let's go see old Frank."

Aubrey knocked on his door. "Frank? It's me, Aubrey."

We could hear grumbling and shuffling, and I almost smiled. Until Frank opened the door and gave Aubrey a mean glare. "Thought you did a midnight runner," he groused. "Was gonna sell your stuff."

Aubrey took a small step back. "Oh, um," he stammered. Clearly, he didn't cope with confrontation of any kind. "Yes, I'm very sorry. We got, I mean, I got waylaid yesterday, and my ankle... I should have come around to see you, and I'm sorry I didn't."

Frank let out an impatient sigh. If he were a cartoon character, he'd be a rickety, cranky old steam train that huffed out steam and smoke all day long. "Yeah, well. You've done good work around here. It's the only reason I didn't make a fuss when Collin came around asking all kinds of questions."

"He came here?" Aubrey asked, paling a little.

"Assured me you've done nothing wrong, but he was being nosy. Typical for a copper. Anyways, I told him I'd seen youse two together, he might wanna try the lighthouse."

"He found us," I added. "Everything's fine."

Aubrey swallowed hard. "Yeah, so anyway, I just wanted to let you know I was sorry and that I'll still be staying on, if that's okay with you."

"Yeah, well, about that," Frank said, his voice softer now. "I might need your van. Got some workers from Stokes Bay. They're working at the pier down where your fella—" he said to me, mumbling something I couldn't hear and waved his hand at the sea in an *off yonder* fashion. We all understood what he meant. "They'll be here day after tomorrow, for four weeks. And I could use the money, and I didn't know if you was coming back. I told 'em they could have it. Sorry."

"Oh." Aubrey stared at him blankly. "Yeah, I guess that's fine. You should let the vans out, yes. The income will be good for you."

Frank frowned. His caterpillar eyebrows sat low over his eyes. "Where will you go?"

"He'll stay with me," I said.

Aubrey shot me a look. "I'll what?"

"You can stay with me." This was incredibly fast and crazy, but the words were out before I could stop them. Like my heart spoke instead of my brain. I gave him a wink. "Tabby would love to have you."

"Oh, and that reminds me. The fellas who're staying said they could use some deckhands. I told 'em you was a real good worker, if you ever came back. Dunno what they're paying, but I figure any money's good money. You could probably get some cash jobs."

Now it was me who was stunned into silence.

Aubrey nodded. "Thanks. I'll be in touch." He pointed his thumb to the van. "I'll just clear my stuff out and strip the bed for you. Thanks, Frank, for everything. And when those guys are done, if Patrick's sick of me, I might come begging for my van and job back."

Frank grumbled some more, and Aubrey went to his van.

I followed with a heavy heart.

I knew he could use the money, and I knew casual deckhands in crab season could make a ton of cash. It'd set him up for six months.

But the idea of Aubrey setting foot on a boat and sailing

out into the Indian and Southern Oceans, just like Scott had done, made me sick to my stomach.

He left his crutch at the van door and hopped inside. I stood outside, not seeing anything, not paying any attention. My mind was swimming. He appeared moments later with a backpack on. "You sure it's okay if I stay with you? I mean, I'm sure I could find somewhere else..."

There was nowhere else to stay in Hadley Cove. Maybe Penny might have a spare room or old Mr McPherson, but he'd have to pay board...

"Of course I'm sure," I answered. "The last few days have been the best I've had in a long time."

"I can pay some money," he offered. "I don't have much. But maybe I can see those guys that Frank mentioned about some cash work. I've never done any work on a boat before, but I'll give it a try."

"You don't need to pay me anything," I answered. I could tell by his face that my reaction was off. So I tried to smile. "Make me breakfast or lunch a few times and I'll call us even."

He held onto the sides of the door frame as he hopped down the stairs. "Well, I have everything." He pulled the door closed.

God, everything he owned was in one backpack. "Then let's get some fish and chips and go home."

He fitted the crutch under his arm, and together we walked out of the caravan park.

How had everything changed in ten minutes? He was going to be living with me! Which was my idea, I will admit. And I was very fond of the idea, of him sleeping in my bed, having dinner with me, cuddling on the couch, making out, making love.

But then the mention of him on a fishing boat put a cold

lump of dread in me. I was blindsided, completely thrown off course.

We were met by Cassy in the takeaway shop. Her usual bright and cheery demeanour made me smile a little, though I'm sure Aubrey saw straight through me. He thanked Cassy for the use of the crutch but kept watching me, like he was waiting for the guillotine to drop.

"Is something wrong?" he asked, once we'd ordered and taken a seat. "Because like I said, I can find somewhere else to stay."

I took his hand. "I want you to stay with me. I promise."

"Then what's wrong?"

I glanced at Cassy, who was standing a little close, trying to hear our conversation inconspicuously. "I'll explain when we get home."

"Okay." He nodded slowly, but there was something close to resignation in his eyes. Not like he'd expected bad news but as though he certainly wasn't surprised it would find him.

It hurt my heart.

"Everything between us is fine, Aubrey. Please don't worry," I whispered as Cassy was busy at the fryer. I squeezed his hand, trying to ease his worry, and when his eyes met mine, I hoped he could see my sincerity. "I promise."

Cassy bagged our order. "Have a good night, guys!" she said as we left.

"Everyone here is so accepting," Aubrey mused with a shrug as we walked up the street. "They just know we're together and there's no speculation or dirty looks. Actually, they're kinda excited by it. Which I assume is their excitement for you."

"More or less," I replied. "I guess they're glad I'm happy

again. But don't be fooled. There is a grapevine in this town that thrives. You and me will be the fertiliser to keep it blooming for quite some time."

He almost smiled. "Well, I guess if they're talking about us, they're leaving other people alone."

I chuckled. "That's what I think too. They don't mean any harm, but not much happens in little old Hadley Cove. So any news is big news."

When we walked up my drive, instead of heading toward the house, I nodded to the ocean. "Let's sit down on the rocks and eat dinner. It's nice out tonight." The wind hadn't picked up yet, and the last of the sunshine would give us about half an hour before the chill set in. Plus, I didn't want to have this conversation with Aubrey with the photo of Scott smiling at us.

He isn't me, Scott's voice said. *What happened to me won't happen to him.*

I can't risk it.

"You can't risk what?"

Shit. Had I said that out loud? "Oh, um, nothing. Can you get down onto that ledge?"

I jumped first and held my hand out for him. He laid his crutch down, sat on his arse, and slid down, dumping his backpack beside us. We sat with our backs to the rock, our fish and chips on our laps, and watched as the ocean crashed onto the small beach below us. "It's too early for the penguins yet," I said. Not that he'd asked. "They'll wait for dark."

"It's safer in the dark," he murmured. "Sometimes things are easier to say in the dark. So if you want to wait, I'll understand.

"If I want to wait for what?"

"To say whatever it is you're going to tell me." He looked out at the ocean's horizon when he spoke.

"It's nothing bad, it's just..." I finished with a sigh. "Will you look at me, please?"

He did, reluctantly. "Then why do I feel you're about to break up with me?" Then he snorted. "I mean, if there's anything to break up. Are we even together? Is there a label that we're tethered to? We're both adults, we can be grown up about it. It is what it is. And I know my secrets are a shadow I can't get rid of. I wish I could. And I know Collin said something today about me that you're not telling me, and if you're worried about where that leaves you, I understand. I get it. I don't expect you to shoulder this burden. I shouldn't have ever expected you to."

My God, he was ranting.

"Aubrey, stop."

He stopped.

"Take a breath."

He breathed.

"I'm not breaking up with you. And yes, there's something to break. My heart, for one. If you were to go, it'd break for sure. And I'm pretty sure yours would too."

His bottom lip trembled, and he nodded. "Irreparably."

I took his hand. "I'm not kicking you out. In fact, I just asked you to move in with me. Which is kind of a big deal. For me, at least. And just so you know, when I blurted out to Frank that you could move in with me, that wasn't my brain talking. It was my heart. But I don't regret it. Not one bit. As soon as I'd said it, I knew it was right."

His gaze bored into mine. "But?"

"But he mentioned that job with the fishermen."

"The cash job?"

I nodded. "And I'd never tell you what you can and

can't do. I realise you've come from a relationship that wasn't good, and the last thing I want is to control anything you do, and I know you need the money, but I..." I shook my head. "I can't go through that again."

He blinked, and I saw it in his eyes the second the penny dropped. "Oh, no." He blanched, then shook his head vehemently. "Oh no, Patrick. I didn't even think... I'm so sorry. I should have known, even when Frank mentioned him... I didn't even put two and two together." He looked pale in the setting sun, and he clambered to take my hand in both of his. "Now I feel like an arsehole. I'm sorry. I won't even follow it up, and if they ask me, I'll say no."

"The money—"

"I don't care about money," he shot back. "I've got by for the last six or seven months without it. This makes no difference. I'll just keep doing odd jobs around town for a box of vegetables or something. Mrs Whittaker needs a lot of work done and she likes me. I think. And I won't take any jobs near any boats or any marinas even. I promise. I'm sorry, I didn't even think. And that makes me a horrible—"

I kissed him quiet. "Boyfriend. A horrible boyfriend."

He stared, then the beginning of a smile tugged at his lip. "I was going to say, person. But boyfriend works. If that's okay with you?"

"It's very okay." I kissed him again. "And you're not even a horrible boyfriend. You're a great boyfriend. A great, sexy-as-hell boyfriend. A great, sexy-as-hell live-in boyfriend!"

"Okay, I get it," he said with a laugh. Then he stared at me some more and let out a long sigh. "And you're a great, sexy-as-hell live-in boyfriend too. Who's a really good cook and who's really kind and has a heart the size of this ocean." He smiled, and his cheeks tinted with the sunset. "I used to think you were this coastline personified. Eyes the colour of water, and your beard is the colour of the brown rocks and grey like the storms, and you were as beckoning and as strong as your lighthouse. So having a heart as big as the Southern Ocean kind of fits."

Now it was me who stared at him. "You really think that I'm like this place?"

He nodded and rested his head on my shoulder. "Absolutely."

I ate some fish and fed him some pieces off my fork. "As beckoning and as strong as my lighthouse?"

He groaned. "You're killing me. It sounded better in my head, okay?"

I laughed, and we continued to eat in silence. A happier silence now, with his head on my shoulder, and to the tempo the ocean beat out, we watched the sun disappear behind the horizon on its way to light another part of the world.

When it was almost gone, he spoke. "I will never tire of this," he said, slowly, reverently.

I kissed the side of his head. "Me either. It's better now with you."

He sighed and looked up at me from my shoulder. "You're okay with the boyfriend label?"

I leaned down and kissed his lips. "Very. What did you call it? Tethered?"

"Yeah."

"I like being tethered to you."

He sat up and put his hand to my cheek and kissed me properly. Soft open lips, the hint of tongue. "Me too."

He shivered then, and I put my arm around him. "Are you cold? Come on, let's go inside."

We got inside and he made us tea while I fixed the fire

and fed Tabby. Then we crawled into bed and made love. Sweet and slow, tender hands and soft cries of pleasure. He whispered my name, like a litany, and we fell asleep in each other's arms.

And for the days that followed, we lived in our perfect bubble of cooking together and laughing together and having incredible sex that strengthened the tether between us.

———

BUT THEN ONE afternoon when I was leaving the light-house, I was met by two cars pulling up at my house. Collin, in his police car, and a government-looking vehicle that followed him. Aubrey came out of the house at the same time I got to the door, and Collin walked toward us. He had his hat on, an official visit. He gave me a sorrowful look, then looked squarely at Aubrey.

"Ethan Hosking. Your game of charades is up."

What? Ethan? Who the hell was Ethan?

I turned to Aubrey, and the look on his face stopped me cold.

He was pale, resigned. Defeated. He shook his head and he tried to speak, but he made no sound. I put my hand on his arm but he flinched, a subconscious habit because he didn't look at me. He was staring at Collin.

I looked to Collin too. "Who is Ethan Hosking?"

Collin's face fell. "I'm sorry, Patrick. But he's not who he says he is." Then he looked behind him to the second car and gave a nod. Then he looked at Aubrey. "You're going to have to come with us."

But then three men exited the car, the sound of their doors slamming ricocheted like rapid gunfire—*bang, bang,*

bang—two men in suits who looked like cops and one man wearing a suit, sans the jacket, shirt rumpled like he'd travelled for hours. And he looked oddly familiar, like I knew him from somewhere...

But then it all kind of happened at once.

"Ethan?" the familiar stranger called out. Shocked, angry.

Aubrey stepped back and stumbled. Or fell. But before I could react or process what the hell was happening, Collin had hold of Aubrey. Aubrey looked... terrified, stricken. He was folding in on himself, falling to the ground in slow motion as Collin tried to hold him. Not restrain him, but support him. I went to him, not knowing what the hell was wrong, when Collin stared at me with wide eyes. "Get him inside," Collin whispered to me.

I didn't argue. I didn't dare. Aubrey was almost catatonic, shaking and white as a sheet. I literally picked him up by the shoulders and lifted him inside. I kicked the door shut behind us, and Aubrey pushed away from me, wild and unseeing. I let him go, and he fell backwards, scrambling on the floor like he couldn't find traction. He backed himself up against the dining table, pushing chairs aside, and he hugged his knees.

I had no clue what the hell had just happened, but I knew, I just knew, Aubrey's past had caught up to him.

CHAPTER SEVENTEEN

AUBREY

MY WORLD TILTED. Slanted. Silent. Slow motion.

Something in my mind screamed at me to run, but I was tethered here.

To Patrick.

I blinked, and he was looking at me like I was a wild cat, injured but needing his help. His face, his beautiful face, was scared, sad.

God, this would kill him.

I was about to break his heart.

No man should endure such obliteration twice in one lifetime.

Tears spilled down my cheeks and I couldn't stop them. I let them fall uncontested.

"I'm sorry," I tried to say. The words wouldn't come. I tried to say it again.

Nothing.

He put his hand up. "It's okay."

But it wasn't. It was far from okay. Because he was outside. Anton. He was here. And men in suits.

This was where it ended.

This was where it all came crashing down.

I should have known. I shouldn't have involved Patrick. This beautiful man whose heart I was about to rip from his chest.

I shouldn't have let it go this far.

It was always going to end like this. I couldn't run forever. I knew it in my bones, I knew this would all crumble, eventually. Just when I had the most to lose.

When I had everything to lose.

Then there was loud talking outside the door, and a new panic set in. I couldn't see him. I couldn't let him see me, touch me.

Never again.

"I can't... he can't... don't let him take me."

Patrick spun at the door as it opened, and two men came in. I pushed back further—Jesus, was I under the table? The door closed behind them, and all the air sucked out of the room.

But it wasn't Anton who came toward me. It was Collin. He crouched down next to me and sat on the floor, and slowly, like I might bite, put his hand on mine.

"It's okay. He's gone. I've asked Mr Gianoli to leave," Collin said, his voice calm and soothing. He nodded toward the man who still stood at the door. "This is Agent Janson. He's with the Canberra police. I hold lead on this case for now, but I've asked him to stay. He's just here to witness, not to act. Okay? You're okay, Aubrey." His fingers slid around mine, holding my hand, and I let him.

I fucking let Collin hold my hand.

Patrick knelt down next to Collin. "Can someone please tell me what's going on?"

Collin answered. "I'm sorry, Patrick. I had no idea. Aubrey's real name is Ethan Hosking. He supposedly died in the Canberra bushfires last year. His boyfriend, Senator Anton Gianoli confirmed his photo. But Patrick, I had no idea. Until I saw Aubrey's face. I've only seen that kind of fear once before." He swallowed hard. "When I came to tell you about Scott."

And for the first time in far too long, I let myself truly cry.

———

COLLIN TOLD Patrick everything he knew about the fires. They'd swept through the national park west of Canberra, which is why the Canberra police were here. The federal police. That I'd been staying in a house in the forest for a week when the fire razed everything in its path to the ground.

They'd found some of my belongings a short distance from the house. Melted and almost unrecognisable. Anton had confirmed a phone call from me, saying I'd been ordered to evacuate and I was leaving on foot. Some of the pieces were missing, but the overall picture was clear.

In the weeks and months that followed, none of my accounts were touched, no traces of me were found online. I was confirmed missing, presumed dead.

They'd buried an empty casket.

Patrick's face crumpled when he heard this. Because he'd had to do the same for Scott.

"I'm sorry," I tried to say. My tears and sobs made it hard to understand, but Patrick's face told me all I needed to know.

He understood, all too well. I'd put others through what he'd gone through.

He spoke to Collin like I wasn't even there. "He told me

his ex beat him, that he feared for his life. He said the man had influence and reach, which is why he had to go into hiding."

Collin nodded and squeezed my hand. He hadn't left my side. "Well, no matter the allegations against Senator Gianoli, Aubrey broke the law. There are crimes associated with faking your own death."

I wiped my face with my free hand, though I could still barely speak. "I never meant to hurt anyone. I just had to leave. I couldn't see another way out. You wanna know why I was at the house in the national park? Because he'd beaten me senseless, and he couldn't risk me being seen with a black eye and split lip. Every time he'd... hit me, he'd take me to his house in the forest and leave me there. No car, no anything. I couldn't leave until he came back to get me." I sobbed. "If I'd stayed in the house, I'd have died in the fire." I couldn't look at the utter heartbreak on Patrick's face. "Maybe I should have."

Collin, still holding my hand, frowned. But he never made me come out from under the table. He just sat next to me with all the patience in the world.

I spoke, still crying, hoping they could understand me. "I was with him for four years. The first two years were okay. I mean, he'd get angry and yell and push me around a bit. But he was making his way up the political ladder; he was stressed and under a lot of pressure. Being the first openly gay politician came with expectations, he'd said. I had to look pretty on his arm, but I wasn't allowed to speak. God forbid if someone asked me questions. He said I should quit my degree because how could I possibly enter in politics? How would that make him look? The first time he hit me was just before his nomination into the Senate. He was so stressed and there was a dinner, but I wasn't feeling well. He lost it. Screaming at me that it was my fault, and he accused me of seeing someone else, which I wasn't! God, by then, I didn't have any friends left. I barely left the house." I scrubbed at my face, wiping tears and snot onto my sleeve. "He drove me to his house in the forest. Told everyone at the dinner that I was on a week's leave, doing some artsy thing, he was so proud of me..." I shook my head. "I was lying in bed with two swollen-shut eyes, a split lip, and bruised ribs. I couldn't see for two days."

Patrick sobbed, and I thought he was going to push up onto his feet and leave, but he squeezed himself under the table with me and pulled me into his lap. He held me, rocked me back and forth, cradling my head against his chest.

Collin let go of my hand, giving me and Patrick a minute alone, and went and spoke to the cop at the door. I didn't hear what was said, but Collin was back a short time later. He crouched down beside us. "Aubrey, those are some serious allegations. I'm not saying I don't believe you, but if we're going to look into that, we'll need proof."

Patrick stroked my hair, still rocking slowly. "Is his word not enough?"

Collin gave him a solemn shake of his head. "Public figure like that? It'll need to be watertight."

"He left everything behind," Patrick said, still rocking me gently.

"I walked away from everything. I left my money, my clothes, my things. The only thing I took was my grandad's telescope. I cut off all my hair, I slept on the streets, doing odd jobs for cash." I felt so heavy, like I was exhausted from carrying this weight for so long. Now it was gone, I was utterly spent. "I'm sorry I lied. I didn't think I had any other way. He wouldn't have let me leave. He told me he'd never let me leave."

Patrick put his hand to my forehead and rocked me some more. I felt like a child in his arms, like a safe and protected child. "Well, he can't touch you now," he said, a quiet promise.

"I'm so sorry, Patrick," I mumbled. I still couldn't look at him. I burrowed into his chest and fisted his shirt and cried some more. "I never meant to hurt you. I didn't want to lie to you. But if you knew, then you'd be in on it and just as guilty as me. I messed everything up so bad. You can hate me, I'll understand. But if you could please just be so kind as to hate me when I'm gone. I couldn't bear it now."

His hold on me tightened, he swayed a little, and then he kissed the top of my head. "I don't hate you," he murmured. "I hate what was done to you. What you went through."

Collin sighed. "Aubrey, you're going to have to come with me."

Patrick's arms went around me, holding me tighter, and I started to cry again. I was foolish to think this could last forever. I was foolish to think I could have this slice of happiness on this rugged, lonely island with this rugged, lonely man under the stars where the Southern Cross had led me.

I sat up in Patrick's lap and finally looked at him. I was a mess, red eyes and runny nose, but he looked horror-struck, heartbroken. I put my hand to his cheek, relishing in the soft wire of his beard under my touch. "I wasn't lying about the Southern Cross. I walked... when the fire came, through the forest. It was dark and I was lost. But I followed the Southern Cross. My grandfather taught me that. Follow it, it will take you south. So I followed it to Melbourne, then to here. It was my compass. To you." I ignored my tears. "I'm sorry I hurt you, but I can't regret it. Because I love you, I'm in love with you, and to regret that would make it wrong, and you're the only right thing in my life."

Patrick's eyes welled with tears. "I'll come with you, wherever Collin takes you. I don't blame you, I don't hate you, Aubrey." Then his face crumpled. "Is that your name?"

"My name is Aubrey Hobbs," I said. "Ethan Hosking died that day. The man who was too weak to leave Anton died in the fire, and Aubrey Hobbs walked out." Fresh tears spilled down my face. "I became a different person that day. Stronger, better. Aubrey Hobbs was my grandfather's name. He was the one good thing in my life I could take with me."

A tear rolled down Patrick's cheek, and he pulled me back against him. He held me, rocking me, as we sat under the table. He kissed the top of my head. "I love you, Aubrey Hobbs."

And instead of his words setting me afloat, they felt like a burden.

I was a burden to him.

These declarations of love from two broken men should have been a revelation. It should have been our very own nebula; the birth of something wonderful. But how could it be when it was all falling apart? I clung to him and ran my hand up to his face, and I kissed him. Our tears mixed, became one. I kept my forehead pressed against his, my eyes closed.

"Hey," he whispered. "This isn't the end of us. We'll get through this."

I dared open my eyes, to look into his. Could I hope? Could I let myself hope, to not lose everything I thought I never deserved?

He nodded, like he could read my mind. "We'll be okay.

I'll go with you to the police station, and I'll make sure that arsehole doesn't get within ten feet of you. But first, you're gonna have to help me get up. I feel like I'm in a box."

I climbed off him, out from under the table, and Collin stood at the same time. I was embarrassed and ashamed at my reaction, at what I'd admitted. I'd never given Collin much credit before. I'd only ever seen him as a jealous man who wanted Patrick, but I saw him differently now. He was kind, compassionate, and a good policeman.

I pulled Patrick to his feet and he quickly stood behind me, his arm around my shoulders.

"You okay?" Collin asked.

I gave a nod and half a shrug; I didn't really have much choice. But something Patrick had said plucked a chord in my memory. "Box," I said. "Dropbox. I had a Dropbox account." I turned to Patrick. "I put photos in it. I thought one day I might need proof. I couldn't hide photos anywhere, like on a USB. He would have found them. So I put them in a storage account online."

Collin spoke first. "You have photos of what exactly?"

"Of what I looked like, after... after he'd had a bad day. He doesn't know. Unless he went through my laptop." I shrugged. "Which is possible. But it had a fingerprint access, not a password, so maybe not?" I was starting to feel a flicker of hope.

"Do you have any photos or videos or witnesses of him assaulting you?" Collin pressed.

Then I was quickly deflated. "No. I don't think anyone saw or even noticed."

"He doesn't know that," Patrick said.

"What?" Collin asked.

"He doesn't know that," he repeated. "Show him a few

photos and tell him you have more. Taking this public will be the last thing he'll want."

Collin made a face, glanced at the federal cop still standing stoic at the door. "Let's just take a look at the photos first, okay?"

Patrick grabbed his laptop and sat it on the table, fired it up, and stood aside for me. I'd kind of pulled myself together, a little. Well, the tears had stopped. "I um, I haven't logged into anything in so long," I said, swallowing hard. "I'm not sure I can even remember passwords. If I open my email, it'll take a month to download all the spam, probably." I searched up Dropbox and tried logging in. "I had three different passwords that I used for everything, so it has to be one of them. If he hasn't found them and deleted them. Or if my account hasn't been deactivated for not being used."

"We can issue warrants to online companies to pull old data," Collin said calmly. "Nothing is ever really deleted."

Okay then.

First password failed. Second password failed. Third password, and presto!

Welcome back, Ethan.

There were six folders in total, dated one year ago, two years ago, and three.

I stood up and gave Collin an *it's all yours* wave of my hand. I stepped away while he took the seat and clicked on the first folder. I went to the sofa and collected Tabby. I sat with her on my lap, purring like she knew it was what I needed to hear, to feel. Like she somehow knew her rumbling sounds and sleepy head-nudges would help me heal.

Patrick stood behind Collin, and he watched as Collin clicked and scrolled. Patrick put his hand to his mouth, the colour draining from his face. A tear spilled down his cheek, and he shot me a look. A horrified look, a pitiful look.

"I had long hair," I said to no one in particular. To all of them. "The longer it was, the curlier it was. It was my trademark thing, what I was known for, photographed for. God forbid if I pulled it back; the Sunday papers wrote about it once. That the boyfriend of Senator Gianoli was easily recognised by his long curly hair. So I hacked it off that very first night after the fire." I sighed and patted Tabby for a minute. Even Collin stopped clicking for a moment. "Kinda crazy that they were right. No one recognised me. No one missed me."

Collin gave me a sorry smile. "I recognised you. You looked familiar, but I couldn't place it. I searched your name, found nothing. Then the senator was on TV, talking about the coronial inquest. They showed a photograph of you. I had to be sure, though."

"I don't blame you," I told him. "I'm responsible for what I did. No one else."

Patrick took a deep, shaky breath. He looked like he wanted to say so much more, but his eyes were drawn back to the photos of me.

Collin sighed and glanced back to the laptop screen. "Can we use these photos?"

I shrugged. "Sure."

"I can't promise they won't be made public, Aubrey," he furthered. "I'd like to think this might go away quietly when you tell your side of the story. But given he's a public figure and a politician, at that, I'd say this is going to be huge. Are you ready for that?"

I sighed. "I can't change what happened. I tried running away from it and just ended up hurting innocent people."

Patrick came over then and sat beside me. He took my hand. "You did nothing wrong."

"I lied, and I hurt you. If I need to pay for that, then I will."

"Aubrey..." He shook his head.

"I'm tired of running, Patrick," I said, fighting new tears. "I'm tired of covering tracks, of looking over my shoulder. I'm tired of keeping secrets. The truth is, I'm exhausted of it. I want my life back. My driver's licence, a bank account. A real job."

Patrick put his arm around my shoulder and pulled me in so he could kiss my temple. He was warm and strong, and if this was my last moment with him, with his heartbeat in my ear, and Tabby purring on my lap, I'd take it.

Collin called the other officer over and they talked, pointing at the screen and squinting, looking for what, I didn't know. But they nodded and agreed, then pointed and squinted some more while Patrick and Tabby stayed with me on the couch.

I had to blink hard a few times to stay awake. "I'm sorry you saw those photos," I murmured.

Patrick's arms tightened, and he kissed the top of my head. "Don't be sorry."

"I'm so tired," I said, my voice mumbled and slurring.

Patrick put his hand to my forehead. "Close your eyes for a bit."

Before I could, Collin spoke. "Aubrey, I need to make copies of these. Because chances are this case will get ugly, and I'm not saying these might disappear, but if they're compromised, we'll have backup copies. Is that okay with you?"

I nodded. "Sure."

Truthfully, I was past caring at this point. The whole thing was blown wide open anyway, so it didn't matter. My game was up, I had been found out. And although I didn't know the extent of the repercussions or the charges I'd be facing, part of me was glad it was over. I was so very sorry Patrick was caught up in the whole mess, and I was so sorry he was hurting because of me. But along with the sorrow came a sense of relief that I was free. If I could shuck off the secrets and lies, then maybe—just maybe—I could deal with picking up the pieces.

Collin and the other officer talked some more, agreed some more, and decided sending the images to two separate destinations might be a good idea. Then he turned to us. "Okay, Aubrey. We *are* going to have to go to the station, there's no avoiding that. But the sooner we get it started, the sooner it'll be over."

———

I GOT to ride in the back of the police car, but Patrick followed us in his car. I was being taken to Penneshaw. It was much bigger and better equipped than Collin's one-man station. Thankfully, Collin had forgone handcuffs.

I wasn't running anywhere. Not anymore.

I was led into an interview room where I was charged with False Representation, and Collin stayed with me the entire time. I gave my statement and was questioned for what felt like hours. I didn't want to lawyer up, because I knew it would only elongate the process, but I wasn't naïve. The truth was, I had broken the law. There was no escaping that. Did I have my reasons? Well, that was for a judge or jury to decide. Collin went out to make a call, and waiting for a lawyer to turn up gave me time to think...

I had no idea if Anton was in another interview room.

Was he being shown photographs, was he being charged, or was he already on his way home with a smug smile on his face?

And where was Patrick? We're they questioning him? Was he in trouble? Or was he sitting out in the waiting room worrying about me? Was Collin keeping him informed?

God, the grapevine around Hadley Cove must be shooting new sprouts all over by now. What would they think of me? Would they still accept me like they had just days ago? If I saw them again anytime soon. For all I knew, I could be charged right now and held until trial. That could take years...

Oh God, Patrick.

The door opened and Collin came in. "Is Patrick okay?" I asked before he'd even closed the door.

"He's fine. He's waiting. Said he's happy to wait."

I sighed and sagged into the uncomfortable plastic chair. "I never meant to hurt him," I said. I had no doubt people were listening to my every word, even recording it behind the mirrored window.

Collin sat down across from me. He gave me a smile that said he knew, but he didn't say it out loud. He couldn't, I guess. "So, here's what's happening," he said. "Your lawyer is on her way. She's been briefed and has copies of your statement and photographs."

He'd no sooner said this before a woman entered without knocking. She wore a crisp grey pantsuit, had a soft face, and, as I was quick to learn, a sharp tongue.

"Sergeant O'Hare," she said, putting her briefcase on the table. "I trust you weren't barraging my client."

He almost smiled. "Of course not."

"I've seen the file and the photographs. What are the charges against Senator Gianoli?"

"Still to be determined," he replied smoothly.

She paused. "But he *will* be charged?"

"I would imagine so. He's waiting for his lawyer from Canberra to get here."

"Good," she said, finally sitting down. "That gives us time."

"Aubrey," Collin said, "this is Kate Pawson, your attorney."

I got the feeling they knew each other well. In fact, I kind of got the impression Collin had chosen her on my behalf. I certainly hadn't asked for anyone in particular.

"Is it Aubrey or Ethan?" she whipped back before I could speak.

"I prefer Aubrey," I said weakly. "It's who I am."

She opened the briefcase and took out a manila folder, opened that, and clicked the button on her pen. "Aubrey Hobbs was the name of your grandfather, yes?"

"Yes."

"And whilst you assumed his identity, you never attempted to defraud any company or persons of information, money, or property?"

I blinked. "Never."

"You never withdrew money, you never made a claim, you never legally proposed to be Aubrey Hobbs."

I shook my head. Jesus. She scared me, and I was at this point still undecided if she was on my side or not. "No. I never even signed my name. Not ever. I couldn't get work, sign a lease, see a doctor. Nothing."

She scribbled notes all the while, and Collin might have even looked amused. Kate didn't even look up when she spoke. "So, you never once benefited from assuming this identity?"

"No... Well, I... I guess if you mean benefited by the fact that my ex couldn't find me, then yes."

She stopped writing and stared at me. "Honey, if this goes to court, promise me you won't repeat that."

"Sorry," I said quickly. "I'm really tired. It's been a long year."

"You didn't benefit financially under this new identity," she added.

"No. In fact, I left all my money behind."

"And your ex, Senator Anton Gianoli," she went on, "wears this ring on his right hand?" She slid a photograph in front of me. It was a man's hand, hemmed by a dark suit sleeve, and a familiar gold ring on the ring finger. It had a squared top with initials engraved with a small diamond. I knew it well.

"Yes," I whispered. "It was his father's."

"Whose father's?"

"Anton Gianoli."

She put other photos in front of me, laid them out like a deck of cards. Me cut. Me bruised, me swollen. The haunted eyes I would never forget. "These markings, here, here, here"—she pointed to them in turn, to the slightly imprinted marking on each bruise—"were kindly pointed out by Sergeant O'Hare. They've been sent to forensics to examine, but he believes it to be markings made by the same ring."

My gaze shot to Collin and he smiled. "He will be charged."

"And as for my client's charges," Kate said like she did this all day, every day, and this was all rather tedious. "As no financial gain or charge of Conspiracy to Defraud has been made, I'm petitioning for a lesser charge of Failure to Disclose. I ask my client not be held. He poses no flight risk, and he won't leave this island until extradition." She shot a well-aimed glare at me. "Will he?"

"No, I won't," I promised. "What did you mean extradition?"

"The incident occurred in another state," Collin answered. "It's more than likely the case will be heard in Canberra."

"So I have to go back there anyway," I whispered. "I never wanted to go back there."

"You don't have to stay there," Kate said. "Once I have you cleared of all charges, you can come back here."

Collin almost smiled again. "I'll let you get acquainted," he said as he stood.

"Can you tell Patrick..." I started to tell him until I realised I didn't know what to tell Patrick.

"I'll tell him you won't be long," Collin said. He gave a nod to Kate and closed the door behind him.

Then Kate turned to me and visibly relaxed. "You holding up okay?"

I gave her a nod. "I've been through worse."

Her eyes darted to the photographs. "I can see that. We'll get this sorted out, don't worry. The fact you assumed a new name isn't a crime. You didn't forge documents, you never profited. It wasn't pre-meditated, and it was done without intent of malice. In fact, you made it decidedly difficult for yourself because you feared for your safety. That will be taken into account. I'll be pushing for you to be exonerated of all charges. If that's okay with you?" she asked with a tug of a smile.

"Can I ask you something?"

"Of course."

"Collin. Sergeant O'Hare, did he really match the photos to the ring?"

She nodded. "I've known O'Hare for a long time. He's very good at what he does. When you asked for legal aid, he put a call into me."

"I wondered," I replied.

"It means he believes you," she said simply. "And if he wants me to take on your case, then he wants the best for you."

And for whatever reason, I believed she was as good as she said she was. "I thought he hated me," I admitted. "Maybe he was just protecting Patrick."

"The guy out in the waiting room who looks worried sick?" she asked. "Beard? Handsome? Pacing?"

Now I smiled. "Sounds like him."

She turned back to her paperwork. "Right, then, let's get this out of the way so you can go home with him."

"Can I really leave?" I asked, not wanting to sound too hopeful.

Kate smiled. "You got me for a lawyer, hon. You'll be going home until I need to see you again." Then she shot me a levelling stare. "You won't leave this island, you won't log into any of your old life online, you won't contact anyone, you won't even blink out of turn until I tell you you can, are we clear?"

I could have cried. "Crystal."

CHAPTER EIGHTEEN

PATRICK

WORDS COULDN'T DESCRIBE how it felt to see Aubrey walk out of that interview room at the police station. I stood as soon as I saw him, and he nearly started to cry again when he saw me. They were tears of relief, not of horror or shame. He looked exhausted, limping on his sore ankle as he walked toward me, and I wasted no time in wrapping my arms around him.

He sagged against me, fisting my shirt like he held on for dear life. "Thank you for being here."

I kissed the side of his head. "I'm not going anywhere."

There was a woman with him who smiled at me, then Collin appeared. "He's right to go. For now. I'll be in touch," he said.

"We'll talk soon," the woman said with a smile, then she left with Collin.

"You ready to go home?" I whispered.

He nodded against my chest, then looked up at me, his brown eyes imploring, wary, and a little lost. "Are you sure?"

Was I sure if I wanted him in my house? In my bed? Or

in my life at all? Was I sure that I was ready to face whatever he was about to face? Would we face it together?

"I'm sure."

———

THE DRIVE from Penneshaw didn't even take an hour, but he was asleep just ten minutes into it. He was utterly exhausted.

I could see it now as he slept beside me, his real face merged with memories of those photographs of him beaten black and blue. I could see the faint line above his eyebrow, a slight nick on the inside of his nose. His perfect imperfections I'd assumed were from childhood camping and running wild in the bush but were from a nightmare instead.

Those photos would haunt me forever. A bloodshot eye, swollen brow, cut cheekbone, bleeding lip. The hollow, empty, utterly profound sadness in his eyes.

Collin had told me he'd sent the photos off to some specialist, along with a photo of Anton he'd got online from some tabloid photograph.

I didn't recognise the Aubrey in those photos. It wasn't so much the long, curly hair I couldn't get used to. It was the sullen look in his eyes. The blank stare, the gaunt sadness that the media had written off as the *moody bohemian* or some such rubbish.

I was angry that no one had noticed. He'd been a victim in plain sight and no one questioned, no one looked twice. Had Anton isolated him so much that no one dared even speak to him? I'd seen that smarmy son of a bitch in the police station. He was being led from one room to the next, and it took every ounce of my self-control not to run through the officers with him and give him a taste of his own medicine. See how he liked getting smacked around for a change.

It was Collin's hand on my arm that stopped me. "It's not worth it, Patrick," he said, low and steady. "He'll get what he deserves. They should be able to prove by those photos and his ring that he did the damage to Aubrey's face."

"Someone needs to teach that prick a lesson," I bit out.

"Karma will. And the justice system."

I sighed and slumped in my seat. "What happens from here?"

"That will depend on how the senator pleads. He's going to want this to be as fast and quiet as possible. At any rate, his political career is over. His community standing is done for. Those photos of Aubrey will hit the media and it'll be a chequered flag for him." He paused for a moment. "It's gonna get pretty hectic, Patrick. Are you ready for that?"

I looked at him and nodded. "Yeah."

"You really love him," he said. It wasn't a question.

"I do."

"I'm happy for you." His smile was genuine. "I've been trying to tell you for a while that I've been seeing someone from Stokes. But it never seemed like the right time, and I was gonna tell you when I called around to ask about Aubrey, to prove in some stupid way that I wasn't acting out of jealousy. I was concerned for you, that you'd get hurt because he wasn't who he said he was." He let out a long breath. "But then I saw his face today and I knew."

"I'm glad you're seeing someone," I replied. "He makes you happy?"

Collin smiled. "Yeah."

"Good. You deserve it. And thank you for what you did today. You were great."

He patted my shoulder as he stood and walked away, and I felt bad that I'd maybe not been too kind in my refusal of his affection. I couldn't change the past, but I could be a whole lot nicer from now on. And as I drove us home, I promised myself I would.

I pulled up in front of my house and left the engine running. Aubrey was still asleep, and I knew as soon as I shut the car off, he'd wake up. I just wanted another moment to breathe.

Everything changed after this. Everything was about to be laid bare and exposed, and we couldn't go back to how we were. We had to deal with everything from Aubrey's old life before we could move forward. I was completely and utterly prepared to do that. Though I had to wonder how Aubrey would react. He was fully expecting me to leave him before, to say it was all too hard, or to tell him his lies were unforgivable.

But they weren't unforgivable.

They were understandable.

There was nothing to forgive. He'd told me from the beginning that he couldn't tell me about things because I'd get involved and he didn't want to risk that. He'd been as truthful as he could have been, given the circumstances.

"Hey, Aubrey." I gently shook his arm. "Hey. We're home."

He sat up, bleary-eyed and groggy. "Oh. Did I fall asleep?"

"You're exhausted."

He rubbed his eyes and sagged. "I really am. I feel like I've been hit by a truck."

I took his hand and squeezed it. "You kind of have been.

It's been a helluva day. How about I make us a casserole for dinner, and you can snooze on the couch. Then you can have a hot shower and crawl into bed, sleep for days."

He slow blinked at me. "Sounds perfect." He rubbed my thumb with his. "We need to talk. You must have a thousand questions. I can tell you everything now. Anything you want to know."

"The only thing I need to know right now, and something I insist you must tell me is, do you want pumpkin in the casserole or mashed on the side?"

He gave me a teary laugh. "I do love you. That has been my one, constant truth."

I kissed him. "That's all I need to know."

———

AS SOON AS Aubrey had a belly full of food and was in front of the warm fire, he couldn't keep his eyes open a second longer. He'd had an excruciating day. We both had, if I was being honest.

But I didn't regret my decision to stand by him. How could I?

I was in love with him.

I took him to bed, pulled back the covers, and crawled in with him. We needed to strip away the surplus, the unnecessary, and just be together. Close. Intimate, not sexual, even though my body reacted to him the way it always did. He needed to be safe and secure, and I needed to know he was.

He faced me, and I rubbed his back and ran my hands through his hair and took in his flawless, sleeping face. I had flashes of his bruises superimposed on his skin as I watched him sleep, and I had to trace the images away with soft touches and gentle strokes along his eyebrow, his cheek-bone, his bottom lip.

His eyes opened. "Hey," he whispered.

"I will never hurt you," I vowed. I pressed my lips to his forehead, pulled him in close, and he nuzzled into my neck.

"I know," he mumbled. "Patrick, if I asked you to make love to me, would you do it?"

I cupped his face. "You can barely keep your eyes open."

"And when I fall asleep, promise you'll stay inside me."

Jesus.

His eyes closed, but he gave the faintest smile. His hand started to work between us; he was stroking himself. "I want to feel good. I want to feel you in me. You take me places I can only go with you." He sighed and rolled onto his stomach, spreading his legs wide. "I want you to replace the bad with the good."

"Aubrey..."

"Please." He slid his hand to his arse and dipped it downward. "Make it slow. Make it good."

I groaned, and he knew he'd won.

By the time I pushed into him, he was so desperate, so damn wanting, he was begging, and there was no place else I wanted to be but inside him.

I ran my hands over his arms, over the back of his head, down his sides, everywhere I could touch. I slid my arm under his chest and lifted him back so I could kiss him while my cock pinned him to the bed.

It was slow and deep and so, so good.

But it was more than pleasure. It was grounding and centring, and if he wanted a front-row seat to some star-spangled galaxy he swore he saw when I made him come, then I would damn well take him there.

I thrust in hard.

"Yes," he groaned.

It might have felt good, but he was never going to come like this. I pulled out and rolled him over, and he was about to protest until I hooked his legs over my hips and slid back inside.

He gasped, sucked back air in short bursts, his mouth open, his eyes wide. I covered his mouth with mine and kissed him because I knew sensory overload drove him wild.

We made love like that, slow and sensual. He pumped his cock and he arched as his whole body went rigid.

"Oh my God," he cried, rasped, whispered, and then he spilled between us. His orgasm wracked through him, he convulsed, his neck corded, and he shuddered.

I wrapped him up in my arms and he was boneless, pliant, and making the most delicious sounds. I stayed inside him, wringing out every ounce of pleasure in him. He was so hot, so tight around me, an absolute perfect fit for me.

Like he was made for me, and I for him. "I love you," I murmured into his mouth.

The way he looked at me, the depth of his eyes, the love within them. I fell so, so hard.

He put his hand to my face and kissed me as I came, then he wrapped his legs and arms around me. "I love you too," he mumbled.

Oh, Aubrey.

"I know," I whispered into his neck. I slowly pulled out and discarded the condom, and quickly settled back down next to him, and by the time I pulled him back in close, he wrapped himself around me and was already fast asleep.

Tabby joined us and curled into the backs of Aubrey's legs. The three of us hunkered down, safe and warm, and despite the day, I smiled.

He's the one for you, Patrick, Scott's voice said.

"I know," I whispered.

You knew from the second you saw him.

"I think I did." I sighed and Aubrey snuggled in, stirring a little. I kissed his head. There was something I needed to know. "Did you bring him here?"

Scott's laughter whispered in my mind. *No, Patrick. He was always going to find you.*

"I love him, Scott."

I know.

"I love you too."

I know. But he is real, and he is your one, Patrick.

I breathed in deep and tightened my arms around Aubrey. "I know."

————

HE WAS STILL SLEEPING SOUNDLY when I woke. I tended to the lighthouse, as I did every morning, then came back to start breakfast. I was pretty sure the smell of eggs, toast, and coffee would rouse him, and I didn't have to wait long.

He came out, sleep-rumpled and bleary. "Still tired," he said, walking up to me and putting his forehead on my chest. "But thank you."

I rubbed his back. "You hungry?"

"Starving."

He ate his breakfast, trying hard not to make eye contact, and it was a little awkward. We needed to clear the air, to talk about what happened and where we went from here, and we both knew it. After he showered, he walked out and stood with his hand on the back of the dining chair while I wiped down the sink.

"Can we talk?" he asked. "We should talk."

I folded the dishcloth and threw it over the tap. "Of course."

He held out his hand, which I took, and we sat on the couch. He studied my fingers for a long few seconds, and I gave him all the time he needed to get his thoughts in order. "This isn't going to be easy, but I need to say this. All of this. So please let me get this out."

He let out a deep breath. "First, I need to say I'm sorry. I really am. I knew it would all catch up with me at some point. I mean, it had to, right? And I knew the risks, involving you, falling for you." He met my gaze then. "But I couldn't stop. I couldn't walk away from you, not then, not now. You are the best thing to ever happen to me. And it was selfish to drag you into this, and I am truly sorry for making everything messy and complicated. I never meant to lie to you, and I'd like to think I didn't, but I did. By omission, by not telling you the truth."

"You did it to protect me."

"And to protect myself. And you, but mostly me. I finally found one true chance at happiness here, and so help me God, I just wanted a taste of normality. I'm sorry I hurt you. I never meant to. I never expected to meet someone so wonderful, someone who understood me. I never expected to fall in love." He looked at me and shook his head, almost in disbelief. "I never expected you."

"Me?"

"To find my one. To find the one who understands me, who makes me a better person, who gets me." He blushed a little and snorted quietly at our joined hands. "I never expected love."

I wanted to say so much, but I knew he wasn't done.

"There is so much I never lied about though, and I want

you to know that. All the important parts, the honest parts, are true. My parents died when I was little, my grandad raised me. He died when I was nineteen and I moved to Canberra to study political science. I wanted to make a difference. I met Anton at a charity event in my first year, and before my third year, he'd convinced me to quit, he isolated me from my friends, and I was trapped in a cycle I couldn't get out of."

"I can't imagine how awful that must have been."

He smiled sadly and stared into that middle space, at memories only he could see. "I'm ashamed, embarrassed that I let him get away with it."

"You're not to blame."

He sighed. "I know that now. I didn't then. And I honestly couldn't see any way out at the time. He broke me down until I could be any shape he wanted. And when I decided to make a run for it, I literally had thirty minutes before the fire reached the house. I contemplated sitting on his sofa, drinking his expensive red wines, and watching as the fire roared toward me. I thought about it. It would have been easier."

Jesus.

"But I remembered something my grandad told me once when we were camping. About fire. That sometimes when the heat was too intense, it made identifying human remains impossible. And I thought... what if they just thought I died? What if I could start over? And in that split second, I thought, *fuck it*. I took a backpack with a few changes of clothes, the telescope, and I walked out into the forest. I dumped my phone and wallet and watch under a fire blanket, thinking it might seem like I'd perished." He took a shaky breath. "I could see the line of orange behind me. It was huge, and I ran south, away from it. I came across a fire-trail road and found a small cattle truck. The driver had stopped to close a gate or something, and I climbed into the back with the sheep and hid. He stopped at a town a while later and I climbed out. That's how I got out of the forest."

He licked his lips and continued. "The first place I went to was a seedy motel and she needed a name. I couldn't use Ethan Hosking, because he'd just died. So I thought of the one person I loved and who I missed terribly. My grandad. His name was Aubrey Hobbs. And you know, it felt right. Ethan was a weak man who truly had died inside long before that fire. But Aubrey was strong, and he used his hands, and he built and fixed stuff and was street smart, and he survived." A tear slid down his cheek. "I am Aubrey Hobbs. The only name you've known me by, that's who I am. I am not the man Anton knew, not anymore. I am the man you know."

"The man I love," I added.

He squeezed my hand and brought it to his lips. "I followed the Southern Cross. That was no lie. I followed it then, I followed it later to get to Melbourne, and I followed it here. To you. You are... you are so good to me. And I love you. I don't know what my future will be, and I can't promise anything, but please know this, Patrick. I love you, and if you ever want to know anything, just ask, and I'll tell you the truth. I promise."

It was my turn to talk now, and after everything he'd said, I wasn't sure where to start. "Don't apologise for anything you've done to get where you are right now. You did what you needed to do to survive. No one has the right to judge you on that, because they weren't in your place. I saw those photographs," I said, then swallowed hard. "No one deserves to go through that. Ever."

He leaned his head on the back of the sofa and looked at me. He was clearly exhausted again.

"But I'm in this with you, Aubrey. No matter what happens from here. We'll cross each road together, okay?" I squeezed his hand. "Collin seemed to think your lawyer had it all sorted."

He smiled. "He handpicked her. Said she was the best. And it was him who recognised the marks in those photos that might match the ring Anton wears. So, he turned out to be on my side after all."

I almost laughed. "Yeah, he's a good guy."

"My lawyer, her name is Kate. She wants me acquitted of all charges. She said that because I never tried to get money or any benefits that it proved I did it out of concern for my well-being, not gain. Apparently most people who fake their own deaths do it for a life insurance claim or to escape big debts, but not me. I didn't do that. I did it for safety concerns."

"Well, I hope so," I said. "And I hope that arsehole Anton gets well acquainted with karma."

He smiled at that, weary but genuine. "Me too."

"What do we do now?"

He shrugged. "I guess we wait to hear from Collin or Kate. I don't have a phone, so I assume Collin will pay me a visit sometime today to let me know what's going on."

"We can get you a phone now. And your ID so you can get a licence or see a doctor." I baulked and blushed. "Not that seeing a doctor for tests so we can stop using condoms is a priority, of course. I just meant that you can do whatever you want now..."

He chuckled. "Not a priority, huh?"

I groaned. "I meant—"

"I know what you meant." He turned my hand over and

kissed my palm. "Yes, I can see a doctor. Or get my Medicare card reissued for a start, then see a doctor. Kate mentioned not logging into my old life just yet, so I'll need to ask what she meant."

"Maybe it's just a precaution," I said, "maybe so she can decide what to tell the media. It'll look better if they don't find this all out first."

He sighed and nodded. "And you know, I don't mind being off-grid. I'm glad you know the truth now, that's for sure. And I'm grateful you didn't run a mile. But I think we should enjoy the anonymity before the press gets a hold of this. Because they will. And they'll flock here, no doubt. Hadley Cove won't know what hit it. So for now, I'm just happy for the peace and quiet, a simple life. That's all I want. Just you and me, we can have picnics in the lighthouse, or on the rocks watching penguins, or looking at the stars. I'd be happy if we could do that forever."

I leaned and kissed him. "Are you saying picnics and stargazing is all you want to do forever?"

He slow blinked and smiled serenely. "Yep."

"Here, on this island?"

"I never want to be anywhere else."

I sighed. His words settled warm in my belly, in my soul. "Forever?"

"Until the stars are no more."

EPILOGUE

AUBREY

THE NEWS BROKE six days later. Anton had resigned from parliament and from his electoral seat, citing personal reasons. The press investigated, the press found out, and it was a shitshow from start to finish. One photo of me was leaked to the media. My bruised and battered face was plastered on every front page of every major newspaper in the country, and it was breaking news for the week that followed.

Anton was never going to get a fair trial, he'd complained. He disputed all accusations, denied all wrongdoing. Until another guy came forward, saying Anton had hit him years ago, then another guy, then someone else.

The short version of a very long story was my charge of False Representation was downgraded but couldn't just be wiped clean. But, because I only told people I had a different name, I never pretended to be someone else for financial gain, hell, I'd never even signed the name Aubrey Hobbs once, the judge deemed it irresponsible, at best, without malice or intent to mislead, and I was given a six-month suspended sentence. The trial itself was highly publicised and long-drawn, but in the end, I was free to go home for dinner with Patrick and Tabby.

That was four years ago. I haven't left the island since.

I have no need, no desire to ever leave.

I changed my name by deed poll and I was now, legally, Aubrey Hobbs. I got my driver's licence, a new Medicare card, a perfect bill of health by the doctor, and I got to have Patrick in bed every night. Well, he had me. And for work, I got a small ute and registered a handyman business, and I got busy real quick. I was still paid in the bartering system by most Hadley residents, which I kind of loved, but everyone else paid me in actual money.

I also got engaged.

During the many times we were in Canberra for hearings and meetings with lawyers during the trial, Patrick had taken me to Mount Stromlo Observatory and Research School of Astronomy and Astrophysics. I'd needed a break, so he suggested some stargazing. What I didn't know was that he'd booked us in for a special viewing.

The high-powered telescope allowed us to see much of the galaxy. He'd specifically wanted me to see the rings of Saturn, and I was awed, amazed, and completely blown away. So close up, so surreal, so perfect. I'd never seen anything so incredible.

Until I pulled away from the eyepiece and saw Patrick down on one knee with a ring on the palm of his hand. "I will love you every minute of every day for as long as there are stars in the sky," he said. "Aubrey Hobbs, will you do me the extraordinary honour of marrying me?"

I cried and nodded, and while everything was a mess in my life, with the court case and the media, he was my one true thing.

Like the lighthouse he tended, he kept me safe, my course steady. He navigated me home.

Which was why the lighthouse was the perfect place for our wedding.

One hundred and two steps.

We each dressed in our suits. I helped him with his tie; he helped me with mine. And holding hands, we walked up the spiral aisle and met the minister and our closest friends at the top of the lighthouse.

Penny, Collin and his boyfriend Robbie, and Cassy, and even old Mrs Whittaker had made the climb. And Scott was there, his memory, his spirit. He was a part of Patrick's life, and over the last four years, he'd become a part of mine. We talked about him often and his photo still graced the mantelpiece, alongside Patrick's old family photo and a picture of my grandad. And his telescope, of course.

One hundred and two steps.

Right on sunset, before the calm and beckoning ocean, as the stars began to shine, we stood before each other and promised each other forever.

"As it's written in the galaxies and oceans, I promise my heart to you," Patrick said. With shining eyes and tender hands, he slid the ring on my finger.

I blinked back happy tears, my heart completely full. "May the stars forever guide us, and may this lighthouse bring us home."

THE END

ABOUT THE AUTHOR

N.R. Walker is an Australian author, who loves her genre of gay romance.
She loves writing and spends far too much time doing it, but wouldn't have it any other way.

She is many things: a mother, a wife, a sister, a writer. She has pretty, pretty boys who live in her head, who don't let her sleep at night unless she gives them life with words.

She likes it when they do dirty, dirty things... but likes it even more when they fall in love.

She used to think having people in her head talking to her was weird, until one day she happened across other writers who told her it was normal.

She's been writing ever since...

ALSO BY N.R. WALKER

Point of No Return

Breaking Point

Starting Point

Spencer Cohen Book One

Spencer Cohen Book Two

Spencer Cohen Book Three

Yanni's Story

Free Reads:

Sixty Five Hours

Learning to Feel

His Grandfather's Watch (And The Story of Billy and Hale)

The Twelfth of Never (Blind Faith 3.5)

Twelve Days of Christmas (Sixty Five Hours Christmas)

Best of Both Worlds

Translated Titles:

Fiducia Cieca (Italian translation of Blind Faith)

Attraverso Questi Occhi (Italian translation of Through These Eyes)

Preso alla Sprovvista (Italian translation of Blindside)

Il giorno del Mai (Italian translation of Blind Faith 3.5)

Cuore di Terra Rossa (Italian translation of Red Dirt Heart)

Cuore di Terra Rossa 2 (Italian translation of Red Dirt Heart 2)

Cuore di Terra Rossa 3 (Italian translation of Red Dirt Heart 3)

Cuore di Terra Rossa 4 (Italian translation of Red Dirt Heart 4)

Intervento di Retrofit (Italian translation of Elements of Retrofit)

Confiance Aveugle (French translation of Blind Faith)

A travers ces yeux: Confiance Aveugle 2 (French translation of Through These Eyes)

Aveugle: Confiance Aveugle 3 (French translation of Blindside)

À Jamais (French translation of Blind Faith 3.5)

Cronin's Key (French translation)

Cronin's Key II (French translation)

Au Coeur de Sutton Station (French translation of Red Dirt Heart)

Partir ou rester (French translation of Red Dirt Heart 2)

Faire Face (French translation of Red Dirt Heart 3)

Trouver sa Place (French translation of Red Dirt Heart 4)

Rote Erde (German translation of Red Dirt Heart)

Rote Erde 2 (German translation of Red Dirt Heart 2)

Galaxies
and Oceans

N.R. WALKER

Printed in the USA
CPSIA information can be obtained
at www.ICGtesting.com
LVHW091258250823
756177LV00001B/174

9 781925 886184